Guru
with
Guitar

Guru
with
Guitar

Vikrmn:

Srishti
PUBLISHERS & DISTRIBUTORS

SRISHTI PUBLISHERS & DISTRIBUTORS
Registered Office: N-16, C.R. Park
New Delhi – 110 019
Corporate Office: 212A, Peacock Lane
Shahpur Jat, New Delhi – 110 049
editorial@srishtipublishers.com

First published by
Srishti Publishers & Distributors in 2015

Dedicated to
My family and teachers... my inspiration;
My friends and fellows... my respiration.

Prologue

Life is like a Guitar

"I *used to doze off for a dream and get up with a hope. One day I dozed off with a hope; next morning I got up for a dream. That day I got to know: Hopes may vanish, but dreams never die,"* he said.

The auditorium resonated with applause.

It was 10.00 p.m. in Sydney. A tall, herculean man clad in an exotic black kurta and frayed denim made an imposing presence in an auditorium. A red muffler tied around his neck did some good in betraying his age of sixty that his folds on the skin visibly showed.

His dark eyes conveyed a strange confidence that seemed to contagiously reflect in the audience that he faced. As he braced the people and shifted from one side to the other, he never lost eye contact with the masses that packed the auditorium and cheered endlessly.

A few cameras were focused on him as his colossal image was projected onto a huge screen on the stage. The glaring lights rotating around an exquisitely carved ceiling fell upon him but his experienced eyes never flinched at their audacity. Multi-hued chandeliers clung to the roof of the hall and bathed the entire hall in their dazzling glory. The place had turned into an unintended rejoicing hall where people had gathered to peep into the brighter side of their lives.

Viktor adjusted his microphone and addressed the enthusiastic audience, "*Every vision has its own rainbow*. The day you realize your vision, you will find yours." A thunderous clapping punctuated every sentence that came out of his mouth.

"Thank you everyone…for believing in me for making others find their rainbows," he said, bowing to express his gratitude. The audience returned the favour with an approving ovation.

Two people scrolled a long box towards the stage and placed it in front of Viktor. He walked towards it. Glancing at the carving on the box, he touched it, moving the hand towards center of lid, "*Life beyond living*" etched on the bob. He touched the letter and then lid corners as if there was a treasure lying in that box.

"Mr. Viktor! Wait a minute," said a gorgeous lady, coming on the stage, an anchor-woman, "Let's keep the suspense a little longer."

The hall echoed with hooting and whistling.

"Any guesses please!" asked the lady aloud.

The people in the audience started yelling one by one, "Novel! Paintings! Guitar!" They started guessing and a guy said aloud, "Balance Sheet!" People roared in laughter.

"Well!" said the lady controlling her laughter, "Though Mr. Viktor is a Chartered Accountant, he won't do the auditing here as of now."

The very next moment, everyone started jingling in chorus, "Guitar! Guitar! Guitar!"

The lady smiled and turned towards Viktor saying, "How does this overwhelming response make you feel, Mr Viktor?"

Viktor smiled, or at least that was what he thought he was doing, and his eyes fluttered slightly. In an instant he was in a daze, lost in his thoughts and infinite memories.

∞

"What the hell do you think of yourself?" she yelled at a guy sitting in front of her.

The whole restaurant was suddenly quiet as people started to look at them, but she no longer seemed to care.

"You are lost in your own imaginary world. You have no idea what everyone in the real world is saying behind your back."

All he could do was sit there, stunned. The silence was deafening.

"You are a failure, Vik," she said, her eyes cold. "And I can't take this anymore."

∞

Viktor stood under the bright lights, struggling between his past and present.

"I just believed in myself and my dreams," he managed to say. "Because I knew... *Every TODAY has a better version... called TOMORROW.*"

"Viktor?" the anchor said, interrupting his thoughts. He looked at her and gave her a smile. She asked again, "We would love to know how you found the way towards your dreams."

He opened the buckles of the box, looked at the audience and said, *"You are born the day..."*

"...the day you find yourself," the gallery echoed with a unanimous clap as he ended his sentence.

"Amazing! I have to say that's one of my favorite quotes from your novel *Life beyond living*," said the lady.

He smiled and opened the box.

∞

Viktor opened the door of his house and was greeted by a courier guy who was in a hurry to drop his packet and rush for other deliveries. He received the parcel and scribbled on a page for a signature before the courier guy fled off. The door slung close behind him as he walked towards his bedroom focusing on ripping off the packet's cover.

It was a small velvet box, one very familiar to him. After all, he was the one who had kept it in his pocket for weeks, waiting for just the right moment to get down on his knee.

He knew what was inside, but he dreaded seeing it nonetheless.

His heart racing, he opened the box to find nestled inside the beautiful ring he had so carefully chosen. Tucked beside it was a note, and all it said was, "We are done".

Shattered, he found himself on his knees. He threw the box. It hit his guitar that was lying in the corner of room. It felt like the guitar cried out loud.

∞

The box was open. The audience tried to get a glimpse. The camera on a robotic arm captured the glimpse inside and as it flashed on the screens, the audience gasped. It was indeed a **Guitar**.

Viktor touched the strings as delicately as a father touches his baby's fingers, yet it was as firm as a warrior's grip on his sword.

Viktor picked up the guitar and pulled the thick strap over his shoulder. He strummed the chords of the guitar to a tune so soulful that it mesmerized everyone present there.

"Life is like a guitar," he said. *"Tune. Play. Repeat."*

Facing Problems?

Good, that's cocoon stage

It was the sound of a familiar rock song that woke Viktor up. Not bothering to turn off his alarm, he got out of his bed, only to realize that it was already 7:00 a.m.

Bleary-eyed, he made it to his bathroom, ready to face a rather mundane Monday morning. He knew he had to bear another bout of Monday blues, a side-effect of office monotony that had become his way of life.

He looked into the mirror, and gazing back at him was a man lost deep in his thoughts. For a minute he didn't recognize himself.

His life had appeared to be in stasis for the past five years, his enthusiasm and personal life seemed to be buried under the long and busy nights at the office.

"Am I the same person I was a few years back?" he wondered while getting ready for work.

"Why am I not feeling myself anymore?"

The corporate world seemed to have swallowed his dreams, hopes and passion, all at once.

His ride arrived an hour late; the journey to work was just another excuse for Viktor to get busy sorting out his thoughts. "Where did I go wrong? Why do I feel so incomplete? I have fantastic degrees, a great career, my bills are paid on time. I have it all, but why am I still not satisfied?"

He was looking for some sort of hint that would lead him to what he was really looking for: fulfilment. It seemed like all his life, the only thing that remained constant was tediousness. Apart from a few promotions, there was nothing much happening in his life.

"May be I should give some time to my hobbies? Or maybe pursue a joint venture with my friends? Try something new... what are my other interests?" His thoughts continued to occupy him even after he reached the office.

He stopped in front of a mirror, staring at himself, lost in thought, washing his hands, "Where am I? What do I want?" he muttered.

"Looking for something?" someone asked.

He turned to find Christine, one of his colleagues, walking towards him.

"Oh, hi Christine," he replied looking at her through the mirror.

"I asked, are you looking for something?"

He murmured, "Yes, I am looking for *something*."

"Sorry? What are you looking for...especially in the ladies' room?"

Snapping out of his reverie, he looked around to confirm where he was. Sure enough, behind him were two women, neither of them pleased by his presence.

He turned bright crimson. "Oh. Erm. Hello, ladies. How are you? I mean...Hi...no...sorry...bye."

They looked at each other, amused, as he rushed out.

A quick apology to Christine and he dashed across to the men's room. But in his hustle, he ran into someone else; a gorgeous lady, blonde hair, beautiful eyes, charming, the one he had never seen before in his office.

She seemed as flustered as him, rushing out of the men's room, embarrassed.

"Oh, I am very sorry," said the lady raising her hands.

"Hi! It's OK!" he replied confused and subconsciously raising his hands just like hers.

They looked at each other like they knew each other from ages. He was lost for that moment, in the blonde hair beauty, the same ways she was lost in his dark eyes.

"Hey, Kimberly!" said Christine peeping out of the door. "Don't worry about him. He entered here by mistake. Trust me, he is a true gentleman otherwise." She said with a hint of sarcasm.

"Yeah...I just..." she smiled, about to accept her mistake that she too had just come out of the men's washroom, but he interrupted, "Oh yeah! She just got scared while entering."

"Yeah," said Kim, acknowledging his attempt to save her embarrassment.

"Oh never mind," said Christine. "Hey, do you remember asking me who sends across those soul-lifting quotes every day??"

Kim nodded, "Is it him?" she asked glancing at Viktor.

"Smart!" said Viktor raising his eyebrows.

"Why?" giggled Christine. "Because he is standing his hands up and indicating inverted commas?"

They laughed, but with their hands still up.

"Are you guys taking an oath? What's with your hands?" Christine chuckled rushing back inside the ladies' room followed by Kim. "We'll catch you later Viktor."

Viktor's day had just begun, though a bit differently, he knew there were loads of financial statements to review and settle. But right now, he had to get into a conference call with his team back in India, an extended group that came under his company's shared service model.

Viktor's phone kept interrupting his intense discussions with the team, and agitated, he put it on silent without giving it a second look and continued working.

It was indeed a long day; the hours were packed with meetings with auditors, which made him have his dinner at work. Finally he wrapped up and made it home.

Tired and weary, he pulled out his office access card and started searching the frisk point to get inside home. Smiling at his folly, he quickly took out the key, opened the door and threw his laptop on the sofa.

Heading towards the washroom got him cautious. He looked for a sign to check if it's indeed the men's room and then rolled his eyes in contempt. Looking into the mirror, he raised his hands saying, "Sorry". He smiled again, this time at his own light attempt at mimicking Kim.

He smiled and put his hands under the tap, waiting to wash his face. For a second there he didn't realize that he was at home, there was no sensor system, and he had to twist the nozzle to get the water flowing.

The carelessness frustrated him; he just wanted to wash his face and in that attempt perhaps get rid of all those layers that had made him lose himself.

He came back to bed but only after getting his suit for the next day ready. As he picked up a pillow, he found a sticky note under the cover. He crushed it and threw it on his study table before retiring.

The morning began with the same rock song. Again, without bothering to turn off the alarm, he dragged himself to the bathroom, expecting it to be yet another boring morning.

Without a doubt, this time he was dejected with the Tuesday blues. While getting ready he noticed the sticky note lying on floor that he had thrown on the table last night.

He picked that up and opened. It read, "Birthday-Mom".

Wondering how he could have forgotten his mom's birthday, he checked his mobile and found multiple snoozed alarms, thirteen missed calls from his mother's number, and numerous messages from his cousins.

He quickly called back to greet his mom, but a few rings later he realized, back in Delhi, it was 11.00 p.m. and way past her bed time.

He grew restless, frustrated with himself. For a moment he forgot he had to get ready for office. He remembered putting away a photo with his parents on his study table. And right now, he wanted to see it.

His desk was cluttered with coffee mugs, sheets of paper, charging wires, and books that he had bought or borrowed but never found the time to read.

One by one he cleared everything off the table. When he found the photo frame, it was lying face down in the corner behind the table lamp. He picked it up and smiled, slowly wiping the dust off the glass with his fingers.

The photo was taken at a surprise party that he and his father had once planned for his mother's birthday. On the wall behind them was a collage that his friends had helped him make.

Maa to Maa hai...

Door ho tum... jo ghar se apne...
To sochte hoge... office mein baithe...
Maa kaisi hogi?
Ghar pe hai, to theek hi hogi.
Kaam mein doobe, tum sochte hoge...
Maa jaagti hogi... ya soti hogi?
Maa to maa hai...
Jaag hi rahi hai... soi nai...
Shayad roti hogi.
Sochti hogi tum aaoge...
Dhoondhti hogi kaunsi raah se...
Tum door ho na... samjhoge kaise?
Darti hai vo... khali ghar ke kone se...
Jhule ke khali hone se...
Mausam ke badalne se.
Tumhare ghar se chalne se.
Poochhti hai fir kab aaoge... bata dena...
Saansein thodi hain... hak apna jata dena.
Ik baar to din mein baat kiya kar...
Neend achhee aati hai... teri awaz sunkar.
Teri hasi, teri khushi ke vaaste...
Kare sab kurbaan vo tujhpe.
Duaayen deti hogi;
Maa to maa hai... roti hogi...
Fir chup chaap soti hogi.

∞

A tear rolled down his cheek and fell on the photo. He touched the glass and let himself cry, a sense of loneliness and guilt taking over.

He remembered the words of his father who had passed away three years ago, *"Be a master of your dreams, not the slave of your sorrows."* After his father's death, his mother decided to return to India. Her words echoed before she flew back to India for good.

"Your dad always dreamt of opening a school for underprivileged children back home in Delhi," she said. "I have to make that happen; that's the sole purpose of my life now."

"But Mumma, why do you want to go there and face problems?"

She smiled replying, "I was facing problems when I shifted from India to US with your father and I complained to him about this. He said, *Facing problems? Good. That's cocoon stage. It makes the wings stronger, you know."*

After that, nothing he ever said could make her reconsider staying in the US with him.

Suddenly, his cell phone beeped. He quickly reached for it, hoping to see a message from home.

He was disappointed to find that it was only Christine's text. "Are you on leave today? I heard your boss making some spiteful remarks about you."

"Will be there in an hour," he typed and started getting ready.

∞

Heavy traffic clogged the roads of Delhi, India. Viktor was in the office cab, determined to isolate himself from the world outside with his head tilted back, eyes closed, and earphones secure.

A grinding machine seemed equally determined to disturb his peace, incessantly making sharp noises that managed to distort the loud music he was trying to enjoy.

Growing more and more irritable, he pulled out his earphones and opened his eyes. He noticed a young boy, probably a locksmith mending a key with his filer.

Viktor's cab was moving slowly, which allowed him to study the young locksmith and notice how engrossed he was in his work.

The boy seemed truly interested in what he was doing. Dressed in rags, the young boy looked so content working, oblivious to the noises behind him.

Viktor was surprised, he couldn't help wonder how the boy could ignore the endless cacophony of the city.

Suddenly the boy looked up and saw him watching. He offered a smile, and Viktor smiled back. The boy quickly grabbed a packet lying on his table and ran towards the cab.

Still smiling, he stood by Viktor's window, quietly presenting a packed set of two pens. Realizing that the boy was trying to sell the pens to him, Viktor shook his head, refusing his offer.

But the boy refused to leave just yet, raising his merchandise against the glass, his eyes imploring. Viktor put a hand on his chest apologising and finally looked away.

Disappointed, the boy took his packet and began to leave. From the corner of his eye, Viktor thought, he saw the boy heave a sigh of resignation. He rolled down his window and called out. "Hey! Hey kid! Chhotu! Wait!"

The boy didn't turn his head. "Oye ladke!" Viktor called out again, pulling out a hundred rupee note from his pocket. But the boy still didn't turn.

A passerby tapped the boy's shoulder and pointed towards Viktor. The boy looked back quickly. Seeing Viktor holding the money in his hand, he beamed, came back running, gave the package to Viktor, and took the hundred rupee note.

The boy started digging through his pockets, and the disappointed look returned to his face as he failed to find what he was searching for. Defeated, he reached out his hand as if to return Viktor's money.

Viktor said raised his eyebrows asking what was wrong.

The boy opened his mouth and let out a groan, shrugging and moving his hands in the air, then finally turning his pockets inside out to let Viktor understand that he didn't have any change.

It then dawned on him that the boy was deaf-mute. He gestured for Viktor to return the pen set, handing him back his money.

When Viktor took the hundred rupee note from his hand, the boy gave him a faint smile and shrugged, as if to say, "Maybe another day!" But Viktor saw the disappointment in his eyes.

He raised a hand, asking the boy to wait, pulling out his wallet, Viktor handed him a five hundred rupee note. The boy looked at Viktor, eyes wide with mild exasperation, and again turned his pockets inside out.

Viktor nodded his head and put a hand over his heart, telling him, "I liked your work."

The boy stood there, stunned. The traffic finally moved, and as Viktor's cab began to drive away, he smiled at the boy and waved goodbye. In the rear-view mirror he caught a final glimpse of the boy standing frozen by the side of the road, staring at the note in his hands.

Viktor sighed, sliding the pen-set into his laptop bag without checking its contents. He rested his head, returning to his thoughts.

"Show me," a voice said from the back seat. It was a colleague from his office who was also in his cab rostered for Viktor.

Viktor spent the entire ride so lost in his thoughts that he hadn't noticed someone else was in the cab with him. He handed over the pen-set.

"That boy wasn't mute, Viktor," his colleague said, peeling off the polythene cover. "They pretend to have disabilities to fool people into letting them keep the change." He burst out laughing, "Nice label."

"No, I know when I'm being fooled," Viktor said, smiling. He took the box, wanting to know what was so funny about the label. His smile faded as he saw the words written in gold:

"Writer's Dream."

A blaring horn woke Viktor up. He realized that they had almost reached office. The dream about his office life back in India a few years ago compared with his office in US was almost the same, except the fact that he was earning in dollars.

Gentle Reminder

Smile please

Viktor immersed himself among the scattered files on his table, numerous tabs in his desktop's internet browser and pending deliveries while the forgotten remains of his personal life remained unattended.

Christine and Kim passed across his desk and exchanged pleasantries, but his unwavering devotion to his work was not affected even once.

It was evening when Christine reached at his desk at last. "Where are you lost these days, Viktor?" she said snapping her fingers in front of his eyes.

"Sorry?" he looked at her startled by the sudden gesture, "Oh, hi Christine! Bit busy with work," he said taking his glasses off and rubbing his eyes.

"I was messaging you on the system. I think you didn't check messenger."

Viktor quickly scrolled through the numerous windows on his system to check messenger, but couldn't find it. Christine leaned on his table, took the mouse and clicked on it, "See! Coffee! Coffee! And Coffee!" she said clicking on the desktop screen with her finger.

"Well, I would love to join you but...." he said rubbing his forehead. "Come on! Since morning you are occupied in these spread sheets and you don't even bother to reply to my Hi."

"Hey Christie!" said Kim approaching them, "Three-thirty! Let's go for coffee and come back quickly. I have to leave early today. Hi Viktor!" she said enthusiastically.

"Hi....amm," he raised his hand in air to return the wish but failed to recall her name.

"Kimberly!" replied Christine staring him in anger and then turned to Kim, "Let's go."

"Oh, yeah! Sorry, hi Kim!" he said smiling and trying hard to undo the damage.

"Never mind, we are going to Circle Café. You wanna join?"

"Yeah but..." he uttered hesitatingly.

"Nope!" said Christine standing up. "He is busy."

"Oh come on! Look at yourself Viktor," said Kim. "Get a break and some smiles too."

"Ohkay!" he said sighing.

"Ahem!" Christine smirked. "Even I had invited you a while ago but you had refused. Point to be noted." She winked at Kim.

"Noted!" Kim smiled back and they left for Circle Café.

They ordered a hot cappuccino and settled in the cosy chairs of the roof top café, enjoying the cloudy weather and the soothing cool breeze.

"I come here often whenever I need a break," said Christine.

"Whenever I need a break, I go to office," said Kim. Christine gave her a high five laughing, but Viktor looked at her as if he didn't understand what she had said.

"So what are the plans for weekend?" she asked Christine.

"Laundry and grocery," said Christine with a sad face.

"Saturday office," said Viktor, checking his appointments in his mobile.

"And Sunday?" asked Christine. Viktor was blank. He shrugged. "No plans," and resumed browsing through mails in his indispensable device.

"Viktor!" said Kim.

Viktor turned his neck towards her while his eyes still somehow focussed on the mail he was typing.

Giving no response till the minute he was done with his mail, he finally asked her after typing the last word, "Yup! Tell me."

Both the women were staring at him with rage-laced eyes. Realising his mistake of earning their well-deserved wrath, he put his mobile in his pocket, "Sorry! That was an urgent one."

"Here is a mail from me too," said Kim.

"Sorry?" Viktor raised his eyebrows without looking at her.

"*Vik!*" she emphasised.

He quickly looked as he heard his nickname.

Kim looked straight into his eyes and said, "*Gentle reminder! Smile please.*"

Viktor looked at her in surprise at the unexpected comment. Christine again started laughing. He turned his neck towards her, and then back to Kim. She smiled back.

That was the magical moment when he felt a strange connection with Kim. He could not help but realize that she had struck a chord in his heart because it was not every day that he felt the deep pang of emotion that paralyzed his senses. The eye contact between the two had said it all.

∞

Coffee Song

Coffee... Coffee pe hum dono jab they mile;
Coffee... brown sugar vo tere hothon se;

Cup cake ke saath... sip sip karke;
Aakhon se fisal... dil mein utarke.
Chhoti chhoti yaadein... hazelnut si;
Jo tune... di thi humein.

Coffee... Brownie jaisi lage ye smile tumhari
Coffee... Butter scotch se mithi baatein pyaari pyaari
Vanilla si... awesome simple style,
Choco pie se deep aankhen tumhari...
Black forest se bhi zyada dark
Julfein mathe pe latakti pade dil pe bhari!

Coffee... heart shape ki cookie jo hai rakhi...
Coffee... dil ka mere haal ye byaan hai karti...
Machine bhi dekho... sneeze kar rahi hai...
Usko lagta hai love ki steam chadh rahi hai...
Bhaiya ji, vo kahe, no ice-cream...
AC mein baith ke meri kulfi jam rahi hai!

Coffee... Agli baar milne ka promise abhi karo...
Coffee... Office office ki baton ko zara door rakho...
Tumse milke... acha lagta hai...
Saara din ek dum mast nikalta hai...
Coffee... coffee... kya ye jaadoo karti hai...
Jo bhi hai... cheez ultimate badi hai!

∞

"O Hello!" said Christine, but they were still lost.

The tower clock ticked 5.00 p.m. with a bang and they flew back from their imaginary world, getting cautious of the reality surrounding them.

The half an hour that he spent in the company of those two lovely ladies had such a tremendous impact on his overall demeanour that his morose expressions broke into smiling curves and relaxed his tensed facial muscles multiple times.

As they reached their office premises they strolled back to their respective departments. While the ladies left at 6.00 p.m. in the evening, Viktor was still drowned in his sea of work.

The clock ticked 9.00 p.m. and Viktor was still busy with work. He grabbed a burger at 10.00 from a nearby café and glued himself back to his computer.

After a video call with his team back in India, he reached home at 1.00 a.m. and dozed off immediately after reaching his humble abode that resembled a shanty.

Late night work had become a norm that he never forgot to not follow. The next day he reached home at his usual time but pleasantly was welcomed by a friend request from Kim.

He smiled and could not resist accepting immediately. Though she was online, he did not chat with her.

Kim was awake and she checked her mobile as she got the notification that he had accepted her friend request. But she too didn't reply.

Third day too, at office, he sought apologies for not being able to join them for coffee. Kim and Christine left for the cafe but Kim looked back at him as she neared the exit gate.

He opened the door of his house and smirked to see the hands of his wall clock strike 1 at night. He prepped his bed and lay flat on his cot, struggling hard to sleep a wink, but there was something in his mind that was keeping him from giving in to slumber.

Suddenly the image of his last dinner with his parents flashed in his mind, "Soon I'll go to India and have my dream school project completed," said his father holding Viktor's mother's hand.

Viktor, aged 16 that time, was busy with his phone, playing Ninja fight.

He looked at Viktor and said, "Viktor! You also *Follow the dreams that your heart visualizes, as what you actually see is just an illusion of temporary contentment.*"

Though Viktor heard what his father said, but he didn't bother to reply, except nodding his head.

The happy moments faded to the memories full of sorrows the next day itself when his father had a severe heart attack.

When Viktor and his mother went to ICU after surgery, his father seemed to have burdens of regrets. Even after getting shifted to general ward the next day, his father shared remorse with his mother for not fulfilling his dreams for so long.

That night, his world shattered the moment his father passed away. Since that day, he concentrated on his education and then job. After that, he never looked back.

But today he was not aware what he was running for. The purpose of his restless life was unclear to him.

His mobile blinked. He pulled his handset to check for the notifications.

"Hw R U?" It was Kim on chat.

He paused for a while and put the phone down quickly.

Another message blinked, "There?"

He was wishing to talk to someone, but was not sure if he should reply to her. The next moment, he quickly picked up the phone and typed, "Good, tanxo. U?"

"Gud. Saw U still online," she wrote. "Unusual 4 U, so thought 2 chk if U R fine."

He went to the terrace and called her, "It's unusual for you actually, not me."

"Was doing some college project work for my sister but what happened to your voice? You are sounding low."

Viktor shared what exactly he was going through. Kim tried to console him, empathizing with his state of mind.

"I have no time for myself or my family," he said. "Everything I hoped for as a student... it's all gone. I can't even remember the last time I went home before midnight. All I have is my office schedule and my arrogant boss."

He heard Kim sigh on the other end of the line. "But that's the culture, Viktor. You know that."

"It's not even just about work anymore, Kim. I am not happy, about anything. I've never risked anything or taken any chance about pursuing my dreams. All I worry about is making ends meet, and how much I'd lose if I fail. I've been spending so much time worrying about the future that I don't even know what I'm working for anymore."

"I understand, Vik," she replied. "You know I do. We're all just money-minting machines here, nothing but an asset for the company. And even then, we're all expendable to them.

Viktor was quiet for some time. "Hey," Kim said, "Why don't you write down your feelings? It might help you feel better."

"Maybe."

Kim continued, "You know those motivational articles you e-mail us sometimes? Do you know that lots of people in the office actually look forward to receiving them?"

"Including you?"

"Especially me! You write really well, Viktor. Do more of it. It's never too late to start."

"Hmm."

"Decide. What do you want? Life full of years or years full of life. Now."

He felt his tears coming back and looked towards the sky in hopes of holding them. He noticed something. "Wow."

"What happened?"

"You are right." He nodded. "There is only one star in the sky."

"What are you talking about?"

"Is this a sign?" he wondered out loud.

"What sign?" Kim asked, sounding very confused.

"You said I should write, and that exact moment I noticed this lone star in the sky." Viktor smiled, trying to explain.

"Yes! You should definitely write."

"You know, we often get so confused, burying ourselves in office work. We don't notice the universe creating such a beautiful view right outside our windows."

Kim was silent on the other end, listening as he continued sharing his epiphany.

"We earn money, but that isn't real happiness. I thought these things would make me happy, but I ended up missing phone calls, birthdays, family functions. I actually missed *life*."

He heard the smile in Kim's voice. "You should probably get some sleep, Viktor."

He went back to his room, but couldn't sleep. He tossed and turned, holding his pillow tight.

He tried to go back to sleep, but his mind refused to stay still, returning to the image of that lone star he had seen. Was it really a sign, or was it a mere coincidence?

"I'll figure it out soon enough," he thought to himself. He rested his eyes on his cluttered desk across the room, and studied the contents of all the junk that he had allowed to accumulate over the years.

"*Live life full-time, work just part-time.*" Viktor carefully inscribed the lines on a sticky note and smugly pasted it on his wall before sleeping peacefully after a really long time.

You are Born

The day you find yourself

The next morning seemed a little different to Viktor. After his conversation with Kim last night, he had understood that he needed to take charge of his life and steer it the way he actually wanted.

He got up with his old rocking guitar tune and again put his alarm on snooze for ten minutes like his customary practise. He went to work on time with life showing up on his face.

He worked enthusiastically, meeting all his deadlines and attended late-night video calls with offshore team, just going through the motions.

He couldn't meet Kim or Christine that day but he felt a strange zany energy that he didn't feel the need for any breaks. He had already made up his mind to find out exactly what he wanted to do with his life.

Whether he was meant to find it or create it, fight it or make peace with it, he was finally prepared to deal with his destiny once and for all.

That day onwards he began the habit of keeping a journal on his computer so that he could practice his writing while exploring his ideas.

"Sometimes," he said to Kim and Christine when they both were sitting at Circle café, "*Life is like a vacuum cleaner. You know what it does. All you need to do is to kick the power plug and take the charge.*"

The hands of the tower clock struck 5.00 p.m. "Wow! What timing?" Christine was amazed, "Where did you copy it from?"

"You wrote this?" asked Kim.

Viktor nodded with an affirmative smile. Christine was surprised, "This is a surprise! You know him so well...ahem."

She started teasing Kim by kneading her shoulders.

Viktor was occupied with his train of thoughts even while sipping coffee. Vaguely staring at the tower clock, he mumbled, "I am living a dumb life devoid of any substantial passion or goal. I exhaust my life to earn money and then invest my wealth to have a semblance of a life." Christine and Kim were silent, enjoying the setting sun but alongside Kim was noticing the pool of thoughts going on in Viktor's mind. She didn't want to disturb him, so she kept Christine busy in talks about people roaming on amphitheatre near the clock tower.

He reached home by midnight and settled to jot down his ideas. As he saw Kim online, he pinged her.

"U wr lost in ur thots," she said.

"Oh! U noticd?"

Next moment Kim called him up asking, "Tell me! What were you thinking?"

"Nothing as such."

"You can share if you think you should."

"Actually," he said with a sigh, "I am stuck in this facile cycle; I have no space left for myself, or my family and friends. I have no time for finding the purpose of my life."

"So search it, research it."

"But certain limitations, boundaries, responsibilities," he cribbed.

"You won't know your limitations until you soar high and give it a try," said Kim.

"Wow! I am impressed," smirked Viktor.

"There is only one way to live your dreams... and only one person can lead you there... you."

"Goodness! You are so good at words."

"I love reading quotes, that's why I feel connected to you."

"Means?" he chuckled.

"I mean I feel connected to quotes you send daily in office in spite of your busy schedules. That's passion, Vik. Don't let it die."

"Hmm," he nodded. "I feel determined to change everything that led to hollowness in my life. I will make up for the lost time."

∞

Next morning, while walking back to office, Viktor's gait and determined composure revealed his ambition to change his destiny.

He wrote a long list for his plan of action and penned down his hobbies and interests, making several additions to the record every single day and including even the tiniest of his longings.

He started bringing more order to his life, keeping his calendar organized and often sending notes to himself to keep track of his ideas.

He began calling his mother every morning while on his way to work. With his schedule being choc a bloc with appointments, he started managing his time more wisely, avoiding avoidable social networking activities on the internet.

"I want to make a collection of quotes," he said to Kim over the call at night.

"How will that help? And why would people buy it?"

"I'll do it differently. I mean old wine in new bottles, like writing quotes in a beautiful way in a pocket-sized book."

"Doing differently what's already done is old and boring. Do something new, that's yet to be done," she said.

"That's a good idea, let me sleep over it."

He started working on how to change his fate, connecting the dots of his destiny. Now that he had the chance to explore his options, he began a mental list of things he was passionate about or interested in – music, writing, sculpting, photography, swimming, salsa dancing, etc.

He realized he had a myriad of things that he had always wished to do but never had the courage to try. Now the possibilities were endless.

Viktor's office was going on as usual, but his days used to always end with a discussion with Kim over call. She guided him which hobby to pursue first.

"I want to make my hobby my profession," he said to Kim.

"But you can't leave your job."

"You know, *happiness is doing something you love and loving something you do.*"

"Great!"

"Yup! So now I have started loving my office work and doing alongside the things I love."

"That's the spirit, and innovate something new. I know you can."

"They say," Viktor said, *"Tough is to innovate; else you are just competing with photocopy machines."*

"Exactly, don't be a photocopy machine. *Be different...be yourself.* You are different from crowd, Viktor. Not everyone realises that he or she is becoming part of a silly, boring and dull life where nothing is new, where people don't realise that *joy is temporary, happiness is permanent; for it comes out from positive a mind and is an art of a tension free heart.*"

Viktor was taken by her words, "I am speechless Kim." He had tears in his eyes and Kim sensed that.

"Hey, Vik!" she consoled, realising that he was silent and sobbing. "I am sorry if I said something wrong that hurt you."

"You said something right," he said wiping his tears, "and *right is right, no matter how wrong the time is.*"

"Right time will come buddy," she said lovingly.

"Yup, I will make it happen."

"Good! Hope you are fine now."

"Ha ha! No I am going to jump from the roof." He chuckled.

"Silly you. Get back to bed and doze off. You have to go early tomorrow. It's BD 5 tomorrow (Business day). Your closing day."

"Hmm! Good night."

"Good night."

"Hey listen!"

"Yup."

"Thanks," he whispered.

"Thanks for?"

"Making me feel light," he whispered again.

"Hah! Now go and sleep tight," she also whispered.

"I'll try. Good night."

Viktor came back to his bed, thinking, smiling, and looking at his study table that was full of unwanted papers. Despite that, his vision of a clean desk was clear to him.

Pankh Parinde

Pankh Parinde... ke na they jo! Khwaab udaane... oonchi dekhe!
Gir gir sambhle chalne-pe bhi jo!! Maksad bana jis... use kaise paale!!

Teri koshish hi taleem barabar! Na rakh sirhaane darr ke bahaane!
Zindagi kya kyun dikhlaaye!! Jeene ka sabab... kaise aur kab!!

Kaun hai tu... bhool ja ye! Kis rukh samay ruk paayega!
Jis din uda tu us lamhe... soch zara Duniya to kya!
Aasmaan bhi jhuk jaayega!!

∞

Another month passed. He was getting even busier at work, but with his new take on life, everything became easier to tackle and Viktor was brimming with new-found enthusiasm.

At the onset, Viktor found it increasingly difficult to deal with the anxieties that his workplace posed in front of him. It had become a norm for him to burn the midnight oil in his professional settings, but be rewarded with darkness in his personal life.

He had sunk deeper into the mire of work pressure, immersing himself in the world of debits and credits. The deep furrows on his forehead and dark pits below his eyes made him look like a stereotype browbeaten specimen of the corporate jungle.

He often had dreams where he saw himself wallowing in the fields of his motherland, but woke up to his maternal-care-deprived abode.

Near his bed post Viktor had treasured a photograph taken years ago that depicted his family, hale and hearty, smiles on their faces, being the perfect picture of happiness on a holiday trip.

Viktor was just a kid then, but his bright eyes still sparkled with the same innocence that defined his personality now. Thought his pristine face was wrought with some wrinkles brought about by work pressure and stress, he was never distraught with grief. But of late, something within Viktor had changed for the better and it divulged itself from all his facets.

When asked about work, he would find himself responding with more zeal than usual. But even as he began to find more appreciation for the most tedious tasks, in his heart of hearts he knew that he had to find his fulfilment elsewhere.

"May your profit and loss account of humane deeds be in profits; for you have to present your Balance Sheet on the Judgment Day." He posted a random thought on his public profile from his mobile app as he got up and went for a shower.

As he came back, he found an orange flickering light on his cell phone and took it up casually to check out notifications. A beam of smile spread across his face when he saw the welcome notice of 300 likes on his post and a few comments.

"Awesome one," Kim had commented and he liked her comment along with liking others'.

That day onwards, every time he was on the way to office, he started surfing the web rather than listening to music or taking a power nap.

He was often asked to report to work on weekends, but one Saturday evening he was fortunate enough to make it home before midnight. He took advantage of this rare luxury by spending some time surfing the web before going to bed.

He logged into his online profile to check notifications and status updates from his real and virtual friends.

"Happy Teachers' Day!" one notification read.

He smiled, remembering his former English teacher, Mrs Elissa, who would later have a defining role to play in his life.

She was unlike the other teachers Viktor had the opportunity to be a pupil to during his school days. She was a woman in her late forties who always wore a charming smile on her face and greeted her students just the way the mother of a soldier receives her son on homecoming.

A nun from a Catholic church, Mrs Elissa was a profound believer in righteousness and propagated the message to her students. The greatest capacity of a teacher is reflected in the way he or she imparts the most complex of matters in the simplest of ways and Mrs Elissa was one such veteran. She not only instilled in children knowledge that mattered, but also them inspired with thoughts that fuelled their ambitions.

She held an iconic importance for Viktor who trusted her as an inspiring figure. He reflected on the time he spent with Mrs Elissa, intently listening to her philosophical take on life that he grasped and related to instantly.

If it were not for her, Viktor would have never become a successful person. She was more than a teacher to him; she was like a messiah who showed him the path to individual fulfilment.

Next day, on the way to Circle Café, he shared his memories of Mrs Elissa in intense vivacity with Kim and Christine.

"Give her a call," Kim suggested instantly.

Viktor replied otherwise with a nod, "I always want to talk to her, but I fear my unexpected call might disturb her."

"Why?" asked Christine.

"She used to say I am so innovative and creative. She would not be happy to see me doing a back office job leaving all my dreams behind."

"Vik," said Kim stopping there while Christine kept on walking while talking to someone on her phone.

Viktor stopped and looked back at Kim.

She said, *"May you live long, but, for a second, suppose it's your last day on earth. Have you done all you wanted to do, you always dreamt of? If the answer is NO, your time starts NOW."*

He kept looking into her eyes. The time in the tower clock gonged 5.00 p.m.

"This is the time Viktor!" she said, "Call her up *now!* She would be happy to talk to you."

He was still in doubts.

"A leader is not born; Teachers make the one," she said. "Do it now. Come on."

After this profound encouragement, he dialled Mrs Elissa's number and waited eagerly for her to pick up simultaneously mumbling, "If she would be able to remember me at all."

"Hello! Could I talk to Mrs Elissa?"

"Hello, yes! Who else would speak on an old woman's phone!" she said wittily.

"Hi Mrs Elissa!"

"Hi! Who am I talking to?"

"Guess!"

"Well, my son, it's tough for me to guess at this age."

"Ok! I'll give you a hint!"

"One second, Chalksmith?" she said.

"My goodness! Mrs. Elissa! Your memory is awesome."

"Oh! Viktor, my son! It's only you who can do this guessing trick on call. You used to steal the imported coloured chalks from my desk, right? How can I forget you?"

"Oh yeah! And you used to ask me, 'Do you smuggle chalks?' Ha ha... funny were those days."

Kim was happy to see extreme happiness on his face.

"Yes my son! Funny indeed! And you used to ask for more chalk saying 'I need to write quotes and messages on black boards.' Isn't it ? And I named you Chalksmith."

"Oh, you remember that too?"

"Yes my son! I do, and in fact, I always thought that you'll be a writer someday."

"You don't know how much it means to me, ma'am."

"Yes boy! I always told you, that whatever you want to be, be the one others can look up to. But, it's true that I always wanted to see your name as the writer on the cover of a book that I would buy someday." A faint smile broke out on Viktor's face.

"So," she asked, "Mr. CA, do you still get time beyond your balance sheets to pay heed to your beautiful ideas?"

"Oh, that was just a hobby ma'am," he said, humbled by her regard.

"Cultivate your hobbies as your profession, my boy."

"Yeah! Maths was my hobby in school and you guided me to be a CA. The day I failed in my favourite subject MICS (Management Information and Control System), you made me realise my dreams and priorities. Thereafter I never looked back. Five years now and today again I need your advice."

"Son!" she said taking her spectacles off, "You know I am always there to guide and show you the right path. Your call is a pleasant surprise. But I hope everything is going well at the family and health front."

Suddenly moved to tell her about his latest undertaking, he added, "Yes ma'am, matters are great, although these days I've been considering my life a bit more seriously. God knows how hard I've tried to find my passion in the corporate world; unfortunately this company simply doesn't love me back!"

While on the call with Mrs Elissa, Viktor didn't realise that he was walking down from the Café towards the amphitheatre. Kim was waving to him from the terrace of the café.

She chuckled. "Well, I am certainly glad to hear that you have been constantly challenging yourself even when you achieve something, but consider writing again. *Bless you for you never stopped learning.*"

"Of course." He smiled. *"The day I stop learning would be the day I stop growing."*

"Now why does that sound familiar?" He could hear the smile in her voice. "I always suspected you might eventually end up as a writer. I would be happy to see this hobby of yours turn into a book someday."

Viktor felt a chill run down his spine. Was this that one big moment, like the Big Bang, he had been waiting for? A confirmation from the cosmos itself that he was on the right track?

He remembered the time when he was awarded a trophy by Mrs Elissa for his contribution to a writing competition held annually at his old school. But today there was no one to cheer him up. He felt alone as he stood in the vacant ampitheatre.

"Hey Viktor!" yelled Kim from the terrace.

He felt someone waving at him, encouraging him, though she was just indicating that coffee was ready.

He came back to the terrace and settled with Kim.

"You seem to be very happy and relaxed, right?" she asked. Viktor nodded. They had coffee in silence as Viktor was in an ecstatic trance to speak anything.

In the late hours at office, as Viktor sat at his desk, he felt overwhelmed by Mrs Elissa's words of encouragement and kept thinking about their conversation.

As he came back home at night, wishing to somehow re-live his glorious school days, he started searching for his old trophy.

He checked his drawers, finding nothing but dusty sheets of paper and old office supplies.

"How the hell did I get so much junk?" he muttered to himself. He started pulling out all things from his drawer.

As he placed the pile of papers from the drawer on his desk, a black box fell on the floor.

The box aroused in him a sense of familiarity and as he bent down to pick it up, he recognised the words embossed on its surface. It was the same box that he had bought from the boy he had encountered in India.

The words glinted in the yellow light from the table lamp, appearing as if they were written in gold, "Writer's Dream".

Viktor's eyes glittered; he quickly ran and looked at the sky outside his window. He was growing tired of waiting for signs. He simply had no way of determining what the universe intended for him. Only he could decide for himself.

"Had I ever dreamt of becoming an author?" he asked looking at his reflection in the window pane. Then, looking towards the street and without anything to lose, he decided, "If I hear a car honking, then this is the moment I was always looking for."

A few minutes passed, and he heard nothing. It was the middle of the night after all. He returned to his desk.

"What am I doing in my life?" he murmured. "I can't let chance decide my future and probabilities shape my destiny. I shouldn't rely on happening or non-happening of events. I need to rely on my instincts; I must have faith in myself."

He switched off the light, leaving his desk and drawers, past and present cluttered in the darkness of his room.

In his mind he painted the images of his destiny, the path that he would follow for the rest of his life.

∞

"And the winner is…." a voice in the background announced. A young man walked towards the stage. With every step he grew older, and when he finally reached the platform he was a thirty-year-old man. The hall filled with applause.

As he proudly took his next step, a sharp honk threw him off balance and he fell off the stage.

The blaring horn of a passing truck woke Viktor from his dream. He felt for his phone in the dark and quickly texted Kim.

"Av u evr thot if I wntd 2 b an author?" He wrote and desperately started waiting for her reply.

About 5 minutes passed, then 10 turned to 30 but no reply came from her. At last he dozed off while staring at his screen for the coveted reply.

∞

"Vik!" said Kim while Viktor was pulling the skin of his nails. "Your life definitely has a purpose." They were sitting at the café circle.

The clock struck 5.

"In fact, everyone's life has a purpose, and I've always believed that the day you find it, that's when you become the real you. After that, everything else in the universe will appear secondary to that purpose," she kept saying.

Viktor pondered on her inspiring words.

"You know," she continued, "*Your date of birth is just the time you begin to exist, and life only truly begins the day you realize what you're here for.*"

She ended her sentence but Viktor was still lost in thoughts, taking time to absorb the wisdom in her words.

"Wow, when did I get so philosophical?" Kim joked, breaking the silence.

Viktor was still silent, designing something on newspaper.

"Show me," she said pulling the paper towards her, "Wow! It's shadow writing! It's your name! Right?"

"Nope!" he shook his head. "My signature!" And they started laughing.

Viktor chuckled, "What you said actually makes a lot of sense, though."

"It's something my parents used to tell me when I was younger," she smiled.

"That's an interesting thought! Then I should probably meet them someday," Viktor quipped. "Get myself some sage advice."

Kim suddenly became silent.

Viktor noticed her fading smile and added, "I am sorry if I asked something wrong. I mean…"

"I lost my mother when I was ten years old. She had cancer." Kim said grimly, trying to overcome the tears in her eyes.

"Oh! I could not be sorrier, Kim. I honestly didn't know."

An awkward silence hung in the air for another moment, before Kim retorted, "Dad couldn't bear it, and he took to alcohol. He began drinking to cope with the grief of mum's death, giving in to sorrow and doing away with his health. His liver stopped functioning after a while and one day as I returned from school, I found his corpse on the floor."

Viktor didn't find appropriate words to console her, but he held her hand tightly and tried to comfort her spirit.

"Since then, I've been living with my aunt and uncle."

"I understand how difficult it must be for you to deal with everything!" he said looking straight into her eyes.

"Anyway!" Kim resumed her preaching mode, "I see you at work every single day, watching you guide the team like a real leader. But I didn't realize how strong you really were."

He found himself saying. "You've been through so much, and yet here you are now, a self-made person."

"Well, if there's anything I've learned, it's that sometimes you have no other option except to be strong," Kim said.

"Strongest is," he replied, *not the one hard at heart, but the one tough at heart, to endure the hardest situations of life."* "But once in a while," she sighed, "I still ask myself why all these things had to happen to me...if any of it was my fault somehow. I mean, I couldn't have done anything about my mom's illness, but I could have helped my dad survive after her death. Instead, I let him succumb to his sadness, and I still hate myself for it sometimes."

"But you were just a kid," Viktor pointed out. "You were grieving too. While you had to take care of your father, you also had to take care of yourself."

"You know," he added, "I learned a while back that there's nothing wrong with prioritizing your needs sometimes. *You have to love yourself first, because only then will you be able to love everyone else.*"

"Oh, so we're talking about love now?" she said, laughing.

Viktor couldn't help joining her mood and letting out a big laugh .

"Hey!" she asked, "By the way, are you engaged with someone?"

"I was," he answered. "But she married a rich guy. All I know about him is he was getting thrice the salary I received."

"Oh! Practical girl!"

"Yeah, most girls are." He sighed. "How about you, got a boyfriend?"

"Oh, you mean that rich guy I dated a couple of years ago?" she joked. "I'm pretty sure he's the same guy your ex ended up with." They burst into guffaws of laughter.

Kim asked him about his education and his family back home. She hadn't spent as much time in India as he had and she was curious to know more about the mother country.

Their talks continued for another hour and it seemed they lost track of time discussing their hobbies and passions, likes and dislikes and everything that mattered.

The sun was beginning to set by the time they were done with coffee, but the talks were on. While on the way back to office, it seemed they were about to begin the journey they were destined to.

That night Viktor wrote another page in his mobile diary before he dozed off. *"You are born the day you find yourself."*

∞

The next day on the way to the office, Viktor had a different view about life. He seemed to have found the first step towards discovering his true purpose.

In fact, he felt as though he was finding himself, something no one else could have done for him. He had to do it himself.

"You can only get guidance from others, but they can't make everything happen for you," he thought.

He felt reborn. The purpose of his life appeared clearer to him. He had found himself. He had found a dream.

When he reached his workplace, he rushed for a video conference, the first task for his day. Though he tried his best to remain attentive, in the back of his mind he was busy making other plans: "How do I start writing?"

After the meeting got over, he caught up with Kim at the usual Circle Café, excited to share what he had felt the night before.

"I guess I should write more, something that makes connections," said Viktor, designing something on the news paper.

She showed genuine appreciation for his realisations and newfound enthusiasm, "I'll help you in any way I could."

As Viktor was done she pulled the paper from him, "Show me" and read, "Writers' Dream?"

He nodded closing his eyes. She smiled, "Bingo!"

When he reached home that evening, he searched online for some tips on how to start writing or how to fulfil your dreams. He wanted to make his dreams come true rather than wait for luck to hand it to him.

He was still busy doing research on his computer when the system shut down unexpectedly.

He had learnt a long time ago that every event, whether good or bad, had the potential of teaching an important lesson, only that he didn't have the means to learn from this particular disaster without access to the internet.

He called up a friend, a IT engineer. After hearing the problem, he told him that all he needed to do was to "defrag the system."

"Explain like I'm five," said Viktor.

"When there is too much clutter in the hard disk memory," he explained, "Your system gets confused. You need to arrange it to allow the system to jump through the files easily rather than having to go through a junkyard."

"Well, this condition resembles the status of my life," Viktor thought, bemused at the explanation.

That evening, Kim joined him once again for coffee. Viktor told her about his computer in need of a defragmentation process.

"My sister Amber is an IT champ," she said.

"Sister?"

"Cousin," she smiled. "I told you I am staying with my aunt and uncle."

"Oh! Sorry! Yup, you told."

"I call them Mom and Dad."

"Oh! That's nice."

"Yup! They are. Anyhow, Amber is busy with her finals right now, but I could ask her to have a look at your computer. Hold on, let me give her a call."

Grateful, Viktor waited as Kim called up her cousin on her mobile.

When she hung up, she said, "Would you mind joining us for dinner sometime? She said it's the only time she's available. But she'll set your system right, and by the time it's finished we'll be done with dinner."

Viktor considered the offer. "I'm a little busy arranging some stuff at home these days, but I have to send e-mails over the weekend. I really need get my computer fixed soon."

"No problem. Then we'll catch you for lunch at your place this weekend?" she said, smiling. "Amber can repair your system during that time."

"The plan couldn't be better!"

On his way home that day, Viktor considered the need to defrag his mind. He wanted to rid his brain of all the trivial issues that were of no consequential value.

He wanted to clear his thoughts so that he could arrange his writing plans and organise his daily life.

By 1.00 p.m. that weekend, Kim and Amber were at his doorstep. As Amber taught him how to set the system on defrag mode, Kim started setting the table for their celebrated lunch.

While they enjoyed their food, Viktor shared the thesis he was developing, that in order to start afresh, one's mind-set had to be free of tension, just like the raw mind of a child.

"Defragging means only defragging," Amber said suddenly. "No processing."

Viktor and Kim gave each other a grave look shrugging their shoulders, unsure of what she meant.

"Never mind, I should have known I am dealing with technically handicapped people. Let's eat, we will discuss this later," Amber quipped in her usual sarcastic way.

"Okay, granny," Kim chuckled, winking at Viktor. "And you," she added, punching Viktor's arm playfully, "She is my sweetheart, so don't you dare tease her, got it?"

"No way, I've got too much to lose. My precious computer is at stake," Viktor quipped. "Besides, I think I'll be learning a lot from you, Amber. You, miss, are going to teach me how to be a kid all over again." Kim and Amber laughed.

Even when they were done with lunch, their talks continued for an hour where they discussed their plans, laughed along, and meanwhile Viktor's laptop was ready to rock again. In the meanwhile, Kim and Viktor started arranging the cupboard.

"Aw! So this is the one that you wrote on newspaper that day we met," asked Kim holding the pen case that read 'Writer's Dream'."

Viktor nodded and told them the story how he had got it.

"Amazing!" Kim was amused, "So this is your starting inspiration, right?"

"Yup!" Viktor chuckled and looked at Amber. "Granny! Do you think I can be an author."

"*It's your life, paint it the way you want,*" she replied coldly.

Kim looked at her being a bit rude, but Viktor indicated with his eyes that it was fine.

"Hey! You play guitar too?" asked Kim as she saw guitar lying in a corner.

"Sort of," he giggled. "I can entertain just myself. It's a great stress buster for me."

"Show me," said Amber and Kim gave that to her.

Amber tried like a kid and played the strings one by one.

"Happy birth day tune?" asked Kim, "Awesome."

"I learnt it in school."

"You played it for me?" Viktor said with a smirk. "Thank you."

"Is it your birth day?" asked Amber.

He looked at Kim, "*You are born the day…*"

Kim smiled replying, "*…the day you find yourself.*"

Viktor smiled nodding, "I found myself recently."

"Crazy," added Amber making faces. "Where were you lost if you recently found yourself?"

"Amber!" said Kim with a serious note, "You are helping him, but it doesn't mean…"

"Shh!" Viktor interrupted, indicating with his eyes for Kim to be quiet. "Amber! I recently learnt how to paint my life the way I want."

Amber looked at him with a serious look and said, "That sounds good."

Viktor smiled as if he noted something in Amber's behaviour and said, "*Your are the best at life and shine when you just be* yourself. *Let nobody tell you that you are not capable of doing what you believe in.*"

Amber looked away as if she was avoiding him.

In the evening, he dropped them back home and collected clothes from laundry on the way back.

That night before sleeping, Viktor looked at the pen case for a while and thought of beginning the plans of his learning process. He wanted to forget all the unnecessary things that he had stored in his mind. His worries were occupying a lot of space.

Suddenly he had an epiphany that perhaps meditation is the thing that could come to his rescue and help him defrag his mind.

He looked for ways to reflect on his intentions and instantly grabbed his laptop and created a new document. He let his mind wander, looking for the right words. He saw his guitar lying in the corner, and he imagined the fret board as a musical staff, with notes running along the strings.

"*Life is like playing a guitar,*" he wrote, "*and meditation is like music. Daily rehearsal sessions won't show much at first, but you're sure to rock in the long run.*"

∞

Viktor spent the next week learning many meditation techniques, incorporating these new habits into his lifestyle. He continued searching for a technique that would help him pursue his goal with a full passion and without any fear, just like a child.

"*To grow up, be a kid again,*" he wrote in his wall post at his public profile and left for office.

Over lunch, he met Kim.

"Amber is done with her exams," she told him. "She expects me to take her out for a picnic. Do you know any place we could try?"

"Try Jurassic Inn," he said quickly. "It's amazing."

"Why don't you join us?" she asked, "Amber would love it."

"I don't know," Viktor said. "I've got a lot of things to do. Organising my place, sorting through all the drawers, cleaning out my closet… I'm defragging, you know." He winked.

She rolled her eyes. "But that's so easy. We'll help you. Got another excuse?"

He pretended to groan. "Alright! It serves no purpose to argue with a girl! Even worse with a pretty one, I'll be your tour guide."

"You know," Viktor added, "I think we have met before, same time, same place."

"What?" Kim was surprised.

"Déjà-Vu, I am having that feeling now."

"Oh! You know I used to think I am the only one who grapples with this feeling, but I learnt about it in my psychology syllabus.

"No!" Viktor nodded, "It's magic, some hidden power giving indications."

Kim's smile faded away seeing Viktor's serious expressions. They were looking into each other's eyes.

"It was destined to happen," Viktor whispered.

She rolled her eyes to his eyes and face, getting nervous, as if Viktor would bend forward and kiss her.

"We are destined," he added. Kim was entirely lost in him.

"We are destined to eat Hakka noodles," he completed.

Kim was surprised again and he burst into laughter, "I was joking, order some Chinese please. I am bad at reading menu cards and I am famished."

Kim was still looking at him, unable to take her eyes off his charming visage. She ordered Chinese food and was amused during dinner to see Viktor happy.

∞

In accordance with the plan, the trio met during the weekend at Jurassic Inn and regaled themselves with no limits. They went on all the rides they came across, and Viktor took the opportunity to try everything he never got to do as a kid.

"You know kids play with toys in their childhood," Viktor said as they settled on a Toy Train. "I enjoyed my childhood by making my toys first and then playing with them."

Soon enough he found himself forgetting his stressful life, all the regrets of the past and the worries of the future. For the first time in a very long while, he found himself actually having fun.

He grabbed his cell, clicked a funny selfie with them and posted on his wall as, "Let the pain of past not ruin the happiness of present and dreams of future. Move on."

Amber, in spite of having a serious disposition, enjoyed Viktor's company. He made her enjoy most of the rides she liked.

"Let's try this one," yelled Viktor, pulling Amber towards the roller coaster.

"Nah, Kim's afraid of roller coasters."

Viktor looked at Kim and put his hands on her shoulders with pretentious gravity to calm her down. "*If you think you can, then you should. And if you think you can't, then you definitely should,*" he said glibly.

"Fine!" she yielded, crossing her arms. "I accept your dare, but you have to fight with us in paint ball, got it?" She winked at Amber who jumped in joy, "I love paints."

Viktor looked at her, analysing, connecting her previous conversation at home and got to know something about Amber's liking.

Both the girls walked briskly towards the queue leading to the roller coaster ride followed by Viktor.

"Wow, who would have guessed," Amber said wryly.

When everyone was settled and buckled up their safety belts, the ride finally started. The roller coaster slowly began to climb up a slope.

Viktor looked at Amber, who was thoroughly enjoying herself, but she pointed towards Kim who had her eyes shut tight in fear. She was paralyzed with apprehensions and didn't open her eyes in spite of repeated requests by Viktor and Amber.

"Hey, that's not fair!" Viktor yelled, laughing. "Open your eyes! The world looks beautiful from up here!"

She shook her head vigorously, tightening her grip on the safety bar.

"Just try it," Viktor pushed. "Believe me, you won't regret it."

"Noooooo!"

"Trust me! I am with you."

She relaxed her tight shut eyelids. Finally, she managed to open one eye. She caught a glimpse of the setting sun, burning red-orange in the horizon.

She smiled and opened other eye, "Wow!"

Viktor was pleased to see her smile.

"We're about to fall!" Amber yelled gleefully.

Kim made the mistake of looking down and immediately began to panic. "No! No! Stop! Stop! I'm too young to die!" She started squirming in her seat like a kid, her knuckles white from grasping the safety bar.

Viktor relished the sight of sweat on Kim's forehead and broke into peels of laughter. "Kim!" he said. "No one's dying, calm down!"

She shook her head, keeping her eyes shut.

"Hey, it's okay," he assured her more gently. "Look at me."

She shook her head again.

"Look into my eyes," he insisted.

Finally, she looked at him. Viktor wasn't wearing his eyeglasses as was advised by the ride operator, and he did his best to maintain his focus while the roller coaster sped through the track.

"What do you see?" he asked.

"Kohl!" she exclaimed, and started laughing. "Do you really use Kohl? Look, Amber, he uses Kohl!" Amber turned to look at him and started laughing as well.

Viktor groaned. "I've been hearing that from everyone since childhood. My eyes are naturally like this, alright? I don't use eyeliner!"

"Oh, really, Mr. Royal-eyed King?" giggled Amber.

"Indo-Viktor-ian King," added Kim. The girls pretended to bow, still laughing. Viktor shook his head in amusement.

"See, the world looks amazing from here," said Viktor as they reached the top of a steep slope. Kim's eyes widened as she saw the sun about to hide behind the seas, and the people and vehicles below them looking like tiny ants.

"And you're not scared anymore," he said to Kim.

"Let's just say that I'm beginning to see the appeal," Kim said, glancing at him. They looked into each other's eyes. "Thanks, Viktor."

The roller coaster finally took its dive from the top of the hill. Kim started screaming while Viktor and Amber waved their hands in the air, hooting and laughing. Eventually, Kim let go of the safety bar and joined in, yelling and enjoying the ride.

As the ride was over, Kim came out yelling, "Yess! I did it. Yess! See! Amber! I am not afraid of anything."

"Thanks to Viktor," she replied.

"Yess! Where is Viktor?" she turned back. "Oh Viktor! Thanks a ton," she said and hugged him tightly. He was standing with open hands looking at Amber.

"You can hug her back," said Amber. "I am not watching. You can even kiss her. Who cares."

"Silly," said Kim getting back ad thumping her head. Viktor stood there with open hands.

"Release your hands and take us to paintball," said Amber.

As they entered the Paint ball area, it was marked by paint splattered over huge dummy walls that were designed for cover during the game.

The moment they put on their paint suits, they did not stop a second before attacking one another with the paint gun that plastered the walls in multiple hues.

Suddenly Amber backed off from firing at her worthy opponents and instead went to the wall opposite her that resembled an artist's palette with a motley of colours.

She observed the mute wall for a few seconds before using her hands to smear them in defined movements. Using several strokes of her fingers, she used the paint to create magic.

Kim and Viktor were busy drenching each other with colours before Viktor found Amber near the wall and indicated Kim to look her way.

What they saw mesmerized them completely, for it was a painting of a heart shaped rising sun, spreading its rays piercing the clouds and lighting up the door of a hut.

The creativity and the blend of hues were so ingenious and original that they could not believe that the quirky Amber was behind that amazing creation.

Everyone around them began applauding the painting and cheered Amber for her genius art. She looked at Kim and Viktor, with tears in her eyes and came back to them running and hugged them tightly.

Viktor hugged her tightly and said looking at Kim, "I was right. Now I understand why she said *Paint your life the way you want.*"

At dinner table in the food court of Jurassic Inn, Viktor nodded, "So! Lady Amber wants to be a painter. Hmm!"

He looked at Kim who indicated him to keep quiet. Amber was silent but she looked at Viktor furiously.

"*Gentle reminder, Smile please,*" he said.

"Very funny!" replied Amber.

"Oh! Amber in Anger," he added. Amber couldn't contain her wrath, and Kim put a finger on her lips indicating Viktor to keep quiet.

"*True happiness is...,*" Viktor added, "*...when you find all dark coloured socks in a pack of 5.*" Viktor completed, looking at them, but they didn't laugh.

Amber whispered in annoyance, "Pathetic joke!"

"At least it was a joke," Viktor said and burst in a huge laugh by tossing on his side, unaware that a waiter carrying wine was coming along the way. He hit the waiter accidentally which made him to tumble down the wine flask that went straight on Viktor's head. The red liquid spilled over his head and Viktor was drenched in it.

The sight of wine dripping from Viktor's hair to the forehead was so funny that the girls roared in laughter, falling on their sides while Viktor sat in embarrassing quietness.

After the dinner, as Viktor was on the way to drop them home, Kim and Amber craved for sweet seeing an ice cream parlour. Unable to resist her whims, Viktor got them two ice-creams each.

Viktor told Kim about his parents and their dream to start up a school in India while Amber was busy sitting on the bumper of the car, enjoying her favourite white mischief ice creams in both her hands.

"I want to do important things while I am still strong and healthy, while I'm still alive," said Viktor. "I loved my dad a lot.

He always inspired me to live my dreams, but he never could. I don't want to bury my life at the office and regret not having time for my family, seeing my dreams die slowly."

"Amen," said Kim and gave him a warm hug. "You still have plenty of time to do plenty of wonderful things."

Viktor closed his eyes, finding comfort in her embrace.

"You got me to face my fears today, convincing me to ride that god-awful roller coaster," Kim said, pulling away. "Granted, it's not that big a deal because I totally handled it like a pro, where any brave guy would pee in his pants."

He laughed uncontrollably.

"But what I'm really trying to say is that you got me to do it. So I know that you can get yourself to do it, too. And then later on, once you've reached your goal, you'll do the same for so many others. Like you tried to do for Amber too, right?"

"You know in India, it's auspicious to donate mustard oil on Saturdays as that's Lord *Shani's* day," said Viktor.

"Ohkhay!" said Amber giving her ice-cream to Amber and getting ready to listen carefully as she was interested in Indian culture a lot.

"During the days I was preparing for CA exams in India," he continued, "Mumma used to come to my study table every Saturday with a bowl full of mustard oil. She would place it in front of my face and ask me, 'Can you see your face in the oil?' I had to say yes, else she won't go. Then she would ask me to dip my fingers in the bowl. I would put my left hand in, the right one being busy solving questions and sometimes intentionally. She used to thump my head saying, 'Dip the right hand,' and then she used to donate that oil to the pundits who go door to door for collecting oil. She would ask them for blessings for me. She never asked anything for herself."

He looked at Kim, "Opening a school is the sole dream of my mom now, and I am unable to make it happen for her."

Kim put her hand on his shoulder, "The day will come."

Viktor couldn't help but get a little teary-eyed by Kim's sudden earnestness, and he pulled her back into a hug.

"That means a lot to me, Kim," he whispered.

For a minute they just stood there, in a tight but soothing embrace.

Amber let out an exaggerated cough. "Hi, just wanted to remind everyone that I'm still here, but I can take a taxi home."

Laughing apologetically, they finally let go. They sat there for another half an hour enjoying the calmness of the night.

Viktor dropped them home. Her parents saw them from the window.

As he was about to go, Amber said, "Vik!"

He stopped and looked back. Amber went to him and hugged him tightly. "Thank you. I know that you now know that I know how to paint."

Viktor laughed, "You know, I knew ever since the moment I started knowing you."

"Good one," she said. "But don't talk about it with me anymore." she said with serious expressions. "Bye."

Viktor just nodded.

She turned back and Viktor said goodbye to Kim too.

Amber again turned back to him, "Don't even think about it, especially in front of mom and dad."

"I knew it," smirked Viktor.

As Viktor left and Amber went inside the house with Kim, their parents asked, "You guys should have dropped a text."

"I sent it to mom," said Amber. "Check her cell."

"Is he Viktor?" their father asked Kim.

"Yes dad. He is my colleague," she replied.

"And he is very good dad," yelled Amber, ascending the stairs.

"Make sure you guys are safe when out," said their mother.

"He is a gentleman mom," Amber yelled from her room upstairs.

"Good night mom." Kim kissed them. "Goodnight dad." And she went upstairs.

Their parents could hear the girls giggling and fighting upstairs.

Viktor came home and landed straight on his bed. He felt a strange amusement and there was music in his heart, for his entire body sang in happiness.

He looked at his photo lying beside his bed. He felt like he had become the Viktor in the photograph; the Viktor who always knew how to see the best in things and find something funny to laugh about. He was a kid again and his mind defragged.

Every Vision...

...has its own rainbow

It was business as usual in office. As always, work had Viktor tied up again. But now he had learnt to find time to do the usual with a twist, to work on the same old things in new ways. He was far more focused and found time in his busy schedule to work on his dreams too.

It began with simple tasks, simple yet effective. He switched off his computer and set out for a fifteen minute stroll into the human world, away from the hi-tech gadgetry.

He was generally accompanied by Kim and Christine. There, in the open air away from their computers and out of their cubicles, they felt better connected.

Perhaps this was evident for all to see. Soon other colleagues followed them. Many began to take a walk into the park or at least get off their seats, away from computers for a while, or go for a post-lunch walk to find a better connect with other colleagues from different teams.

The connections between Viktor and Kim grew naturally, with effortless conversations.

"It's Amber's birthday this Sunday," said Kim as the three were out for their walk after lunch.

"Wow! Great!" Viktor stopped. "Where are you taking her to celebrate?"

"No, it's a House party, and you both are invited," she replied.

"Awesome, that sounds like fun!" Christine replied quickly.

"Amm!" Viktor contemplated. He opened his mobile and said, "Let me check my calendar."

"Cool!" Kim interrupted, "Thanks for ensuring that you would join!" she quipped.

"But…" Viktor looked at Christine in disbelief.

"Get a good gift, all right?" Kim continued.

"But…" Viktor hesitated

"Ok, then. I'll let you know the timings," Kim said, as if to conclude.

Viktor looked at her and just smiled. Kim too beamed a smile right back at him.

The next two days Viktor and Kim stayed busy at work, unable to catch up in their strolls. However, on Saturday, Kim called Viktor and Christine and made sure to confirm the timings for Amber's party.

∞

"Happyyy Birthday to youuu… Happy Birthdayyy too you… happy birthday dear Ammberrrrrr…!!" The chorus was accompanied by applause as Amber blew off the candles.

No sooner she blew "Whoop!" Amber was surprised as candles sparkled back to life and were alit again. She gave Viktor a knowing glance; it had to be him, as he had bought these magic candles to tease her, she thought.

She blew off once more, but 'whoop' the candles got alit again. Sensing play, Viktor joined her to blow the candles off.

Kim and Amber's parents took the cue and joined in to blow the candles too. Whoop, whoop oopsss...

Amber at last managed to cut the cake and went around offering everyone. The celebration jingles continued to grow louder and louder, they sure were not stopping soon.

When it was Viktor's turn to taste and toast the cake, Amber offered a bite and he decently pecked a bite, "Ummm yummy, these decoration on cake are awesome and the colour combination is just out of the world," commented Viktor.

"It looks like a painting. Where did you guys order this from?" he enquired.

Kim smilingly said, "Amber did it herself."

"No ways! Is it?" Viktor said knowingly. He held Amber's hand and said, "Gosh! You are amazing at colours. Why don't you try your hand at painting?" and he looked at her parents.

Kim's smile turned into a serious look. Amber looked at him, then at her parents, and said, "I have to be an engineer, not a painter."

Viktor sensed something not right and to avoid any serious situation further, he took the rest of the cake piece from Amber's hand and playfully offered her a bite too.

The moment Amber stepped ahead to take a bite, Viktor held her head and smeared the cake on her nose followed by her full face, taunting her, "Birthdays are not supposed to be such proper affairs, my dear."

Soon the party was crackling again. All the family members were laughing while her friends well behaved until then, joined the fun. Kim too got into the cake sledging act and grabbed a big piece of the cake to join Viktor in smearing it on Amber.

Amber was a funny sight, coated in the colourful delicious cake. As she stood wiping the cake off her eyes and hair, Viktor and Kim kissed her. Christine was busy clicking photos, and then everyone followed the same like a tradition.

Amber looked at Viktor in anger while Viktor and others couldn't help laughing.

"Guys!" said Amber, "Either you bear my anger or hold him tight."

Viktor was shocked as all her friends jumped on Viktor in a blink. Amber came pouncing on him and smeared the rest of the cake on his face and head. Kim was busy recording the whole scene in glee.

Viktor got up searching for tissue papers. Christine offered him the tissue box. As he headed towards her, she threw it towards Amber. Amber grabbed the box and ran to her parents who joined in the fun. They seemed to like Viktor, as he had changed the mood of the party in a blink.

"Aw! My baby!" said Amber pulling Viktor's cheeks, "Looking *cho chweet*!"

"Vik!" calls Amber's Mother, "From your face, it seems it's your birthday."

He smiled as he heard the nickname being adapted in Kim's family.

"Actually," agreed Kim aiming for a close up shot of his face now.

Post clean-up routines, every one settled down with conversations and soon guests began to leave. Christine and Amber's other friends also took leave, whereas Amber's parents invited Viktor to stay back for dinner.

Viktor agreed and to occupy himself better, he took Kim and Amber to a nearby mall for bowling and shopping.

"How is this one?" asked Viktor pointing towards an easel in the showroom. "I want something for my nephew, he is really good at painting."

"Not good!" replied Amber, "This one has no space for putting paint tray and brushes. Take this one." She pointed at another one placed at a distance from them.

"Which nephew?" blurted Kim confused.

"*Chintu*, you know," Viktor replied, winking at her.

"I want to gift these four colours too," he said picking up the oil paint tubes and showing them to Amber. "Good contrast, right?" he asked.

She curved her lips upside down and replaced two of the tubes with other ones, "This is the best contrast ever."

"Wow!" said Viktor holding the tubes up high, "Good colour sense."

Amber smiled feeling contended and got busy checking other canvases and colours. Viktor asked the store helpers to gift-wrap the things he had bought.

At home, celebrations continued at dinner time and everyone had a good time. Amber and Kim sensed that their parents seemed to like Viktor and his sense of humour.

Viktor and Amber were fighting like kids over dinner table. Kim took note of this changed behaviour in Viktor towards life. She was happy and smiling to herself, seeing him enjoy the moments.

"*To grow up, be a kid again,*" once she had told Viktor and he seemed to be following that now.

Viktor left for his and on the way back, he felt a sense of completeness.

He switched on the voice recorder on his mobile and said, "*If you want to fly, you need to grow up; to grow up, you need to be a kid again. To be a kid again, you have to just be yourself; so come out of your cosy comfort zone, yell out and break the boundaries you are stuck in... then only you can fly.*"

The next day at work, Viktor and Kim were having coffee at his office.

"Mom and Dad didn't like that you gifted her painting accessories," said Kim.

"I knew it. That's why I had asked you to slip them into her room without telling anyone else about it," said Viktor.

"But you don't know...Amber was crying, you made her cry." said Kim.

Viktor was stunned. "But I thought she likes painting, and she is great at it."

"Yeah! I know, but they want her to be an engineer; and she has accepted it now."

"But why?"

"Oh let it be, it's an unending debate... let's talk about something else. What's up on your dreams front?"

"Ohkhay, I have this new idea. I am thinking I should start writing on something."

"Something like?" said Kim.

"A story!" he said pouring sugar into the coffee. "A novel may be!" He put another packet of sugar into the coffee. "Or a saga!" He poured the third one too, "Whatever you call it."

"Sweet!" she noted grinning.

"Thanks."

"No! Silly, you eat so much sugar."

"We are Punjabis,' he winked.

"So let me tell in your language Mr. Punjabi; more the sweet, better is the taste. Then all you need is to read a few novels, create the story by adding bits and pieces from each of these and voila!!! Your novel is ready."

"Being a copy cat is not my cuppa-coffee," Viktor remarked.

"But copying is tough, you know," she pressed.

"No! *Tough is to innovate. Else you are just competing with photocopy machines.*" Viktor said firmly.

"Copy the structure," she winked.

"*Every vision has its own rainbow,*" Viktor replied, a little lost, as he grabbed a cookie.

But Kim had a sparkle in her eyes. Excited she added, "See! I was just searching within you. Actually you know everything, but you are not implementing it."

Viktor looked at Kim.

She continued, "*The day you realise your vision, you'll see your rainbow.*"

"But it's complex." he added.

"*Complex means simply difficult, not impossible,*" Kim replied.

Viktor turned his head down, agreeing.

"That's like Viktor; Viktor the thinker," she winked.

Back home that night, Viktor began his exploration, he began exploring a thought process to get into action.

The very next day onwards, he jotted down a list of interesting things he could write about; anything that caught his attention, any idea he was interested in exploring, just about anything he felt like and Kim helped him with suggestions.

∞

The process eventually turned into a month-long research work, and when he was done, they both set some time away from their busy office schedules to meet and discuss the dream project regularly.

Every brief free time was invested into this dream project. Evening coffees at office soon extended to discussions over lunches; weekday lunches grew into weekend evenings.

On Saturdays, Amber too accompanied Kim as her bodyguard and soon they ended up in suppers and ice-cream parties... and discussions grew on...

∞

"I have a problem," said Viktor to Kim over a call at night.

"Cool!" she replied smiling, "*Got a problem? Good that you know you have one. Otherwise people either don't know that they have one or they don't accept the fact that they have any.*"

"Ha ha! Mine is serious." he said.

"Thinking to wax your chest?" she quipped.

"God! Ha ha! No! Actually I've started talking to myself," he confessed.

"I think that's perfectly fine," Kim replied. "*Thinking in loneliness and speaking in public are the two things leaders are masters at.*"

"Is it? Is it healthy?" he was surprised.

"I do think it is. I mean, *no one else can understand you better than you yourself, right?*"

He smiled knowingly, because he sure knew she was right.

The conversations seemed to seamlessly connect themselves around them, all the time.

"But it's strange," he said as they were strolling in the park. "I'd look at the ceiling and talk to myself out loud even while I am working," he laughed.

Kim chuckled. "There's nothing wrong with that! Look, I studied psychology, and I know for a fact that what you are experiencing is perfectly fine. Unless you're beginning to see things as well, like the rainbow-coloured elephants!! Are you seeing rainbow-coloured elephants?" asked Kim mockingly.

Viktor laughed, "Heck no!"

"Then you're fine," Kim mused as they sat sharing a cup of coffee at Café Circle the next day. "Besides, this way you'll be able to guide your subconscious into focusing on the things you want to pursue," she added.

Viktor was lost in thought.... as "Bang, Bang, Bang, Bang, Bang!!!" the tower clock clanked 5.00 p.m.

∞

The next weekend Viktor organised all his drawers. He arranged his books and glued his special black box to his desk. "Writer's Dream", the label read. He thought it was a nice reminder.

He thought to connect with his old friends.

"Hello! Could I talk to Rahul please?" said Viktor dialling up his chuddy-buddy.

"Rahul speaking. Who is this?"

"This is *Akash* from SCT bank and we…"

"*Kamine* (Rascal)! You…" said Rahul interrupting, "Try these tricks on your other a** friends, not me, ok."

"Oh!" Viktor was surprised, "You got me."

"*Saale Laddu! B*******, k******, b*******, ch****… Aa gayi yaad dost ki?*" Rahul was fuming out.

"Sorry *yaar!* I was badly stuck up."

"*Kamine*…you rascal! Stuck up for five years, hmm? Richa is angrier than me. You didn't even come to our marriage? You'll be killed the day you meet us."

"Sorry yaar! Things happened so quickly. I was after something I now realise, would get me nowhere."

"It's ok! Sala emotional blackmailer. Are you in India?" Rahul was a bit relaxed.

"Nope! Would meet you the day I come."

"Hmm! And, how is life there? Get married soon bro and join the gang of married people like me."

"Why are you after my happiness? Let me enjoy some more years of bachelorhood."

"Enjoy my boy, enjoy. I'll ask your mom to get you married to a *dehati* (village) girl. Saale NRI."

"Ha ha, yup. Mom suggested many, but I never followed up. Anyhow, how is Rix baby?"

"Richa is more dangerous than before. But getting married to your best buddy gives you the liberty of expressing yourself. Else you think ten times before even farting in bed. Ha ha ha."

"Ha ha ha. You and your *desi* fundas. Come to US some time."

"Will come some day; the president has asked me many times to meet his daughter."

"Ha ha! You are the same as before," smirked Viktor.

"But you have changed," replied Rahul. His tone was more serious than Viktor could ever imagine him capable of. "You know you used to call me Rahu (planet)."

"Hmm!" Viktor's voice changed, "and you called me Vikku the moment you got that it's me on call. Life has changed many things."

"Vikku, you only used to write on the blackboard," said Rahul, "*Work is just a part of our life, not vice versa, so live life full time, work-work, part time.*"

"I know."

"And you only wrote, *if life gives you nuts, then be a nut cracker.*"

"I know."

"What I know?" Rahul blasted. "Actually you don't know, had you known you would have implemented."

"I know."

"Sala! Again I know."

Viktor sighed, "I am trying to know it."

"There is only one funda to know life, and no one knows it," added Rahul quickly.

"That I didn't know," smirked Viktor.

"That's my original quote, you rascal," Rahul giggled. "Don't dare to copy it."

"Ha ha, I will."

"Go to hell!"

"Just reached."

"Oh yeah! I think you have reached office. Ok then, see ya, it's dinner time. Rix is not home, I have to cook. Bye."

"See ya *Rahu!* Catch you once I am there. Take care, Bye. Good night."

That day onwards, he connected with his other friends as well to know their whereabouts. Well aware that some were married and some had settled in different cities in India, he still was amazed to see how life had changed this past decade.

∞

Dosti ke pal

Dosti... ke pal... gajab sab yaar...
Yaaron... ke sang... jab hon har baar...

Dosti... ke pal... yaad aate hain...
Tanha se baadal... baarish ban jaate hain...

Ab kahan hain... vo pagal lamhe...
Dabe puraane... sir phire vo kisse...
Dhoond rahe hain... Dil khol jinhein sab...
So gaye... kahin kho gaye... aa dhoondh lein chal...!!

Dosti ke pal... Vo desi jugaad...
First crush se dil tute to... emotional attyachaar!!!

Milo kabhi to... kuch share karo to...
Jaayen kabhi... fir us duniyaa mein...
Karo dobara... nukkar pe party...
Time nikaalo... wohi jhooth bolke...
Le aao... fir se waapis... apna dhundlata kal...!!

Dosti... ke pal... vo maar aur pyaar...
Yaadon... ko sambhaale... senti sab yaar...!!
Dosti... ke pal... gajab sab yaar...
Yaaron... ke sang... jab hon har baar...!!

∞

Another day, Viktor went to meet Amber's parents when she was out at college and Kim was on client site.

"I am sorry that I gifted her the painting stuff," he apologised to her parents.

"Her grandfather was a painter," said her father, "and I didn't see him ever make a living out of this."

"I believe she should not be stopped to pursue her hobby," pressed Viktor.

"There is no value addition from that," butted her mother, "and we want her to concentrate on her studies."

"And what if she scores a good grade in her exams?" Viktor insisted.

"Then she is free to do anything she wants," replied her father.

"But what's the point if she doesn't take engineering as her profession later but decides to become a painter?" Viktor enquired.

"Sense of security," added her mother coolly. "We are not against her wishes, but we want her to be self dependent and then she can do whatever she wants."

∞

Viktor met Kim and told her that he had started to write. It was a story of his childhood friends from school.

"How are you progressing?" Kim enquired.

"I am talking to them one on one to know how they progressed," replied Viktor.

"How many friends have you selected?' sought Kim.

"Ten."

"And how will your writing be unique from others?"

"The whole novel will be in dialogue form, like a movie script," he replied with a spark in his eyes.

"Sounds good!" Kim noted, "but will the audience like it?" she asked worriedly.

"That's just a fear of failure. I am ready for it," Viktor confided.

Kim smiled assuringly, for she was sure that Viktor was ready for pursuing his dreams now.

Viktor too had begun interviewing his friends. He pursued all aspects in his novel, beginning it right from the school days to college, then work life and progressing to first job and love life too.

Viktor had changed all his office, bank and other passwords to include the words "Writers Dream" so that he gets a reminder every time he logs in that there is another target of his life that he has to complete along with his professional responsibilities.

His days and months were slipping from the pages of his calendar quickly. Few instances narrated by his friends were taken directly as is in his novel, whereas for a few others, his imagination would connect the story back on a single track.

∞

Ten months had passed by, it was so quick, thought Viktor. He couldn't recollect how he had managed to cope with tight deadlines at office and still be his enthusiastic best to complete the novel at home. His first novel was nearing completion.

As usual, Viktor and Kim met after dinner with Amber in tow. Lost in their own world, with each other, they were lost to the world outside.

"The thing I couldn't do in five year of easy life, I did in the last ten months of a hell of a busy season," Viktor said to Kim with excitement.

"I am happy for you Viktor," she said.

"Happiness is?" he snapped fingers to which Kim just raised her shoulders.

"*Happiness is… when someone says I am happy for you,*" he replied and they laughed.

"I actually have found the purpose of my life," he said looking into her eyes, "Thanks to you."

She closed her eyes smiling.

"And thanks to Amber!" yelled Amber sitting in the car, enjoying her white mischief ice-cream.

They looked at her and laughed. Viktor recollected his toddling the first month of his realisation with tiny and tough steps. He knew without any doubt that Kim's care was always with him.

She noticed them for a while but she was getting impatient to go home now.

"Are you guys done kissing?" she yelled, "If not, then hurry up please, we are getting late."

"God!" Kim gushed, looking at her smilingly; trying to get angry but failing miserably. "I won't get you here the next time," she said.

"Go to hell baby!" replied Amber, "*Viks* will take me."

Kim got into the car and the two started soft kick boxing at each other.

Viktor dropped them home. Amber's parents saw them.

"I am happy," said their mother to father, "that they are with a trustworthy person."

Their father smiled, putting a hand on her shoulder, "You brought them up well to know whom to trust. Thanks to you." And he hugged her.

Bemused by the events, a contented Viktor traversed his own journey of warmth and discovery with Kim.

"Kim!" said Viktor as he was about to leave, "You have been a source of my motivation." And he kissed her.

"Oh God!" cribbed Amber, "Not again." As she went inside, she saw her parents hugging each other and she couldn't help saying, "God! You guys too! Huh. Good night." She smiled to herself fondly and left for her room upstairs.

As Kim entered, her father asked, "How is his novel going?"

Kim smiled. "Near completion."

"You guys thought about something?" asked her mother.

"He is a bit busy with finalising the novel," replied Kim. "After that, I guess."

"Great! Good night!"

"Good night Mamma," she said kissing her. "Good night Dada," she quickly gave a peck to her father too and went upstairs.

The old couple again heard them whispering and giggling.

"This guy has changed Amber, no?" said the father.

She nodded. "And Kim too."

Austerity...

if I were to define... It's YOU.

Viktor and Kim now found new excuses to spend more and more time together. They were accustomed to each other's presence and had grown comfortable in each other's company.

"Vik! let's go for a walk," Kim said as they finished up their lunch in office.

They strolled together, with their pinky finger entangled, something no longer unusual. But today Kim was being extraordinarily coy.

Viktor noticed her blushing. "Umm is something special today?" he asked

She nodded, "Let's walk a little more, a few more steps ahead and then I'll tell you."

A few more steps ahead, Kim stopped. She turned to him, stared deeply into his eyes.

"Whaaat?" Viktor asked.

She took a deep breath and whispered, "Do you remember this place?"

"Yup! We come here almost daily," he whispered back "What's so special about it?" he quizzed.

Kim did not answer, but kept walking. After a minute, she stopped.

"You remember this bench?" she asked again.

"Yeah!" he whispered grinning sheepishly. "It's Circle Café property."

"That tower clock?" Kim tried had to draw his attention to the memory with details.

"God! Yup! That's government property," he smirked.

"You remember this time of the evening then?" she went on.

"Are you all right?" asked Viktor suspiciously.

Kim only responded with more intensity. She leaned closer, held his hands tighter, still beaming, she explained, "One week from now, it'll be almost a year that we have been together."

"Oh… Ahem!" Viktor nodded in ignorance, but quickly added, "Oh Yeah! One year approx! Wow time has flown so fast, slipped like the sand… No?"

Kim blushed in acknowledgement, still beaming.

"But what does that have to do with this place?" Viktor asked with a straight face.

Kim, surprised by his nonchalance, opened her arms wide, "This is the same place where we met for the first time! Remember?"

"Oh… Okay, great!" Viktor paused, raising his eyebrows, still with a confused look on his face with regard to the connection drawn. "So?"

"Oh Vik!" exhaled Kim, held his hand and began, "I want to tell you…"

"Wait," he interrupted pulling his hand back and grabbing her by her shoulders instead, "I'm sorry. I didn't understand what you just said, but before you say anything else, I want to tell *you* something important."

Kim was taken aback by this sudden outburst; but she continued to smile and anticipated his next words, almost sure that Viktor was about to say the very same thing she was thinking.

"I..." Viktor began. Kim held her breath, her eyes glittering as she waited to finally hear those three words she had been dreaming of. She closed her eyes, blushing.

"I..." he cleared his throat, "I am going to Japan," he whispered.

"Hmm? " Kim's eyebrows curved, eyes still closed.

"I am going to Japan," he whispered again.

Kim opened her eyes. She stood still, wide-eyed. But her thoughts were on a spin. "Did I hear him correctly? Japan? Wasn't it another country?"

Viktor nodded, smiling in his head, "I am so happy; they chose me for this project."

Kim remained frozen in her place, crushed by the weight of what she had just heard.

"One year project!" he added enthusiastically.

Kim heard and her head said, "One year? 365 days?" She could feel herself getting lost and drifting farther and farther away from reality.

"Kim?" he said, jolting her out of her thoughts. "Where are you lost?"

"Amm! Sorry! Yeah!" she tried to gain composure.

"Did you hear what I just said?" asked Viktor.

"Yeah! It's... gooood... I mean... not good."

"What? Not good?"

"Amm... I mean... not just good, its best. Yeah... It's the best," she replied in a daze.

"Cool! Thanks. I knew you would say so," said Viktor happily. "Now your turn. Tell me what is it, that you were about to say?"

She tried to feign a smile, but couldn't. She just couldn't open her mouth. "Yeah. I was just that...umm...yeah...the same thing."

"You mean you already knew?" he held her hands in happiness.

"Yeah, I mean, I...I overheard someone talking about the Japan project, and they mentioned you, so...I...I thought to tell you in advance...b...but I guess you... you found out before me...yeah," rattled Kim.

"Oh Kim!" he smiled and hugged her tightly. "You can't believe how happy I am to get this project."

Kim tried to give him a smile, her eyes shut tight. She tried to hold back her tears and struggled to speak, "I am...just...so... so happy for you, Viktor," she managed.

Her hands were trembling. She tried desperately to control her emotions as she returned his embrace.

"Bang! Bang! Bang! Bang! Bang!" The tower clock struck 5.00 p.m. Kim looked at the clock and was startled in surprise to see it.

"This clock is awesome," Viktor commented. "Always chimes at the right time. It's time to go," he said, still holding her in his arms. "They are sending me this weekend, you know. I'm really excited."

Kim felt another jolt. It seemed as though every word he spoke had caused a heavy ache inside her chest. She couldn't quite grasp everything that was happening.

Her thoughts began to wander again. "How far was Japan from where they were standing? He was always absorbed in his work, what if he never made any friends? Who would invite him for coffee during breaks? Who would tell him to go home and get some rest? What if he got sick there?"

Viktor gave her another squeeze, "Thanks. This is why you're my best friend."

"Best friend?" she was stunned again.

"Yeah! But I need to stop hugging you because I still have lots of paperwork due today. I'll see you inside!"

With that, he let go of her and left.

Kim stared at the clock, her arms hanging limply at her sides. How apt, she thought. He had always been so reasonable. How very typical of him to choose, however obliviously, this very day, a week before, the exact time and place to leave her.

∞

For the next two days, they hardly saw each other, barely even had a word over the phone.

Kim tried calling him a couple of times, but got mere text replies from Viktor: "I am driving." "@ VISA office." "Video call with Japan Team." "In a meeting."

Kim was sure that things were going great for Viktor, but for her, everything was a disaster. Her world of hopes and expectations had come to a shattering end.

It was Sunday, the day Viktor was leaving, and it was almost time for him to leave for airport too. Viktor called Kim, hoping to ask her to accompany him to the airport, but she ignored his calls. He decided to go by her home with his luggage and hoped to say goodbye.

"I'm busy with some work," said Kim as an excuse from upstairs. She simply wasn't ready to see him go. Amber and her parents insisted, but Kim pretended to be busy arranging her books.

At last Amber went to her and pulled her arm, gently saying, "Come on. It's Viktor. Let's go."

"Last night, the office party was awesome," said Viktor as the three of them left for the airport together.

The air was thick with their silence. He looked at them, "Why are you guys sitting like frozen mummies? I am going to Japan, not Egypt. Ha ha ha." He laughed at his own jokes.

Yet no response. Only Viktor was laughing.

Viktor was the only one talking throughout the drive. He talked endlessly whereas Kim and Amber remained silent, kept on looking outside the window. He cracked bad jokes and desperately tried to make them laugh, but all in vain.

When they finally reached the airport, he quickly bid them farewell.

"Take care, Kim," he said. "You were a great support to me."

Kim seemed like a lifeless teddy, waiting for him to hug her but he was in a hurry, he didn't. Amber was holding her hand.

"You can cry if you want to," Viktor giggled, but no response on that from either. Kim was staring at him for his silly joke.

He tipped the driver to drop them back home. They climbed back inside the cab, watching Viktor as he walked towards the entrance.

Before entering the gate, Viktor looked back and waved. Kim held Amber's hand tightly, curled her lips inside, trying not to cry. Viktor was still waving standing between the automatic sensors of the doors. The security guard approached him, asking him to move either inside or outside the door.

Viktor was still looking at Kim. Amber waved and raised Kim's hand to wave at Viktor and ensure to him that she was happy. Kim closed the window of the car showing she didn't care, but she was still looking at him from behind the glass. "Please don't go! Please! Please!" she said, touching the glass with her fingers. "I need you Vik! Please come back!"

Viktor waved and moved in. She looked at the closed door.

In a blink the door opened, Viktor came back running, without his luggage, holding something in his hand, followed by a security guard.

Kim got down from the car, hoping that he would express something. He came to Kim and hugged her tight and she too held him so tight as if wanted him not to go.

He held her from the shoulders saying, "Don't miss me."

She was silent, just looking into his eyes.

He turned back. Kim was shocked again. He hadn't said anything she expected him to, so she decided to not let this chance go and say herself how much she loved him. She said raising her arm towards him, "Vik!" but her voice was so low, she couldn't speak properly.

Viktor again turned back, "One more thing," he said giving her the packing.

The security guy who was following Viktor came and asked, "You left your luggage there? What is this you are giving her?" he said pointing to the packet held in Viktor's hand.

"Sorry officer," said Viktor, "I'll take just two minutes." He said to Kim, "Open it."

Kim quickly opened and found a rose with a card.

Viktor came closer, held her face in his hands and kissed her head, "Happy Rose day! Give it to the one you love."

Kim was shocked, she stood frozen. Viktor hugged her without getting a hug back from her.

"Let's go officer," he said and followed him running.

Kim was still in shock. Amber got her in the car and closed the door.

Viktor went inside, this time without even waving at her.

She quickly opened the card to check if he had written something there, but nothing . There was a song with a message,

"Give it to the one you love." He hadn't even signed it, nor was addressed it to Kim.

"Vik! Please!" Kim broke down to tears, "Don't go!" she whispered at her loudest.

Amber held her from the shoulders and signaled the driver to start the car. She hugged Amber tightly, "I loved him, more than anything. I want him back."

"Shhh!" Amber wiped tears off her cheeks.

"He has no feelings for me. He says give this rose to the one you love. He just loves his work and dreams," she sobbed.

Amber rubbed her back. "Honey," she said softly, "He said he'll visit within six months. You'll see him again. Nothing's going to change." But she couldn't stop her from sobbing aloud.

"One sec," said Amber taking the card from her, "Let me check what he wrote."

The Rose Day

"Rose… if it is…
for the one whom you miss…
and you want to say a lot…
till now that you have not!

Then just go and dare to say…
for that moment is today…
beyond the earth and sky above…
Give it to the one whom you love!!

And sing your heart out…
to the universe aloud…

O girl, O girl, O... O... girl... you be mine...
You are more than this rose to me...
You be my... Valentine.
Just be mine... O O... Valentine!!!"

"Awesome," said Amber. "I didn't know he is so romantic."

Kim took the card from her, "He said give it to the one you love. It means he doesn't love me and neither expects the same from me." And before Amber could guess or stop her, she tore the card into pieces saying, "He didn't sign it, nor did he address it to me." She broke down into tears.

By the time they reached home, Kim's eyes were red. She went to her room, shirking eyes from her parents.

She spent that evening browsing through Viktor's old photos and videos and kept crying.

∞

"Kim! Dinner!" yelled Amber from downstairs. Kim opened her eyes. Though she was able to hear her sister clearly, she ignored the dinner call and shut her eyes again, trying harder to sleep.

"Kim!" she heard a voice, someone patting her head, "Kim! Get up!"

She opened the eyes half and saw someone patting her head, "Kimmmm! Gettttt upppp!"

The voice echoed in her ears. She tried to see and was stunned to see Viktor waking her up.

"Oh my God!" Kim jumped with joy on her bed, sitting down on her knees, "Vik! You!"

"Shh!" said Amber, "It's me...Amber!"

Kim snapped out of her illusions and her smile turned to curves on her eyebrows.

"What's wrong with you?" Amber asked caressing her eyes with her thumbs, "Look at your face, go wash your face and come down for dinner."

The silence at the dinner table was horribly unpleasant. Kim tried smiling to show that she was fine, but *mothers will be mothers*, and Kim and Amber's mother was virtually psychic. Their father had asked her to talk to Kim in private. She agreed that to be a good resolve and indicated to talk after dinner.

After dinner, Kim helped Amber and her mother to put plates back to the kitchen. Her mother held her hand and asked, "Let's go for a walk."

"Have faith in your love, honey," said her mom, while strolling in the park. She put a hand on her shoulder. "*Patience is the turpentine for the painting called love,* you know."

Kim tried to smile. She did her best to appear calm and nodded in appreciation at her mother's words of comfort, but she was too tired to have a long conversation and she burst out hugging her, "I loved him Mom. I want to spend my life with him."

They sat on the bench, and Kim put her head on her mom's shoulder. Amber and her father joined them after a while to add their strength and support to her.

Kim felt light in her heart, but she still was missing Viktor a lot. After this family gathering, she went straight to her room, locked the door and climbed into her bed, without asking Amber to sleep.

She must have been staring at the ceiling a while, when she heard a knock on her door.

"It's me," said Amber, her voice muffled. The doorknob rattled as she tried to open the door, but it was locked from the inside. "Are you okay?"

Kim ignored her.

Amber continued knocking, this time a little louder. "Kim?"

She sighed. "I am fine, Amber. Please go to sleep; you have office tomorrow."

"And is it you who'll go to my school?" Amber asked, laughing softly. "You are not fine baby. Open the door!"

Kim felt her eyes begin to water, "Everything was one-sided," she sobbed. "And I'm a big time fool for not realizing it sooner."

Amber tried to console her through the door and repeated her request to be let inside. When Kim still refused, she said, "Fine! I will sleep at your door if you don't open up."

Kim saw her cousin's shadow through the crack as she positioned herself on the floor.

She got up, opened the door, came back to her bed and sat there holding her pillow tightly.

"I knew you wouldn't let me inhale all that dust!" Amber said triumphantly.

Amber looked at her, then her Viktor's photo on her PC, and then looked back at her. Kim sat still for a while, staring at her. Amber reached out for her hand, pulled herself, and then pulled Kim into a tight hug.

She broke down. Amber consoled her and suggested she take a good night's rest. "Silly girl, you'll have to go to my school if you keep me awake like this," chided Amber. Kim smiled, wiping her nose, and promised to go to sleep soon.

"I'll sleep here today," she said pulling a pillow from her lap and laying it in her lap. They both lay down together and slept.

After an hour, their mother came up to check on her girls followed by their father. She covered them with blankets, ensuring they were warm for the night.

"I am proud of you," said their father to their mother "You kept them connected so well that Kim never feels the absence of her parents," he whispered.

She smiled hugging him in response and said, "But now she really needs Viktor, may be more than us."

Kim had her eyes closed but was listening to this conversation all along. A tear rolled down from her left eye, and her parents on their way out of the room didn't notice it. They had already turned their back to go out and closed the door.

Kim slowly opened her eyes; she looked at Amber fondly, got closer to her, gave her a kiss on her nose, wiped her own tears, and murmured, "I love you."

And she closed her eyes giving her a hug, trying to doze off, "And I love Viktor too," she whispered and lost herself in his memories.

∞

Teri Aashiqui

Ik nasha hai jo teri saason mein...
Ik sama vo jo teri baahon mein!
Ik choti si chahat tere liye...
Rahe mere paas tu umar bhar
Teri ashiqui... meri zindagi!
Teri ashiqui... meri zindagi!!

Ik tu... aur main bas koi aur ho nahi...
Ik aasmaan ik aasmaan, na ho ye zamin...

Teri ashiqui… meri zindagi!
Teri ashiqui… meri zindagi!!

Ik khwaab hai jo teri aakhon mein
Ik jahaan vo jo teri baton mein
Ik raah jo chalun tere sang… mere liye vo khuda ka darr…

Ik jannat main aashiyaan…
Ik dooje ke hoke…
Aa kho jaayen kahin…
Teri ashiqui… meri zindagi!
Teri ashiqui… meri zindagi!!

∞

The next morning, it seemed to Kim as though everything around her was moving in slow motion; right from the cheese melting on her toast to the leaves falling from trees she passed on her way to the office.

It was as though every single particle of the universe was sympathizing with her.

She reached the office, but more than the Monday blues, she was feeling a stark emptiness from within.

She happened to walk by Viktor's old desk and paused. A small card was pinned on his wall. It read: "*Irony of the world is that it wants to simplify the complexity and complicate the simplicity.*"

She took the card, went back to her workstation and tucked that onto her corkboard. Still staring at the card, she propped her elbow on the desk and rested her chin on her palm. In a brief moment, a string of words came to her: "It's not that complicated; don't let him go."

She thought of calling Viktor. She was determined, and with a few quick pats, she searched for her phone in her pockets, realizing that she had forgotten it at Viktor's desk.

She ran back to his old station where she found her phone, blinking. Kim heaved a sigh of relief, picked it up, and noticed that she had seven missed calls from Viktor and two from Amber.

With extreme happiness, she was about to dial him back but got a message from him, "Battery and balance low, will call once reach hotel."

She dialed Amber back in a hurry.

"Kim!" Amber exclaimed, her voice heavy with worry. "Where are you? Is everything okay?"

"Nope!" Kim replied. "Nothing is okay. I need to talk to Viktor."

Amber snorted. "Oh, please. Don't disturb him. He hasn't even gotten himself settled yet."

"No," said Kim firmly. "I want to talk to him."

"Calm down, baby!" said Amber. "I understand. But do this one thing first, okay? Go to Circle Café. I'm sure that will improve your mood."

"What?"

"Try it!" you said you met him there the first time, right?" Amber forced.

"Fine. I'll catch you later, have some work to finish," she quickly ended the call and stood still, remembering about the place. A tear rolled down her cheek. She wiped that and brisk-walked to her seat.

She didn't want to go anywhere, especially the Circle Café. So instead she decided to spend time with her spreadsheets.

At some point, Christine came by. "Hey, sweetie," she said, perching on the edge of her desk, "Let's go for coffee."

Kim looked at her, yet another devil who was daring to take her to the dreadful café that caused her nothing but misery. She shook her head. "Thanks Christy, but I'm still a little busy with work."

"Oh, really? Jumping up and down the cells on your computer is hardly called work." She laughed and leaned over to lock Kim's system and pulled her by the arm. "They're shooting a movie at Circle Café! Come on, it'll be fun!"

After a little more pushing and prodding from Christine, she finally had no choice but to go to the café.

When they reached the café they saw a few people setting up music systems. Seeing Kim nearing, the café guy cleaned her favorite seat and asked her smilingly, "Two cappuccinos, ma'am?"

"No! Just one," replied Christine. "Sir is not there today, so one Dark Devil for me please."

The café guy looked at Kim and Kim looked at Christine.

"Get me two," quipped Kim.

"Two?" asked Christine with surprise.

Kim was lost in her thoughts murmuring, "If he can't love me, it's fine, I can love for both the sides."

"What?"

"Nothing, not to you," replied Amber.

"Ok! Your choice," Christine winked. "I'll be back in a while, see those handsome guys there," she said and trailed off the table.

Christine was more interested in standing amongst the crowd of on-lookers to watch the shooting; whereas Kim stayed in the lobby, lost in her own world as she recollected the precious time she had spent there with Viktor.

She looked at the amphitheatre in the middle of the park near the café. She remembered Viktor was there that day and she had waved at him to ask for coffee. Again a tear rolled down her eye.

A few men were busy there, in the amphitheatre, checking if the speakers worked fine. The cool breeze laced everything with a romantic touch. A few passersby were gathered there, a few of the young ones were seen skating on the concrete and some of the elderly were shuffling along with their walkers.

"Sound check, sound check, cash, demand draft," the guy said, checking the microphone.

"Hey, you in pink!" he called from the sound booth. "This is for you, young lady!"

Kim looked at him, suddenly embarrassed that she had to pick her brightest-colored top to hide her unhappiness. But then she realized that he was referring to someone else.

"Action!" a person shouted who looked like a director.

A young man who was wearing a mask came onto the stage of the amphitheatre. Kim stared at him intently. She thought if it was Viktor, and then he stepped up to a wireless microphone, holding an acoustic guitar. He strummed a chord.

"Austerity...
If... I were to define...
it's you... yoo hoo!"

He started to sing.

For a moment Kim thought that it was Viktor's voice. Then she looked away and tried to ignore him. Was the universe trying to send her another message? She was beginning to grow tired of its messages. She felt more and more self-conscious as the lyrics flowed through her and invaded her heart.

"Happiness is what...
that makes me feel divine...
smiling you... yoo hoo!!"

The singer moved to another line of his song. Kim felt chills running down her spine, and she checked her arms to find them covered with goose bumps.

She stood up from her seat, and as she lifted her gaze, she noticed that the cameraman was capturing her reactions, and only hers.

"What rose is in flowers..."

The singer completed a third line and began walking off the stage towards her. She took a step back. There was something eerily familiar about his walk . . . his voice . . .

"What moon is in stars..."

It was Viktor.

It had to be.

The more he sang, the more she grew certain that it really was Viktor singing to her. She looked to her left, and then to her right, seeing that everyone's eyes were on her.

She had never felt so warm all over, and it felt as though most of her blood had gone to her cheeks. She didn't know whether to laugh or cry. Had she fallen asleep? Was this a dream? He kept on singing.

"That you are to me..."

He was now heading towards Kim. The crowd started clapping and cheering wildly.

"You and I will be we…"

He turned his guitar behind, jumped over and climbed the wooden platform that she was standing on. The crowd continued to hoot, urging him on.

Kim drew her hand to her face, unsure of how to react. The three cameramen were now surrounding her. Christine was busy dancing and hollering nearby. Kim looked at her and realized that she too had been a part of the plan all along.

Viktor continued his song and walked around her as he sang:

"You're my life… I… I…
I love you… yoo hoo…"

He took off his mask, adjusted his microphone, and pulled out a small box from his pocket. The crowd's cheer grew even louder. Viktor started singing again, placing a hand over his heart.

"O girl, O girl, O… O… girl… you be mine…
I love you… yoo hoo…
You be my… Valentine.
Just be mine… I love you…
O O my… Valentine…
I love you… yoo hoo…!!!"

He went down on his knee as he finished the song. Then he opened the box, and took out the most beautiful diamond ring Kim had ever seen. The rock sparkled in the warm sunlight.

"I love you, Kim," Viktor declared.

Kim was numb for that moment.

Holding the ring in his right hand Viktor offered it up to her.

She put her trembling hands on her lips.

"I'm so sorry I made you cry," he added softly, his earnest eyes glistening in anticipation.

Tears rolled down her cheeks.

"Say YES!" the crowd was shouting.

Still in a daze, Kim shook her head slightly, half-convinced that it was all just a dream.

"O Lord! This is a dream! This is a dream!" she whispered, her lips trembling.

"It's the most real thing that has ever happened," he replied tenderly.

Kim saw tears welling up in the corner of Viktor's eyes as he struggled to hold them back.

She came forward and touched his eyes and shouted, "O God! It's real!" People started laughing.

She quickly bent down on her knees, joining him, and touched his face. She kissed his forehead and his tears finally fell.

"You remember the day you made me laugh in the middle of a terrifying roller coaster ride?" she said.

"Yupp!"

"That day I wanted to kiss your eyes in public."

"Hah? Crazy!" Viktor smiled, "Who stopped you?"

"Your kohl!" she smirked, "It would have ruined my lipstick. Haha."

"It's natural, Ok!" he said wiping her tears.

She bent forward, kissed his eyelids, and then his wet lashes, "I know, you *junglee.*"

Then she stood up, and like a queen she extended her arm towards him. Everyone started cheering them up.

Viktor slid the ring on her finger and held out his arms. As the crowd applauded, Kim finally surrendered and sank into his embrace.

"You are a big-time rascal," she said, wiping her teary face on his sleeve.

"What can I say, I love surprises," he quipped, immediately receiving a punch in the arm.

"So why did you go to the airport?"

"Mom was coming!" he happily replied.

Kim's eyes widened and she gave him another punch, "I can't believe you made me go through all that! And… you didn't even tell me that she was coming. I'm so curious to meet her." She started crying again.

Viktor planted a kiss on her forehead. "If I tell you again how sorry I am, will you stop punching me?"

"Ring ceremony, baby," someone interrupted, lightly pinching Kim's waist.

"Ouch!" Kim turned to find Amber beaming at her. "Amber! You! So you're really all part of this conspiracy, hmm?" Kim almost ignored what she said about ring ceremony.

"You should have seen her, Viktor," giggled Amber. "She wouldn't stop crying all the way home."

"One sec!" Kim was surprised, "What did you just say? Ring ceremony?"

"Come!" said Viktor taking her inside the Circle Café as all surprises were over.

Kim was stunned to see her parents sitting there with a lady waiting for her, "My God!"

The lady was Viktor's mom. She quickly went forward, greeted her parents and started crying with happiness, "You all were part of the plan?"

Then she saw Viktor's mother and quickly touched her feet, "Hello!" she fumbled and was feeling very shy too.

"My daughter!" His mother hugged her. "In India, girls don't touch feet of elders before marriage."

It was here that Viktor disclosed his plans for the night, which he had meticulously planned for and arranged with close friends and family, who were all part of his grand scheme.

∾

That night, all the arrangements were made for the traditional Indian ring ceremony. Viktor was in a black *sherwani* embroidered in golden threads, with a red turban on his head. He was on the stage, sitting on a chair that resembled a throne, talking to his friends and relatives from Canada.

The moment Kim appeared with her friends, straight from the beauty parlor, Viktor was stunned to see her dressed in a chiffon sari with a beautiful black, pleated border.

He noticed a familiar design embroidered on the sari; it was a traditional patch he had seen numerous times whenever his mother told him about her courtship with his father. It was the same patch she had worn on her own ring ceremony, handed down from Viktor's grandmother.

He looked for his mother in the crowd, and when their eyes met, she returned his smile as if saying, "Now it belongs to Kim."

Kim looked dainty and delicate in the sari, like a flower from the gardens of heaven itself. The blonde hair queen looked awesome in the folds of the red sari resting slightly on her lower back, showing off the sensual curves that Viktor loved.

She reached the stage and was about to climb the steps when Viktor took a microphone and cleared his throat, "Freeze!"

Kim, with everyone around, looked at him.

"This is a roller coaster," he said. Viktor got up from his royal chair, and everyone started cheering and hooting. Some were smiling and some, like Kim, looked perplexed.

"Do you remember?" he continued. "The day I asked you to ride the roller coaster with me?"

Kim smiled warmly at him, blushing.

Viktor continued, "I know you're a tough lady, so you can go ahead and punch me later. But your irrational fear of roller coasters is an important part of our story."

Kim, now a bright shade of pink, pretended to threaten him with her fist as the audience laughed.

"Yes, my dear, you were always afraid of heights and fast speeds," Viktor continued, grinning. "But you took the plunge and came with me anyway, saying you were not afraid because I was with you."

She smiled at his words and began blinking her eyes to keep herself from tearing up all over again.

"Today," Viktor said, descending the steps, "I want you to board another roller coaster with me . . . the one called *life*."

He walked closer towards her. "Will you join me? And be mine forever?" He thrust his hand forward, "As I shall be yours."

A pearl-like tear she could no longer hold back finally rolled down her cheek. Everyone started yelling, *"Say YES!"* while some mischievous office colleagues shouted, *"Say NO!"* which made everyone laugh.

"Too late, dude!" Viktor called out to them, grinning. "She already said yes!"

Kim laughed and cried at the same time, and trying to control her emotions, she offered her hand.

Viktor took her hand and escorted her to the stage. He wiped off her tears, held her face in his hands, and kissed her on her forehead. The guests started whistling loudly.

Rituals were started as per Indian customs, led by Viktor's mother and *maasi* from Canada, along with Amber's parents as Kim's parents. Friends and relatives cheered excitedly as Viktor and Kim exchanged rings.

The customary sharing of gifts took place as they exchanged gifts. Discussions were rife about the significance of these traditions and the nitty-gritty of these rituals too.

Kim's friends, who were witnessing an Indian ring ceremony for the first time, applauded tearfully.

Later on, the newly-engaged couple announced their plans to tie the knot the next year.

There was an atmosphere of sheer excitement in the room, and there was plenty of lively discussion about how Viktor had cooked up his plan to propose the way he did. He eventually revealed that he had gathered Kim's close family and a few office colleagues, and planned the stunt with them in strict confidence.

Though it was the first time for Kim and her close family to meet Viktor's mom, it was easy to notice that everyone had quickly developed a comfortable bond.

"Your mother is a great lady, Viktor!" said Amber's mother.

Her father added, "Really, her light sense of humour and amazing Punjabi conversations are just mind blowing, though we don't understand what she says in Punjabi." Everyone laughed.

Eventually, Viktor and Kim returned to their thrones to take a break from all the attention.

"For some reason, I didn't expect that Mom would be so fluent in English!" Kim said.

Viktor smiled. "I love that you just met her today and said 'Mom' instead of 'your mom'. That means a lot to me."

She returned his smile. "I love that our families are just one big family now."

Viktor leaned over and kissed her cheek. "And about her English," he added, "Mom is a Punjabi and Delhiite, but she and Dad stayed here in the US for thirty years."

"That is a long time." Kim held his hand. "But thank you for today. I've never been this happy." She gave him a warm squeeze.

He looked into her eyes and whispered, "You are my life, Kim. I'm the one who should thank you. You introduced me to myself."

They shared a soft kiss, and someone from the dance floor whistled loudly.

After a photo session with relatives, encouraged by everyone's enthusiasm, the happy couple decided to take to the dance floor, where they broke out into the salsa mesmerising everyone with their wonderful steps in sync.

Then Viktor pulled his mother onto the dance floor. She was a bit shy at first, but he would not take no for an answer. She adjusted the loose end of her sari, tied it around her waist, and proceeded to perform Kathak to American hip hop.

The applause intensified from appreciation to awe inspiring soon enough as she was a great dancer. Kim too was amazed as she exchanged a look of disbelief with Viktor. He, in turn, acknowledging her surprise, only shrugged his shoulders with a smug grin full of pride.

"Wow, Viktor! Mom is an amazing performer!" Kim exclaimed.

"Well, after all she is *my* mom." Viktor responded with his smile reaching his eyes to form a twinkle.

Kim spontaneously gave Viktor a warm embrace and added, "And now she's mine too." The two hardly had savoured that moment, when a couple of their friends came and pulled them back to the dance floor.

Viktor let the music take over; he was a contented soul. He danced heartily in all openness. His arms up, hands were open, eyes closed, face lifted high up to the sky, with worries thrown away down under, forgetting the real world.

Viktor was in a reverie of his own, where the universe had bestowed all the happiness of the world upon him. He wanted time to slow down, perhaps stand still so he could enjoy every moment of this momentous occasion with the two women that he loved more than anything else in his life.

The next day, Viktor and Kim went to the airport to see off their mother, who planned to go with the visiting relatives to visit their home in Canada.

"See you soon in India, Kim," said Viktor's mother, pulling her in a tight embrace. She then turned towards Viktor. "And you. You better not tease her anymore, okay, mister?"

Viktor smirked, "Yes, ma'am!" and bowed down to touch her feet for blessings and then shouldered Kim too to touch her feet.

His mother slapped him softly and was about to say something, but Kim quipped, "Daughters don't touch feet before marriage," and winked at Viktor.

10 Alone…

met by chance

Day 3 – Chocolate day

Kim got up and searched for her cell phone with eyes closed. She found a chocolate near her table lamp. She got up with a smile. As she checked her mobile, there was a wish, "Happy Chocolate day, my Choco-life."

She jumped with joy and headed to get ready. She found another small chocolate stocked on her mirror. She pulled that and picked-up her tooth brush and found the next one tied to it.

She came back running back to her room, "Amber! You did this?"

"No!" she nodded while eating a huge chocolate herself. "He told me not to tell you."

Kim's happiness knew no bounds and she texted Viktor, "You are sweeter than these chocolates."

"TTYL" he texted back.

"Huh," she replied and went to get ready for office.

As she got into the cab for visiting the client site, the driver gave her a parcel with a card that read:

Chocolate, dark or light…
Makes me smile bright.
Chocolate, whether speak or not…
If it's love, it conveys a lot.
But when you're… not there with me…
It's just a piece… of sugar candy.
It's you, who makes it sweeter…
I love it with you, even if it's bitter.
So be there always… stay forever..
I can't think of life… without you ever.

O girl, O girl, O… O… girl… you be mine…
You are my choco-life…
You be my… Valentine.
Just be mine… O… O… Valentine!!!

∞

Day 4 – Teddy Day

"Ting tong!" the door bell rang. Kim came out to check.

"Wow!" she was surprised as she opened the door. A life-sized pink teddy bear was there. She leaned to check if Viktor was nearby, but couldn't find him. Rather, she saw a greeting card attached to the heart of the teddy.

She bent down, untagged that, opened and started reading:

"A bear hug for you,
and I would make you forget your sorrows!
I'll be there with you forever,
in all your today and tomorrows!!

The day I am not there,
this teddy would be with you;
So just be fine, you are always mine!!!
My life is yours forever...
O girl, O girl, O you be my... Valentine."

The moment she was done reading, Viktor was in front of her, "Happy Teddy Day Junglee."

She planted a kiss on his cheeks and gave him a tight hug saying, "*I need you forever, for you are my teddy.*"

∞

Day 5 – Promise Day

Life had found a new meaning for Viktor. He had just started a new life, with new found purpose that he passionately adopted. But even then, he knew this was because of Kim.

"How long since I met Kim? One or two years??" Viktor wondered aloud, taking a sip of coffee from a tumbler.

"Years???" mused Kim sharing his coffee, "Nope it's just been few months."

"Hmm!"

"But why are you counting?" she asked grabbing one more sip from him.

"To keep my promises," Viktor replied putting a small greeting card on the table.

"Goodness! Another one!" she picked up happily and read...

"I don't promise...
that I will bring the moon for you, but...

I shall stand by you in the sun!
I don't promise...
that I will not fight with you ever, but...
We shall be together, forever;
and distances or differences would be none!!
I don't promise...
that life will be so easy, and cheesy, but...
when you are with me, I would make sure it's always fun!!!
But I promise one thing;
I'll never make you cry,
and never let you go, so all I need is you to be with me!
Let's make it happen...
Let's make it happen...
and let our destiny shine.
My life is yours forever...
O girl, O girl, O you be my... Valentine!!!!"

∞

Day 6 – Hug Day

Viktor held her hand and pulled her near him and said, "You transformed me in such a short time."
He unwrapped a small greeting card and closed that in his hand. Kim's eyes widened with smile asking, "Another song?"

Viktor smiled, "The Hug Song, Happy Hug day," he said hugging her in his arms and whispered the song softly in her ears...

"Wrap me in your hug...
make me feel happy!

Hold me tight and close...
not like a pillow or a teddy!!
My heart needs you...
You touch my soul,
believe me things shall go fine.
Wrap me in your arms...
and take me to divine!!
My life is yours forever...
O girl, O girl...
O you be my... Valentine!!!!"

∞

Day 7 – Kiss Day

Kim and Viktor met at Circle Café for coffee.

"Hey which day is today?" she asked.

"A day... when the couples don't say; they actually can't, for they remain speechless," Viktor jingled.

"Means?"

Viktor got up from his seat, went near to her, playing with her lovely locks. She caressed his neck and was lost in his eyes. He pulled her close and planted a soft kiss on her forehead followed by a lip-lock.

"To start with a kiss...
I'll first mark... on the top of your head...
just to say that... I'll be with you... forever!
Next two on the eyes...
just to say that... the world is so beautiful...
as I see with you... whatever!!

Then three... on the nose and cheek...
just to say that... I am myself...
As I walk with you wherever!!!
Then a peck on the neck...
just to say that... you are perfect.
and then... final one on the lips...
just to say that... just to say that...
just to say nothing.
Because our love is beyond the skyline!
My life is yours forever...
O girl, O girl...
O you be my... Valentine!!!!"

Day 8 – Valentine's Day

Next Day, Viktor went to Kim's client site in the evening and from there they drove down to a ballroom party in down town where many couples joined to celebrate the Lovers' Day.

Dim-lit yellow chandeliers, candles lit on the tables and a red carpet was adding grace to the party. Viktor and Kim were busy like other couples doing salsa on the soft tunes of lovely music.

Kim placed her head on Viktor's shoulder and said, "Vik! I never knew I'll fall in love with you, so deeply."

Viktor smiled, kissed her forehead and said, "I surely knew I am going to *rise in love* with you."

Then he straightaway went to the orchestra, leaving Kim awestruck and asked the guy for his guitar. Everyone present there started whistling.

"A Valentine song for all the lovely love birds here..." said Viktor and started strumming the love tunes...

"What earth is to sky...
on the horizon...
What moon is to night...
no matter star-studded ocean!

What Love is to life...
above all give and take...
that you are to me...
a rhythm that soulful music would make!

Let's surrender to each other...
for a dream to be woven together!!
You're my weakness and my strength...
wanna live with you...
till the end!! ... and beyond... ;)!!!

Even a dent in the universe...
can't express my Love for you!
My life is yours forever...
O girl, O girl...
O girl... you be mine!!
Not just for this time...
Everyday beyond... Valentine!!!"

∞

Viktor was tuning his life and composing the tracks to his dreams. Determined to walk it all the way, he worked ceaselessly on his dream run – he continued to work on his novel, his dream, all credits to Kim.

"The power of dreams," Viktor wrote that night," *is not measured by the frequency of one's dream, but by the speed of the*

actions that he adopts to make them come true." With that, he closed a conversation of his protagonist.

Being at the office didn't keep him from writing, and he often sneaked away from his spreadsheets to jot down a few lines here and there, be it on tissue paper or a notepad or his mobile.

"You won't know your limits until you soar high and give it a try," he wrote.

He felt that he was going in the right direction. He edited his novel after lunch at the office, sometimes at home before going to bed. To save time, he employed a driver and started editing in the car too, on the way to office and back home. Occasionally he would send some of these lines to Kim, who would respond with her comments.

Kim reviewed his edits, and they would often discuss his manuscript over the phone. Amber extended a helping hand as well, but on the condition that she would get free scoops of White Mischief ice cream as a perk.

"What will be the title of your novel?" asked Amber one night perching on the hood of Viktor's car, licking her ice cream off its cone.

"That's her job," replied Viktor, pointing at Kim.

"Oh! Is it? Ohkhay!" Kim replied, "You have to give me options. It's still your novel."

"How about *The One?*" Viktor suggested.

"Sounds boring," said Amber. "And too *God of the springs* or something like that."

"*Single?*" Kim asked.

"Yuck," Amber made faces.

"Friendship?" she added.

"What? Girl, we need to be creative. It's the title of a novel... you know," Amber complained.

"*Alone!*" Kim said thinking aloud again.

"Hmmm, I guess that's pretty good. Being alone is nice," Amber said. "But why call it *Alone?*"

"Because…" Viktor began…"Well…"

Amber raised an eyebrow.

"Because …" Kim pondered.

"Because," Viktor continued, "No matter how many people we have around us, we're all still alone, one way or another."

"Well, that's not depressing," Amber smiled.

"I mean," Viktor explained, "No matter how many friends or relatives you have, no matter who you're with, you have to achieve your dreams by yourself, alone. No one else can do it for you."

"Hey, what about *10 Alone?*" Kim quickly suggested. "That sounds like a title."

"Why ten?" asked Amber; she paused. "Oh, I see. It's about ten friends. Right?"

"If I didn't know any better I would think you never bothered reading a single page," Kim said, shaking her head.

"But," Amber continued, ignoring her, "How can ten people be alone at the same time?"

Viktor walked over to her, picked her up from where she was perched, and carried her inside the car saying, "Go home and read."

∞

After five months of hard work, Viktor was finally ready with his full-fledged, completely edited novel. The day came when he submitted his book to various publishing houses he had listed down earlier. That night, he took Kim out for dinner to celebrate.

"There's something I want to ask you," Kim said, once they had placed their order.

Viktor began pouring wine into their glasses. "Sure, what is it?"

"Don't you think we're ready to move in together?" Kim asked.

He paused.

"I mean," she continued, in spite of noticing his reactions, "I want to, but only if it's fine with you."

"Well, yeah, of course, but..." Viktor took a deep breath. "I...sort of...need a little more time," he raised his eyes to look at Kim, and she squeezed his hand under the table.

He hated to disappoint her. "It's a big step. I think I need to give my best to my novel first. But after that... any time... any day you want. I promise," he put his hand on the table facing up.

Kim looked at his hand and then his eyes, smiled, held his hand nodding, "I understand; your dream is larger than life."

Viktor placed his other hand over hers, caressed it with his thumb, and whispered, "Thank you. Thank you for understanding and helping me meet my life... my dreams."

She bent towards him and gave a soft kiss on his cheeks, "Junglee! Learning formalities? Ha ha."

∞

Viktor was still anxiously waiting to hear from any of the editors he had sent his manuscript to. Three months had already passed, and he still hadn't received any news on the status of his submissions.

"I am worried Kim," he said as they both settled in a restaurant. "What if they wouldn't even look at my story?"

He slid the menu towards her, "Order please!"

"I don't feel like having anything," she replied, holding her stomach.

"Are you alright?"

"I'm okay, but I've been feeling weird twinges in my stomach since yesterday. It could just be because of the weather, though."

"Let's go to the doctor," said Viktor, immediately dialling his doctor's number.

"It's fine! Just not feeling goo…"

"Shh!" he interrupted talking on phone, "Yes! Six is fine. Book it please."

They reached the hospital in the evening and doctor diagnosed Kim and gave her medicines for stomach infection.

On their drive back home, Viktor got a call. Kim picked up his phone. "It's an India mobile number," she said.

"Pick up."

"Hello? Yes, this is Viktor's phone. He's driving."

"Who?" Viktor whispered, trying to keep his eyes on the road.

"Hello, ma'am! This is Kim. He's told me so much about you. Of course! Yes. Yeah… Oh! Okay!"

"Who is it?" he whispered again.

"It's Mrs Elisa!" she whispered back.

Upon hearing the name, Viktor immediately stopped the car and grabbed the phone, putting it on speaker. "Hello, Elisa ma'am! What a pleasant surprise."

"Hey!" Kim interrupted out of joy, "How does she know me?"

"I shared the ring ceremony photos with her," Viktor replied covering the microphone.

"Ma'am, how did you find my number?" he asked.

"Your mother gave it to me. I had your Delhi landline number."

"That's amazing! You saved my number for so long," he said smiling.

"Yes dear. No teacher would forget a brilliant student like you. Anyhow, I am coming to visit some relatives in the USA, so meet me. I will be there for two months."

"That's a great news ma'am! I'll be happy to meet you here."

"Same here son, same here…and congratulations."

"Thank you ma'am! We are going to marry soon and thinking of settling down here."

"That sounds like a very good plan, Viktor. I'm happy for you. By the way your lady has a very sweet voice." she said.

"Ha ha! She is saying thank you ma'am!" he said looking at Kim while she was blushing as she heard her.

"God bless you, my son! How is life and office going?"

"Hah!" he sighed confessing, "Actually… I've been having a tough time lately, but I feel better now. Thank you so much for calling."

"My boy!" said Mrs. Elisa. *"Education always precedes experience. Your real victory is when you experience something you haven't been educated for…and…you excel."*

When he hung up, Viktor felt the same surge of inspiration he'd always felt after talking to her.

"Why didn't you tell her about your novel?" Kim asked.

"Nothing is sure yet. You know me."

"Yup! I do. *I love taking people by surprise,*" Kim mimicked him.

Viktor started the car, laughing. "See? You do know me." He leaned over and gave her a peck on the neck.

Playfully she pushed him back into his seat, "Concentrate on driving, Mr Viktor! I know you will let her know the day you sign a publishing contract."

"My goodness! You decode me so well," he praised.

Rolling her eyes, she held his arm and rested her head on his shoulder.

∞

Another month passed. Viktor and Kim were at Circle Café, where Viktor sat dejected and crestfallen.

"You've been stirring your coffee for five minutes, Viktor. It's about to be buttermilk," she giggled but no smile came from Viktor.

"Now can you please tell me what happened?" she asked stopping his hand.

"I got rejected." blurted Viktor.

"What?" Kim was shocked.

"I proposed and got rejected."

She raised an eyebrow at him.

"I am sad," he sighed.

"If you had proposed to a girl, then you're lucky that I'm still marrying you," she answered, pulling him close, "and if rejected by a publisher... then..."

"You are so me," he smiled nodding, "Yup! I just got my first rejection letter. Well, I guess that's something sad, right?"

"O Vik!" she said holding his hand, "I'm sure someone will say yes eventually."

He nodded. "Let's hope."

"I am with you always," she held his shoulder.

"Thanks for being there."

She held his cheeks saying, "*Success has doors called failures.*"

He smiled looking at her, "I'll *lock that very door from outside and run...* ha ha. And hit back once I am better prepared." and they broke into laughter.

∞

Within the same week, he received rejection letters from almost all of the publishers he had contacted. It was during those moments when the mail came that he felt just about ready to give up hope.

Viktor had to fight his fears of failure. He told Kim about each letter and the frustration that came with them. She could only console him, but she did so each time happily with success.

"What's that line you wrote in *10 Alone?*" she asked one day. "*Hopes may vanish...*"

"*Dreams never die,*" he finished.

Kim simply kissed his cheek whispering the lines from *10 Alone*, "*The first step to success is knowing that you failed to do something because many people don't even realise. Second step is to take a first step again, to give it another shot.*"

Viktor realized that he had to endure the negativity, but he felt charged with newfound trust that he could face it all, especially that he had her by his side.

∞

"*With the setting in of every defeat, barges in the fear of failure, but...*" said a husky voice.

"No! I can't do it," said a small child pushing the bicycle away and sitting by the roadside. He sat pulling up his pajama and touching the wound on his knees.

"You can!" said a man in his late thirties, "I know you can do it."

The boy looked at him shaking his head, indicating a big no. "See, I fell so many times learning the silly two tyre'd thing."

"It was your dream Viktor," said the man. "You only told me you want to learn riding a bicycle and now when you have it, you don't want to learn because you fell a few times."

"No Dad! Please! Believe me! I can't!" the boy cried.

"Believe me! You can!" said Viktor's father getting up and raised his hand towards him.

Viktor looked at his hand, then towards his father.

"I am not assuring that you won't fall down," said the father. "But I'll make sure you are not afraid of falling. Then only you'll be able to ride."

Viktor smiled, held his father's hand and pulled himself up. With a newfound zeal he went towards the bicycle, pulled it up right, and peddled.

On the straight road towards his home, till mid way, he fell 7-8 times while balancing, but every time he fell, he got up with renewed zeal to learn and win the road.

One fine moment he rode it for a few minutes, without breaks, without fall, making a perfect balanced ride.

"Dad!" he started yelling, "See! I am riding!"

"Great! Go on!" said the father running behind him.

He rode a bit faster and in sheer joy looked back at his dad. "See, Dad! I am flying. Run fast! Catch me."

"No…Don't look back!" yelled his father.

"I am flyyyyy…" and he lost his balance. He raised his palms to save his face and THUDDDD…

...And Viktor got up from his sleep. He was sweating. He looked at his palms if the wound was renewed again.

A tear fell off from his eye on his palm and he looked at his computer table, towards the photo of his mom and dad.

"I can do it Dad! Believe me... I can! And I will..." he whispered.

"With the touch of wisdom, comes the end of fears," completed a husky voice.

∞

A month later, Viktor received a letter from a small publisher called AuthorsOwn. He had sent out so many copies of his manuscript over the past few months that he had forgotten that he had submitted his work to them also.

He called up Kim, who was out of town on an official assignment.

"I received a letter from a publisher," he said in a low voice. "They're the last one. If they say no, there's no one else."

"Vik! Don't worry! You remember, what you keep repeating to Amber always – *The ladder of success is built by nails of patience.*"

Viktor was silent.

"I wish I was there with you today," she said softly on the other end.

"I need you, Kim," he whispered.

"Honey," she firmly answered, "I am *always* with you."

A brief pause hung in the air. Viktor repeated, "No, I *need* you."

He heard her taking a deep breath.

"Okay," she said, "I think I can make some changes to my schedule. I can catch a flight home and fly back from here tomorrow." He could almost picture her flipping through the pages of her planner.

"Not just for today," he said. "Move in with me forever."

"Vik?" she was surprised, "What are you saying?"

"Yes," he confirmed.

"Don't tell me. You got the contract, right?" she predicted.

"Oh lady! Yes!" said Viktor as he burst out in laughter. "I just wonder how you know me so well. Just one word of mine spills the beans."

"Which publisher is it?" she asked.

Viktor could barely make out what she was saying over the noise of traffic in the background, but he could hear the smile in her voice.

"It's a small press called AuthorsOwn."

"Brother's what?"

"Own," Viktor repeated.

"Gown?"

"AuthorsOwn!" he shouted, "A small-sized publisher."

All people around him looked at him and he raised his hand apologising.

"Cool!" she shouted back.

"And you know what the editor said?" he added curiously, "He said in his email that he *believes* in me and my story and that if all goes well, the book could be out by the end of the year."

"Wow! That's wonderful, honey!" Kim paused, "Hold on, I think someone's trying to flirt with me." She looked towards that man.

"Oh, he just came over to close the window," she sighed, "Anyway! I think this certainly calls for a celebration!"

"Absolutely!" Viktor beamed. "When are you coming back?"

"I'll be there in two days," she sighed.

Viktor sensing a little low in her voice asked, "What's wrong?"

"I just think it's strange that we've spent all our tough times together, and now that we have something to celebrate, we're miles apart," Kim responded.

"It's okay. It's only two days." He smiled. "Now go and thank the poor chap who closed the window." They laughed and waited to be together soon.

Viktor came home and at night, before sleeping, he looked at the photo on his side table; then wrote a note and stuck on his wall. He picked up the photo frame, hugged it for a minute and then turned that towards the wall, as if showing something to the photo frames. The note on the wall read, "*I don't think I can... I know I will...*"

∞

Zindagi

Soch to raha tha... Ki jo socha kabhi vo hi milega...
Ha ha... nahi mila!
Koshish ki to bohot... Par sapna to sapna hota hai...
Ha ha... aakhir toot hi gaya!
Laga ki zindagi kya ban gayi? Ya ye meri zid hi thi?
Ha ha... jo maine khud hi bikher di!
Zid! Zid thi kuch hatke karoon... Bas dil ki sunoon...
Ha ha... pagalon sa junoon!

Aur wahi hua... Sadak choti lagne lagi...
Ha ha... Manzil tak jaane wali!
Haara... baar baar haara...

Par us haar ka apna hi tha maza...
Jo de gaya aadat... haar ke baad...
Ha ha... jeet ka jashn manaane ki.
Sapnon ke aakaash tale... Fir se khud ko pane ki...
Soch pe yakeen dilaane ki...
Ki jo socho wahi milega...
Zindagi yun hi jee jaane ki.
Zindagi yun hi jee jaane ki.

∞

Two days later, they met at the airport. They kissed passionately until the world was well aware of their joy.

"Lady luck! You are my destiny," said Viktor.

"No, honey," she said, tucking a pen inside his coat pocket. "I just stood by you, silently. You paved your way and you dared to dream."

He took the pen out of his pocket. It was opulent with a steel body. It was engraved with the letters *VK*. He delicately kissed her forehead by way of saying thanks.

"My dreams have you in it, Kim," he said, sliding a pendant around her neck.

Kim struggled to read what was written on it, and let out a surprised laugh. "*VK*!"

They shared another kiss, still laughing about the pleasant coincidence. They walked towards the parking lot, and as he revved up the car to life, Viktor said, "I want to achieve all that I have dreamt of, with you by my side."

"I am always there for you," Kim said, giving him a peck on the cheek before resting her head on his shoulder, "And I am not going anywhere." In that moment, she felt peace.

"The future is not tomorrow," he thought, *"It is today. It is right now."* He heaved a sigh of contentment at his state of affairs. With that deep breath, he took in the scent of her hair and began the long drive home.

∞

Several months passed. Many letters were exchanged between Viktor and his editor. Many hours were spent on long meetings about the novel – meetings about character development, plot holes, book design, cover art, target audiences, and marketing strategies.

As the weeks went by, Viktor rewrote several sections and added new ones, and he watched as his project evolved until it was finally ready for publication.

∞

"And now," said Viktor delivering a presentation at the town hall meeting of the company, "I would request the CEO to present the company expansion plans."

He sensed his cell phone vibrating inside his pocket, and he did his best to ignore it.

Kim, who was sitting in the audience, seemed to notice that something was distracting him and shot him a curious glance.

After the town hall presentation was over, he immediately left to check his phone. He beamed when he read the new text message.

Kim approached, asking, "All well?"

"Yeah! Just a courier. I need to go pick up a package. I won't be long."

Viktor went to the courier's office and collected the parcel. It was wrapped in a familiar shade of violet paper. His eyes widened as he recognized the logo embossed on the envelope.

Immediately, he picked up his phone and called Kim. "Hey, where are you?"

"I am leaving for the client site. Why?"

"Wait for me. I am coming to the office."

"But I have to go to the audit meeting there."

"Okay, then meet me at Circle Café."

"Anything special?" she asked and Viktor heard the smile in her voice.

"I'll see you there!" he finished smiling.

When Viktor entered the café half an hour later, Kim was already at their favourite seat, facing the tower clock behind the amphitheater.

She got up as she saw him coming. Viktor smiled and hugged her without saying a word. He couldn't help but get teary-eyed, in spite of himself.

"Hey," she said gently. "Honey, what happened?"

He wiped his eyes and hugged her tight again.

"What's going on?" she asked, rubbing his back.

Viktor handed her the parcel.

"Oh my god!" she gasped, reading the sender's address. "Brother's Gown!"

They both broke into laughter, remembering the day Viktor first told her about his new publisher AuthorsOwn.

She carefully opened the envelope, and let out a squeal when she saw a hardbound copy of the novel, its title printed grandly across the cover: *10 Alone*.

"Twannnnnnnnng!" the tower clock went off five times.

"See!" she smiled curiously, "The universe is celebrating your victory."

Viktor nodded curling his lips, he was speechless.

She looked at him. "I am so happy for you." She hugged him again and said, "It's like you were born today and introduced to the world. And I'm the first one blessed to live this moment with you." Her eyes glistened with happy tears. Then she grinned, holding out her palm.

"So, Mr. Author! May I have your autograph, please?"

He took out the pen she had given him and gladly scribbled his signature. Then the other palm was thrust out to him. He signed that too, and then she raised her wrist. He signed it again a third time, a fourth, and a fifth!

"That tickles!" Kim giggled, and Viktor happily kissed them too, topping it with a kiss on her head.

∞

Weeks later, Viktor found himself at a press conference inside a book store, attending a book reading event.

"They say, the size of your audience doesn't matter, keep up the good work," said Viktor with his opening lines looking at an audience of around fifty people. He was standing behind a podium. Although his mother couldn't fly to the US, she witnessed it through live video streaming, thanks to Amber.

Among the audience was Mrs Elisa, who was in town to visit her family.

"What was your first step towards success?" asked a newspaper reporter.

He immediately replied, *"Success is... the day you start loving what you do and start doing what you love.* That was my first step; to get up and start doing what I always loved and wanted to do but never did."

He looked at Kim. "And *none of this would be possible without the people who love you and know you so well; the ones who always knew where you ought to be before you even realized it yourself.*"

Then he turned to a teary-eyed Mrs Elisa. "*The teachers who are next to parents.*" He paused and looked at the video streaming camera."*And our parents, who are our first teachers.*"

"Mr Viktor!" a reporter raised his hand, "Your selection of the cover image is a bit confusing. Any particular significance here?"

"Yes! The cover is of significance. It has so many hidden nuances in itself," replied Viktor picking up the novel from table and displaying it in full view for all. "Here, there are two feet imprinted on sand."

All nodded. He came forward adding, "Check carefully, these are two left feet."

Many people were amazed at that detail they had not noted themselve. Viktor continued, "It signifies two people going in their own different directions."

"Which signifies that, it's not necessary for people, even if together, to always agree to each other's viewpoint."

"Check it a bit more carefully, one of the feet, the upper one, is embossed and other one is engraved." Viktor added to the surprise of all who sat still stunned by the depth and detail of a novel cover.

Viktor went on feeding his rapt audience with more. "It shows different ways of thinking of people, say their aspects of life, though they are together."

"Now!" he pointed towards the title, "The design of *10 Alone* reveals letters as protruding out, right?" Everyone nodded to it, "It's Embossed."

"But check now!" he said turning the cover page upside down.

"How the title is appearing now?"

"Sloped in," replied a girl. "It's exactly reverse of the image, it's like an illusion."

"It signifies that...life is an illusion." Viktor added, "Title seems engraved now."

"Observe carefully," he reiterated and pointed to the feet imprint. "The upper foot seems engraved now and the lower one embossed, which is opposite to the image you saw when I held it correctly."

A secret had been revealed. Everyone was all smiles. They reveled in the discovery and praised him too.

"This is called empathy, seeing things from another person's angle," Viktor completed opening his arms.

The girl started clapping and soon the hall was full of applauses.

"And the credit for bringing my imaginations into reality goes to my sweetheart Amber for her amazing art through oil painting." He gestured for her to come on stage as everyone started applauding.

Amber was feeling shy, her cheeks were red.

"Amber is amazing at canvas, a master at coloring dreams," Viktor added. "It's also her dream to be a great painter."

As he finished, Amber looked at him and the next moment, her eyes welled up in tears. Viktor hugged her and she whispered, "I wish Mom and Dad could understand this." She then went to Kim and hugged her.

"Why is there a dot after every letter in *A.L.O.N.E*?" asked someone.

"How can *10 people* be alone?" mused another, trying to dig deeper?

Viktor smiled at him. "It signifies that... we all are alone, no matter two people or ten. We are the ones who have to complete our dreams in life, taking that first step, all alone."

People were now listening to him seriously. He continued, *"The only person standing between your dreams and your success is none but you."*

He pointed at the audience with his first finger. *"So all you need to do is... push yourself... Towards your goals... to make it happen."*

Silence spilled over. Viktor was standing still, looking at everyone with a pause.

The guy who had asked that question started clapping, followed by a deafening round of applause.

"With the touch of a first step to make dreams true, comes wisdom," Viktor added.

"And with the touch of wisdom, comes the end of fears," he completed and the next moment, there was a standing ovation around him.

"What does your novel teach?" asked a person.

"To teach, you need books; to educate you need a heart." Viktor replied, "So my novel connects to hearts, no teachings."

∞

10 A.L.O.N.E sales were on an increase day by day. However, Viktor returned to his regular life. He was once again busy with his spreadsheets, but this time he made sure to keep a tab on the book orders. Initially, as acquaintances were his first buyers, sales were fast.

Viktor thoroughly enjoyed every part of the experience, but he most especially enjoyed replying to the e-mails received from his readers.

Letters were coming from complete strangers who expressed appreciation for his efforts. Some actually critiqued his work and wrote about the areas for improvement.

Nevertheless, he read every letter and personally replied to every comment on his blog and profiles with joy.

"The higher you step up on the ladder of success... the lesser you need to speak about yourself. Your deeds should do so." Viktor posted on his profile wall.

And so he did his best to carry on with as much humility as he could muster. Once in a while people would recognize him, when he was on his way to the office or during dinners out with Kim.

Strangers would interrupt and ask for an autograph, and he would graciously entertain them, asking for their names and scribbling brief dedications before signing his name. He did his best to treat each rare instance as though it truly would never happen again.

∞

Viktor visited Kim and Amber's house one morning. Kim was busy in the kitchen while Amber was in college. Her parents asked Viktor to join then for coffee in the garden.

"I wanted to talk to you both on something," said Viktor.

"About Kim?" asked the Mother.

"Nope!" he replied, "Amber. How is she?"

"Good! Busy with studies, final exams."

"Great!" Viktor sighed, "How are her paintings going on?"

"Viktor!" said father, "If this is regarding her painting hobby, let's not discuss."

"Sorry!" Viktor nodded, "Let's change the topic. Did you both see the video of the book release event?"

"Yes, Kim had shown us. We were in England that time, so sorry for not coming."

"No worries!" Viktor said, "You saw the story behind the cover page?"

"Yes! So many layers of meaning in the cover design. Amazing!" said the mother.

Amber's father added, "And the colour combination was superb, a divine touch I must say."

"I hope you saw the full video," Viktor mused.

"Of course, till the time you explained about the cover page to the reporters. Then Amber had some work, so she took Kim with her. I hope nothing beyond that."

"Amber pulled Kim away?" asked Viktor with surprise and pulled out his mobile, "Here! Watch the full story," and played the video coverage.

Amber's father took the mobile and replayed the video. Viktor leaned forward, "Let me help you to stream it till the place you have already seen."

Viktor forwarded the video till the time he was about to announce who painted the cover page.

With the progression of video, Amber's parents were stunned and shocked as they got to know that it was painted by Amber. They were amused and happy to see Amber on stage too .

Kim watched that from the kitchen window, a bit worried. Viktor looked at her and indicated with his eyes resting on her, assuring that everything will be fine.

The moment the parents saw Amber crying in the video, they both had tears in their eyes. Kim came closer, put a hand on their shoulders and said, "I am sorry! I tried to show you the full video that day itself, but Amber was scared and…"

"Painting is her dream. Please let her live it," Viktor explained.

The mother's sobs just deepened. Viktor went and held her hand, "You said the cover is amazing. It really is... she only made it amazing."

Her father was quiet; Kim came forward and sat next to him. "Dad! She is doing everything for both of you, your happiness. She is good at her studies because of you. But give her a chance to try her hand at painting. On something she likes and you will see she will excel. She is great at it already."

He hugged Kim sobbing. "Sorry honey."

He turned to their father and said putting a hand on his shoulder, *"Children dwell in their dreams. Get them the wings and they'll fly."*

That evening, as Amber came home from college, she gave her parents the customary evening kiss and went into her room. She was taken aback as she switched on the lights of her room.

There was something stacked in the corner of her room covered under the bed sheet, "Mom! You got the renovation started?" she turned back to door yelling, "Dad! I told you not to..."

She was shocked again, On the back of the door was a note for her. It read, "SORRY!"

Quickly she turned back towards the heap covered under the bed sheet. She gave it a quick pull and beamed with happiness.

Underneath were big gift wrapped boxes perched neatly, and on top was an envelope holding a card. She went for it instantly, opened it and it read...

"We love you Amber – Mommy and Daddy."

This was not written, rather painted with a brush, in red paint, which was still a wee bit wet.

There was a stick she felt inside the envelope. She pulled that out. It was a painting brush, which was still wet, with red color on it.

Amber was engrossed, she quickly unwrapped the first box. It was a full set of different sized painting brushes. Curious, she opened the next one and 'wow' it was filled with oil paint tubes. Now visibly excited, Amber jumped onto the next – this one was stuffed with canvas frames.

Overwhelmed, Amber squealed, "Mom! Dad!" with tears in her eyes and ran to embrace them. Her parents were standing at her door, along with Kim and Viktor.

Viktor was holding a camcorder to capture this momentous occasion. Amber's parents too were moved; they had tears in their eyes. Amber ran quickly and hugged them. The family cried tears of joy, hugging each other tightly.

Kim too joined in, sobbing and hugging them.

"Guys!" said Viktor adding a bear hug to the whole bunch, turning the camcorder on selfie video mode, "I am also a part of this family now. I also need a hug."

Amber hugged him, holding his neck and he started yelling, "Ouch! What did I do now?"

"Nothing!" she sobbed, "Thank you!" and she kissed him on the cheek.

∞

10 A.L.O.N.E sales continued to grow, until about six months later when they finally peaked and things began to settle down.

But in many ways Viktor saw this as a good thing. Now that more people had read the book, a fan base had been established. This led Viktor to more exposure as various newspapers and magazines published more reviews and called in for more interviews.

A couple of months more, and the sales reached their saturation point. They plummeted until they were virtually back to square one.

Everyone who had read the book had given him hope, saying it was a brilliant effort for a first-time novelist. But it all fizzled out when he went by the local bookstore to see their sales.

Despite the good reviews and the enthusiasm of his readers, the book was being forced off the shelves by other fresh, new books coming up in the market. Quickly he learned the reality of the publishing industry.

When Viktor went to the AuthorsOwn office to learn more about the issue, Peter, the company's CEO, explained to him, "My friend, every year, thousands of books are published, and they all face the rise and fall of the times."

"You are right." Viktor sighed. "Sometimes reality hurts, but I have to continue dreaming."

"Absolutely," agreed Peter. "My so-called well-wishers used to tell me to leave my dreams and live in reality, but I always believed – *Work to live up to your dreams and fantasies; to hell with them who ask you to come back to reality.*"

"What can I do to help you in this?" Viktor asked.

"Thanks my friend," he smiled, "The reality is that the reach of your book in bookstores is less; and the reason is, limited distribution due to capital constraints."

"*A friend with seed (capital), is a business-man in-deed,*" said Viktor with a smile. "I am happy to invest some money too."

"Well!" he sighed, "We can enhance the marketing plans, but money doesn't make the story run, public does."

Viktor smiled, *"The moment you think you are out of resources; you still have one thing – the will to win. Ignite it."*

Despite being made aware of this fact, Viktor continued to scour every bookstore he came across for copies of his book. When Kim took him out shopping one Saturday, he went straight to the bookstore as though on an urgent errand.

Not finding his book anywhere near the best-seller shelves, he couldn't help but feel defeated.

Viktor was quiet on the way back home.

Kim, who wanted desperately to console him, rolled down her car window and said, "Look, the clouds are following us."

Viktor was still mum.

"Honey," Kim said. *"Challenges are like vehicles in the rearview mirror. They appear larger and nearer than they are."*

Viktor glanced at her, managed half a smile, and again concentrated on driving.

She continued motivating him, *"Keep your spirits higher than the challenges would allow."*

Still heavy at heart, he offered a small nod and continued to drive in silence.

When they reached home, Viktor went straight to his study and sat down to relax on his rocking chair. He let the silence consume him, and soon it almost felt as though he was invisible.

Kim entered to check the room and thinking he was asleep silently went about arranging his things. Cautious not to disturb his sleep, she moved quietly, dusting surfaces and tidying up the room. She saw a stack of copies of his novel lying on the study table. She picked up one of them, took it to the living room, plopped down on the sofa, and started reading again.

A little later, her cell phone rang. It was Amber, asking to meet up with her. After the call, Kim went back to the study room and checked the time. She was surprised to see that an hour had passed. She quickly went to Viktor, who still had his eyes closed, and planted a soft kiss on his forehead. "Love you, honey," she whispered and left to meet Amber at her college.

When she returned four hours later, she found the house shrouded in darkness. She switched on the lights.

"Vik?" she called. The car was parked right outside, and his keys were at their usual spot.

She decided to check inside the study room and she found him still at the same place she had left him.

"Hey," she said gently, walking towards him. "Are you alright?" She placed her palm on his forehead, checking his temperature. It seemed normal. His eyes opened slowly.

"Feel like going out for dinner?" Kim asked.

He looked around as if disoriented.

"Dinner?" she repeated.

"No thanks," he answered, stretching. He pressed his palms over his eyes and sighed. "I'm not hungry."

"Come on, you need to eat," she said, taking his hand and trying to pull him from the chair.

He stood up from the rocking chair and sat behind his desk, leaning back and closing his eyes.

"What happened," she walked over to him. "Why are you so upset?"

"I'm not upset," he replied a bit too aggressively.

"Yes, you are," she said, standing behind him. She brushed her fingertips against his eyelids and kissed him on the forehead. "I don't like to see you like this."

He didn't reply.

She swung a leg over his thighs and sat in his lap. She looked into his eyes and said, "Let's do something junglee."

Viktor seemed disengaged.

She kissed on his nose. "Tomorrow is the weekend. We'll do whatever you want. But right now, you have two options for dinner; either we go out to try a new restaurant, or I'll cook for you tonight."

He moved her from his lap and rested his head on the table.

"Vik! You were never so unromantic!" she was surprised to see his reaction. "Ok! If you don't get up, I'll tell Amber to come over, and our plan to spend time alone would be ruined."

He still didn't bother to reply.

She went behind again and tickled him.

He held her hand tightly, saying in a serious tone, "Please, Kim. I'm not in the mood for jokes."

"Okay, okay." She went to the kitchen and got a bottle of wine and a glass. She returned to the study room and moved the pile of books next to his elbow.

"See! I served the wine in one glass only. We'll share?"

He was still quiet.

"There is something I remember from your novel," she said, picking up one copy of his novel and started searching for a specific page. When she found the chapter, she started reading out aloud: *"Life will never give you what you want from it."* She looked at Viktor, hoping he would react, but he didn't.

"You will fail again and again," she continued, *"but life will not have mercy on you. You have to try again and again."*

Viktor turned his face away.

"Life gives, but in pieces. It's you who must assemble…"

"Will you please shut up?" Viktor yelled before she could complete the sentence.

Kim was startled and nearly dropped the book. She looked up to see his face contorted in anger.

She had never seen him like this before. With a lump in her throat, she said softly, "I am just trying to help you out."

"I don't need help!" he shouted.

"But...."

"Enough Kim! Just go!"

"I just..." she tried again.

"I said go away," he yelled, swinging his arms in anger and knocking the pile of books off the table.

The glass broke, wine spilled, and books flew across the room. One of the books went flying in Kim's direction. She stood static, overwhelmed with shock.

The book hit her on the lower side of her rib cage, and she cried out, bent over in pain.

Viktor froze, realizing what he had done. His anger faded away and was quickly replaced by concern and remorse. He ran towards her.

"Oh, God! I am so sorry, Kim." He held her tightly. She was holding her side, he gently placed his hands over hers, hoping he could somehow absorb some of the pain he had caused.

She looked away, flinching.

"I am so sorry," whispered Viktor, pulling her close.

They stood still for a moment, and he listened to her shallow breathing. Suddenly she seemed so small in his arms, and he hated himself for it. All this time this woman did nothing but share her strength with him, and he hurt her.

Viktor kissed her hair and then her temple. *"It's you who must assemble whatever life offers, according to your needs,"* he said softly, almost whispering the words in her ear. *"It's you who must realize how you can get exactly what you want."*

She raised her face, and their eyes met. He offered her a gentle smile.

"I learned that from you, you know," he told her. "I've learned so much from you."

Finally, she managed a little smile.

"I am so sorry for hurting you honey," he whispered kissing the tip of her nose.

"It's ok," she whispered back.

"You know, they say," he said playing with her locks over ears, *"Hurting a soft-hearted person would please you, but the loss is yours. You will have true friends less one."*

"Ahan?" she smiled.

"Yup!" He nodded. "And I don't wan to lose a great friend like you."

"Oh! Is it?"

"Hmm! You are like a library with trillions of books."

"Hah? How un-romantic," she made faces.

"Ok! What can I do to make up for being such a jerk?"

"Oh, you'll make up for it, all right," she said, raising an eyebrow.

Viktor rested his chin on her shoulder, "I'll punish myself by making dinner for you."

"No, please!" she said, pretending to gag. "Anything but that! You cook horribly."

"How dare you insult my culinary talent." Viktor feigned a gasp as Kim squirmed out of his arms and fled towards the kitchen, giggling.

He laughed and quickly ran after her. She rushed behind the serving counter to avoid him. Viktor jumped over it, and caught her in a bear hug.

She tried to free herself, but couldn't. He leaned on her and gave her a big kiss. Falling into each other's arms, they broke out into fits of laughter.

Rise in Love

Falling is old school

E ven before their laughter could subside, Viktor came close as if to whisper sweet nothings.

"Let's dine out at that new Chinese restaurant." He said leaning closer and pressed her against the kitchen cupboards.

"Noooooo," Kim pouted, enjoying the physical intimacy, but still pretending to be angry.

"Junglee." Viktor playfully bit the tip of her nose. "What about spending the night at that country cottage we saw before? What was it called?"

"Wood's uphill?" she asked smiling with an enquiry in her eyes, and as Viktor nodded, her joy knew no bounds and she gave him a peck on his nose.

"Let's get going quickly," Viktor said adding to the enthusiasm while sweeping her straight off her feet and carrying her towards the bathroom. Kim still laughing, lovingly nudged him out and closed the bathroom door.

She appeared in front of Viktor. He stopped buttoning up his black ban collar shirt as he saw her in a knee high red drape. She flaunted her heels.

"Mesmerising," said Viktor walking towards her. "Let's cancel the plan and do something at home," he smirked and started unbuttoning his shirt.

"Junglee!" she punched him softly, "Be quick."

Within half an hour they both were fresh and ready for a romantic dinner. On the way to the cottage, Viktor called up the reception to book a room and order their food, he was thoughtful and wanted to make it special for Kim. He chose all her favorite dishes, he knew would help her enjoy.

When they reached their destination, Kim was amazed to see a warmly lit terrace seat reserved for them on the hilltop. The breeze was warm, cozy lightings on the grass, with candles glowing inside their green-tinted holders embossed with flowers made for a perfect setting.

As they settled in, happy with the view, a waitress arranged the cutlery and began turning up the wine glasses. She turned the ladies first and as she moved to turn Viktor's glass, Viktor stopped her midway. "That's fine; we will need only one, please, thank you." He said to the surprised waitress. Kim gave him a knowing look and smiled.

Both sipped wine from the same glass adding a doze of love to the cosy setting. Kim removed her sandals and settled well. During the dinner, she put her feet on top of Viktor's in a way to stay in touch while they ate.

The weather was pleasant, painting their color of love on the sky. They enjoyed every sip of the wine, sharing from one glass and feeling truly connected. Dinner was the right beginning. Kim enjoyed her food specially ordered to her taste and soon after they moved towards the railing of their cottage, holding each other's hands and gazing at the stars, glad to be far away from the chaos of the city, together and happy.

Even the clouds in the sky seemed to be smiling at them and wishing them a lovely life together, they thought. As the clouds floated by, the moon appeared shining like a bright silver ball.

"Hey!" said Viktor, pointing towards the moon. "See that ring encircling the moon."

"O Yeah! Wow! It's so beautiful, isn't it?" Kim responded leaning closer into him with sparkling eyes.

Viktor whispered, pulling her even closer, "Not any more beautiful than you."

Gently aware of their closeness, Kim looked him into his eyes and whispered, "Vik, I love you." She then gently held his neck, caressing his jaw line with her thumb.

Viktor held her face in his hands and pulled her closer, kissed the top of her head whispering. "Love you too, Kim," and gave her a peck on the lips.

Lost in the moment, Viktor bit her lower lip, lightly.

"Ouch!" Kim broke the lip lock, and touched her lower lip with her finger. "Junglee!" she said, hitting him softly in the belly.

"Yes, I am," he said smugly. "So what?" He teased her, bent down and picked her up in his arms.

"Oh, God, you're crazy!" she shouted again, looking down the valley.

"Still afraid of heights, haan?" asked Viktor, going near the railing.

"Nope!" she said. "It's you I'm afraid of, leave me." She pretended to be fighting to set herself free.

"Seriously?" he smirked, "Should I leave you?"

"Shh!" she put her finger on his lips, "No! Never ever you dare to leave me."

"That I can't even think of," he smiled.

"But! Leave me for now," she struggled again. "People are watching."

Viktor held onto her rather tightly. "Sorry, lady luck, I can't and I don't care about people."

He walked towards the railing, taking her with him. Kim looked back down the valley and then straight into his eyes, saying. "Your eyes are saying silent words to me, and my smile is the answer." she beamed with love.

"Ahem," screeched Viktor; smirked at her and turned back towards the room.

Once in their own space, they disconnected from the whole world. Both were immersed in each other, as they looked deeply into each other's eyes. Viktor leaned over and gently set her down on the bed.

As he was about to stand, Kim grabbed his hand. He bent down again and kissed her forehead, then left cheek, followed by right, then chin, and then nose, lastly he kissed on her lower lips and later upper and quickly bit her lower lip.

"Ouch! Junglee," she said. Holding the back of his neck, she pulled him closer saying, "You'll be punished for this," planting a passionate kiss on his lips.

Their lips parted, and their tongues danced and explored each other, devouring the sensation of love.

"Happy to be punished like this, lady luck," smirked Viktor, "What about the capital punishment of love?" he winked.

"You!" she said jumping onto his lap, biting his neck. He bit her earlobe and cradled her. His right hand slipped beneath her T, brushing the softness that was still bound by a violet halter. His fingers fiddled desperately but she didn't allow him to set herself free.

She turned back, put her foot on his shoulder, caressed his earlobe with her toe and said, "Mr Different! Show me your creativity, set me free, a bit differently." She posed like a queen.

Viktor put his right hand on his heart, bowed smiling and headed towards her. He grabbed her from the shoulders in a salsa position, quickly turned her back up, bit her neck.

"Ouch," she smiled. Viktor clipped her lower back drape with his teeth and pulled down, bit the halter hooks and pulled that up.

"Mind blowing! Perrfecct!" she said holding that.

Viktor smiled and bowed again smirking, "Experience makes a man perfect!"

"You!" she clinched grabbing the back of his neck, "What experience?"

"Aao!" he closed his eyes in pain, "Your nails piercing my neck."

She bit his ear and pierced her nails along his back, "Experience, ahem?"

"No!" he laughed and cried altogether, "First experience only."

"Better!" she released him and then hugged.

Viktor leaned over and planted so many kisses on her collarbone in a go and working his way down, buried his lips in her skin, nibbling around her navel.

"Oooh!" she whispered, pushing him back on the bed and straddling his belly. She patted him there, smirking. "Six pack? Your lady luck wants two more!"

Viktor gazed at her, as the moon shone on her face through the window blinds.

Kim noticed his stillness and enquired "What's wrong?" in whispers.

"Nothing," he replied, still a little lost in love, "You are making the moon glitter." He said touching her warmly on her cheeks.

Her lips curled into a smile, her round brown eyes still high on love. She leaned forward and melted into his arms like an impetuous wave. She pulled his shirt wildly, tearing off the first button.

"See! Who is junglee now?" said Viktor, laughing.

She slid onto him, nestling against his shoulder, and giggled. "I am a wild queen, Mr Viktor! I am allowed to do anything."

He pushed her back down on the bed and straddled her, holding her arms tightly against the mattress.

"Leave me, you..." she said, pretending to try and free herself.

"Now who will save you from me, wild queen!" said Viktor, struggling to kiss her as she gave him a good taunt moving her face away, allowing him to chase a kiss.

The fun was full on, laughing, giggling and struggling in a bid to free herself from his strong grip. "Oops!" she said as she hit something off the table with her foot.

Viktor checked to see what it was. "My mobile? Why, you..." He leaned in closer to restart the love fight.

"Wait!" she said. "Switch off the lights."

Viktor got up and switched off all the lights, except for the red colored dim table lamp. When he turned back, Kim was not on the bed.

He walked over to the other side of the bed, hoping to find her hiding with coy, not there. He then bent down to look under the bed for her, but she was nowhere to be found.

As he got up to stand erect, she jumped on him from behind the curtains, pushing him onto the bed. She then quickly nailed him sitting on him, saying, "I love surprises."

"I hate surprises," he smirked looking her right in the eyes.

"Ahem! Liar," she said, and started tickling him. Viktor sat up, held her hands tight, and their gaze met again, longing and loving. He touched her nose with his, and then pressed his lips against hers, then her chin, then her neck….

He pinned her hands behind her back, pulled her onto his lap, and caressed her waist with the tips of his fingers. She kissed his collarbone and shoulders and won her set of hands free, pulling him closer as her nails again pierced his back.

They moved together in an ageless rhythm. She moaned softly as the air around her swelled up with passion. And, outside, the moon obligingly hid its face behind the veil of clouds that drifted slowly across the heavens.

They kissed blindly as the wind whispered through the pines. The ebb and flow of the water outside murmured a sweet serenade. As the waves kissed the shore, there she was, amid a sea of sheets, nestled in his arms.

∞

Kim was lying on Viktor's chest. "I can hear something," she began softly.

"What's that?"

"Your heartbeat. It's like music straight from your heart," she whispered, tracing patterns on his stomach. "You make me complete, Viktor."

Viktor smiled, kissing her hair and pulling her close, whispering, "You made me find myself."

∞

The next morning, Kim woke up to the faint chirping of birds. Viktor was still asleep.

"Good morning?" she whispered in his ear. He took her in a bear hug without opening his eyes and kissed her on her neck.

"You want tea?" she asked.

"Nope!" he whispered from his slumbers, "I want you."

"I am all yours and now our soul is one."

He opened his eyes smiling and looked at Kim. Soft rays of sunshine peeked through the blinds, bathing her flawless body with a golden glow. He ran his fingers on her calm, innocent face.

"Junglee queen," he whispered in her ear.

She stirred, smiling. She pulled him near, and kissed his earlobe.

He moved his fingers along the contours of her upper back and said, "Her highness, you're bathing in gold."

She touched his hair and retorted. "Junglee king! You coloured me golden last night."

He chuckled and took her hand, giving it a kiss. "I am no longer a king. You won me over, madam." he said with a peck on her neck, followed by another on her lower back as she rolled on to her back side.

He continued kissing her beautiful curves. Still enamoured with their lovemaking last night, he let his lips travel slowly down her body, inch by inch, kiss by kiss.

Kim smiled closing her eyes, feeling every single kiss he planted.

Suddenly Viktor broke loose in concern. "Hey, what the hell is this?" he enquired touching a patch of skin below her ribcage.

"What?"

"This blue mark here," he said, touching her skin in that area.

She tilted her head, struggling to see, "Ha-ha, that's a love-stamp, you junglee."

"No Kim, it's not red. It's blue, and it's a big one, like something has hit here." He stroked it softly, "Does it hurt?"

"No. It's not hurting," she shrugged.

Still touching Viktor yelled "Oh God! I think that's where the book hit you. Hell!" He woke up with a jerk, "It's my fault. Oh god! We should go to the doctor."

"It didn't hit me that hard, honey," she feigned a plea. "And it doesn't hurt, anyway."

Viktor ignored her, throwing his cloak on and tossing hers to her, "Get up, quick! We need to move."

She lay back on the bed moaning, "Oh, come on. Come back to me, we'll go later."

Viktor noted the longing in her voice. He walked over to her, pulling her up close to him and lovingly dressed her up, putting the coat on her himself. He then picked her up and carried her all the way to the parking lot, holding her as close to him as possible.

"I'm telling you, it's just a love bite," she said, nuzzling against his neck all the way.

"Shhh." Viktor silenced her sweetly as he seated her down in the car, motioning her to be quiet as he dialled Andy, his family doctor.

∞

"It's probably dermal melanocytosis, a technical term," said Andy, after examining the blue spot where the book had hit.

Viktor still tensed and unable to understand sought to know more. "And what does this dermal something mean?"

"Birth mark," Andy Replied.

Kim burst into a full smiled at Viktor as if to say *I told you so*, but Viktor was still tense and asked, "But she is not feeling pain there."

"There's no need to worry," Andy consoled him. "The skin sometimes is extra sensitive at birth marks. The blue color will go away in a day or two." He wrote a prescription and gave them an ointment to speed up the healing process.

On their way home, they stopped by the pharmacy to pick up the rest of Kim's medication.

"Look, clouds are following us," she said, sticking her head out the window.

"Kim, don't. You have to rest," he said pulling her back in. She tried to protest, but he wouldn't listen. "Shhh! You have to rest."

For a minute there was a heavy silence inside the car.

"I have an idea," Kim snapped her fingers.

Viktor looked at her, scowling, "No outing, only rest. Ok?"

But she continued, "Why don't you take your novel to India and launch it there?"

He didn't respond but for that moment he had instant brightness in his eyes.

"Well?" Kim persisted.

"Yeah, good idea," he muttered unknowingly, "I think I can..."

She turned towards him, stretching her seatbelt. "See!" she smiled, *"It doesn't matter whether you can or cannot. Whether you wanted to or whether you tried is what the whole game is about."*

He considered her words and smiled, imagining the pulse of the audience in India, "Would they be receptive to a story like this?"

Some other thought broke his line of thought "Hey, listen," he said. "That reminds me, *Teetu*, My cousin is getting married next month."

"The Delhi one?" Kim snapped her finger.

He nodded smiling.

"Wow! Yes!" She clapped her hands in delight, "See? It's perfect! You should make both things happen together, no?"

"Not two, but three things!"

"What's the third one?"

"I want to give Mom a present," he said winking at her.

"Aww! My sweetu!" she said, hugging him and cat rubbing her cheek against his arm. "Can I jo…"

"Nope!" he interrupted. "You cannot join me! You stay back and take rest."

"Oh! Your sixth sense works, haan! But I was not asking for this," she chided.

"Ohkhay! Done then, thanks, I'll be going alone."

"Nope! How can you even think like this?" she cried fuming out her anger onto the pamphlet on the dashboard, but Viktor seemed unwavering.

"Okay, how about this?" she stretched. "I'm going to guess what you're going to give your mom, and if I guess right, then I get to come with you. Deal?"

"No way, I bet you already know what it is."

"I don't!" she laughed. "Come on, let me try guessing."

"Nope!"

"It's a sari, right?"

He groaned.

"Come on, pretty please? Let me join you?" she pleaded.

"Why do you want to come with me, anyway?" Viktor asked innocently. "It's just another boring trip."

She crossed her arms, feigning annoyance, "Ok! I don't care. Go wherever you want to."

He looked at her, then back to road and whispered, "We'll go where you want us to, your highness."

She grinned and rested her head on his shoulder. "I want to go where Mom and Dad had met for the first time on their trip to India."

Viktor furrowed his brows in thought. "That I don't know for sure."

"McLeod Ganj. You know, in the Himalayas? I think Mom mentioned it to me one time," she jogged her memory.

"Oh, yeah! I've never been there, and I have heard that it's a really awesome place."

"So how about it, Mr Viktor? Would you like to take a vacation with me?"

"Of course, would-be-Mrs-Viktor. It would be my pleasure."

∞

They spent the next few days planning their visit to India. After applying for leave from the office, they started shopping for gifts to bring home. And of course, Amber was always ready to help them in selecting colors for gifts in exchange for White Mischief ice-cream treats.

Viktor was filled with a renewed vigour. Kim's idea had ignited a new spark in him. He was more than happy to take the chance of releasing his book there as India was close to his heart.

It was the country where he realized his dream of becoming a writer; the moment when a boy from the Delhi street handed him that pen so many years ago. More than that, it was his mother's country, his first home.

∞

Viktor's mother was busy in the kitchen when the doorbell rang.

"Chachi ji!" someone shouted from the door.

She wiped her hands as she walked from her kitchen to open the door. Standing at the door was one of her nieces with a worried look on her face. Viktor's mom asked what was wrong, and the girl replied by pointing towards the street.

The older woman looked outside, and sure enough, a man was standing two houses away, facing the other side. It seemed as though he was searching for someone.

Viktor's mother, famous for her spontaneous and open help in resolving all sorts of conflict, no matter whosoever, immediately asked, "Is he bothering you?" And without waiting for a response, she marched outside in a blazing fury, still clutching her ladle and muttering insults under her breath.

"Road-side Romeo!" she yelled in Punjabi. "*Nass pitta, daffa hona, ruddh jana!*"

She gave him a hard tap on the shoulder, and the man, with the muffler on his face, turned around.

She jumped in shock, recognizing her son. "Laddu?"

Viktor laughed, wrapping her in a tight embrace. "Aah! You can cover your entire face and your mother would still recognize you. *Moms will always be moms,*" noted a bemused Viktor.

Tears of happiness started rolling down her wrinkled cheeks. She swatted his arm for the silly prank and instantly knew that his cousin was in on the prank too.

Amidst this high drama, she caught a glimpse of someone standing on the periphery. Blinking her eyes for a clear view of her face, her face lit up when she realized who it was – none other than Kim.

His mother welcomed both of them with a pooja thali, put tilak on their forehead. Kim looked at Viktor with raised eyebrows, surprised and equally amazed at the welcome, "They are worshipping us as if we are gods."

Viktor smiled, "This is how we Indians welcome the would-be-daughter-in-law as she enters her would-be-in-laws' home for the first time."

His mother gave her a sweet from the *pooja thali.*

"What is this?" asked Kim holding that with one hand.

"Take it like this," said Viktor folding his hands with palms facing up, "This is *prasad.*"

"Ok Mr Laddu," she winked.

Mother laughed turning towards Viktor and gave him the prasad saying, "One laddu, for my laddu."

They entered his home and first went to the receiving area and bowed to a framed photo of Viktor's late father sitting on top of a wooden shelf surrounded by fresh yellow flowers.

The welcome was warm and wonderful. Kim got to experience a dose of Indian warmth as many relatives visited Viktor on the same day and everyone of them treated Kim as if she was a part of the family.

Happy with the outcome, Kim whispered to Viktor "They are treating me like they know me and they are behaving like I am a goddess."

"This is India, my daughter," said Viktor's mother. She stood behind Kim and put a gold chain around her neck. "You are a guest, and you are a woman. That's why you are being treated like the goddess Lakshmi."

Kim was over the moon, overwhelmed by the immense love from Viktor's family. "What is this?" she asked, touching the locket.

"A token of love," replied his mother, "Laddu's grandmother gave me this when I came here for the first time."

Kim looked at her and then Viktor, tears welling in her eyes. Viktor was about to wipe them away but his mother got there first, wrapping Kim in a tight embrace and kissing her cheeks.

"There is only one mother in this world who is the best one," said Viktor, resting his head on her shoulder and smirked, *"The one that every kid has got."*

Kim too smiled, wiping her tears of joy. It had been so long since she had felt the love of her mother, and she felt the same touch in her mother-in-law.

"Kim! You know, our relatives say that Laddu bhai has fled from the US with a gori," said Viktor's cousin.

Kim laughed out loud, winking at Viktor, "I didn't know you had a thing for blondes."

"And I didn't know you understood the Hindi word gori," Viktor said.

"Oh, and I also know what a laddu is, and *who* the laddu is. Cute nickname, by the way," she teased, pinching his cheek.

∞

Later that evening, Viktor and Kim helped his mother and cousins in the kitchen. Kim, being new to the Indian cuisine, felt the full impact of an Indian kitchen at work. She sneezed every time they fried something with strong masalas.

After a five-course dinner, they all sat in the living room to chat. Kim connected a video call with her side of the family in the US, and they all spent a few minutes catching up with Viktor's mother.

In the meantime, Viktor began handing out gifts and varieties of chocolates to everyone in the room. Kim noticed that the notorious gang of cousins first picked up all the liquor chocolates.

"Amma," he said to his mother, "This one is for you." He handed her a present covered in a golden wrapping paper.

As she began opening the gift, his cousins tried to guess what was inside. "An iPhone? Tablet? Camera?" the drama heightened with every guess.

However, tearing off the last of the wrapping paper, his mother let out a delighted gasp along with everyone else. It was a copy of Viktor's novel. She held it gently, running her fingers over the letters on the cover. She wiped a tear from the corner of her eye. "It's your name," she whispered.

Viktor stepped closer, "Mummy, you've given me so much; all my life," he held his mother's hand. "I want to give some of it back to you."

"Proud of you, my son," she said, her voice breaking with emotions, embracing him.

"Something is there," he said. "Open the book."

She looked at the book again, and found a folded sheet of paper tucked inside the book, "What's this?"

"Read it," Viktor said smiling.

As his mother read the contents of the page, her hands began to shake.

"Show me," said Viktor's cousin and read aloud, "Oh my God! License to operate the school?"

Viktor's mother broke into tears.

Kim and Viktor hugged her together. "I know how much you and Daddy always wanted to do this," he said. "You've done so much to help me follow my dreams. I thought it was time you had yours come true."

Kissing his cheek and said, "Thank you puttar."

"Come on Mumma, this is nothing in front of your happiness," Viktor smiled. "Daddy might be smiling in heavens," he said looking up and closed his eyes in content, with tears rolling down.

"Aww! My hero, my laddu!" Kim said kissing him and everyone sitting around them bit their tongues.

"Yes, I am honey, but I was not born one," Viktor giggled. "Mom made me." He turned to his mother, "Now I want her to make a few more heroes in her own school."

∞

The living room bustled with warm notes of conversation. It was getting late, but no one seemed to care about the time. Viktor discussed his plans with his mother; the plans for launching his novel in India, attending his cousin's wedding, and then visiting Ladakh via McLeod Ganj.

The whole family shared stories over many bottles of wine, and everyone seemed determined to ask Kim as many questions as they could think of.

Reena, one of Viktor's cousins, asked, "Bhabhi! How did you and bhaiya meet?"

Kim paused.

"Bhabhi means sister-in-law," Reena explained with a laugh.

"She knows what it means," Viktor said in Kim's defense, ignoring the teasing hoots around him.

"Bhabhi, come on! Tell us!"

"It's actually not that interesting," Kim chuckled.

"Not to mention it's embarrassing," Viktor laughed. "At least for me!"

"Now you really need to tell us!" there was an encore.

Kim looked at Viktor. "Should we?"

He shrugged signaling his vote as everyone egged them on.

"Okay then," Kim said, feigning a resigned sigh. "We met outside the ladies' washroom. He didn't realize he was in the wrong room until he noticed the crowd of angry women forming a circle around him. And then he nearly ran me over on his way out. It was very romantic." She playfully kissed the tip of his nose.

Viktor covered his face with his hands donning an Indian actress and groaned as everyone doubled over in laughter.

"Bhabhi!" said another cousin, "You know once Viktor bhaiya fled from home."

"Oh! Why?" asked Kim controlling her laughter, "He didn't tell me."

"Oye! Shh!" said Viktor asking his cousins to be quiet, "Nothing Kim! They all are joking." All were rolling on the floor laughing.

The cousins controlled their laughter and began to spill the beans, "He forgot to buy vegetables and kept on playing cricket in the street. For the fear of getting scolded from chachi, he fled."

That night, all of the gossips most likely involved plenty of embarrassing stories about Viktor, but everyone seemed to enjoy every single moment.

Later, they played a game of charades, during which, to Kim's delight and everyone else's horror, Viktor was forced to re-enact scenes from dirty Hindi movies. Large bowls of homemade popcorn and fried chips were passed around, and while Viktor declined, everyone else helped themselves to cranberry cocktails and a large selection of wine. Even the younger cousins sneaked a few sips behind his mother's back, which he pretended not to have noticed, knowing very well what would ensue if he said a single word.

By the end of the night, Kim and Viktor's mother found a nook to settle down for chit chat. Seeing that the two most important women in his life finally had the chance to bond,

Viktor felt warmth in his chest. Everything in his life seemed to fit right back into its place, including his determination and belief in himself too… all reignited at last.

∞

At three in the morning, when everyone was asleep except for a few cousins, Viktor caught Kim's attention and gestured for her to meet him upstairs. When his cousins refused to let her go, he bribed them with a few dollars each and some more liquor chocolates.

They met on the rooftop, near the water tank, upon which a small candle, a bottle of champagne, and two glasses sat waiting to be enjoyed.

"Who arranged all this?" asked Kim. "You said you don't drink at home."

"Secret sources," he replied with a wink and a quick embrace. "And I never said I don't drink at home. I said I never drink in front of Mom." He laughed.

They sipped their champagne and watched the stars in comfortable silence. Viktor lay down, resting his head on her lap.

"Look, there's no ring around the moon today," whispered Kim, pointing to the sky.

Viktor raised his hand, touching her wrist and then her palm. "It's here," he whispered back, brushing her wedding ring with his.

"Are you aware of how sappy you are?" she replied before giving him a peck on his nose, then on his lips.

"Oh, am I?" Viktor gushed. He pulled her down and bit her lower lip. "That's why we're perfect for each other."

"Junglee," said Kim hitting him lightly on the chest.

"You too," he whispered. "My junglee queen." And then he gave her the softest kiss his lips would allow.

∾

Viktor spent the next few days arranging his press release event. The city travel brought back all his memories and he somehow wanted to re-live the golden memories of his youth. He used this running around to grab an opportunity to meet up with his old friends.

He took Kim and his mother out for shopping, and they spent their days at a plethora of Delhi markets. Kim enjoyed learning how to eat *golgappas* and trying out a wide variety of saris with his mom at Connaught Place. He also took them to the famous gurudwara Bangla Sahib.

Viktor bought champagne while shopping for groceries and showed to Kim from behind the counter. The moment he turned back to put the bottle in the trolley, he saw his mother who looked at him with a hand on her hip.

"For Rahul," he explained her.

"Grab another one for me too," said Kim reaching there.

"Shhh, Mom's watching," Viktor whispered.

Kim controlled her laughter, "I mean get one scented *agarbatti* packet for me too."

Just then a store clerk came by with a bottle, and said, "Here is the other one you asked for, sir."

Kim covered her mouth laughing as Viktor avoided his mother's stare and mumbled, "Mumma! Come on, that's for Richa, Rahul's wife."

"Rahul! Don't tell Rix, I want to surprise her," Viktor said over the phone while on their way to visit the couple.

"Your call," Rahul chuckled. "You know she'll kill you anyway."

When Viktor and Kim reached his friends' house, he whispered to Kim at the door, "Watch this." He cleared his throat and rang the doorbell. "Courier!"

"Rahul!" Richa yelled from inside, "Door!"

"I'm in the washroom!" trailed Rahul's voice.

Hearing her footsteps coming closer, Viktor hid behind the wall, pulling Kim towards him. Richa opened the door and looked around. Finding no one there, she went back inside, muttering, "Silly people!"

Viktor rang the bell again. She returned to see who it was, and finding no one there, she shut the door, a bit more roughly this time.

Viktor seemed to enjoy the prank and moved to ring the bell one more time, but before he could, the door swung open, revealing a very disgruntled Richa. "Who the hell...." she stopped in her tracks, surprised to see Viktor.

"Hey... Hello Rix!" Viktor greeted with a wide smile.

She slammed the door in his face.

"Hey, Rix!" he called, knocking on the door. "Remember me? It's Viktor! Viktor the mutant!"

"Mutant?" Kim repeated, raising an eyebrow.

"That's what they used to call me," he explained, rolling his eyes.

"Rahul! Buddy, open the door!" he yelled, knocking.

"Go to hell!" Richa shouted from inside.

Viktor looked at Kim, who still had an eyebrow raised. "They love me; she's probably just having a bad day." He squirmed sheepishly as an explanation to all the drama that unfolded.

After a few minutes, the door opened quietly, Rahul peeking out.

"Rahul!" Richa yelled again. "Don't you dare open that door!"

He ignored her and stepped outside, quickly hooking his arm around Viktor's neck and yanking playfully. "Saale! I told you she doesn't like surprises."

"She'll get over it," Viktor grunted. "Now stop embarrassing me in front of my wife."

Rahul turned around, finally noticing Kim, who was watching them with an amused look on her face. He let go of Viktor, exclaiming, "Monkey! You got engaged to this gorgeous lady?" He grinned and offered a hand to Kim. "Hi, I'm Rahul. Sorry, didn't see you there."

"Kim," she said, shaking his hand. "Vik has told me so much about you."

"Vik?" he looked at him with surprise.

Viktor straightened his collar and smiled at Kim. "See! I told you they love me."

Kim laughed, shaking her head.

They went inside, finding Richa sitting in front of the TV with a remote in her hand, furiously changing channels without really watching anything.

"Come on, honey," Rahul said to her. "So he missed our wedding. But he's here now, isn't he? Forgive and forget."

Richa crossed her arms.

"Aww, Rix, I said I was sorry," Viktor said. "I really wanted to be there, you know."

She huffed.

"Well, at least say hi to my wife?"

Richa turned to face Kim, still avoiding Viktor's eyes. "Hey," she said, "Nice to meet you, and sorry for ignoring your would-be-husband."

"Hi," Kim said. "Sorry, he is a terrible best friend."

"Hey!" Viktor protested. "You're supposed to be on my side!"

"That he is," Richa said to Kim with a smile. "I like you already."

Kim smiled back, and then looked at Viktor. "Sorry, honey, but you did miss your best friends' wedding."

Viktor rolled his eyes. "I said I was sorry," he muttered. "Hey, where's Chintu?" he asked Kim.

"Who's Chintu?" asked Rahul.

"Chintu, our baby boy," Viktor replied casually.

"What? When?" Rahul asked.

"Kamine!" shouted Richa at last, jumping up from the couch, towards Viktor. She began hitting his arm. "You're so infuriating, you annoying piece of..." She gave in one final slap.

"Ow!"

"You didn't even bother calling us up after the wedding!" She yelled, pulling his hair.

"Ah, Rix!" Viktor cried in pain. "Didn't you read any of my e-mails?"

"E-mail? Wow! Thanks for sending one," she continued. "You don't attend my wedding, and you apologize by sending me an e-mail! Rascal!"

"Not just one, it was more than one e-mail!" Viktor protested.

"You're unbelievable!"

"Okay, honey, how about we let go of Viktor's hair..." Rahul pried her fingers off of Viktor, "and take a seat for a second, okay?"

"I had to go to Japan for an assignment," Viktor explained, rubbing his head. "I swear I did everything I could, but they wouldn't let me leave. I really missed you both... especially during the midnight margaritas." He grinned lopsidedly.

Richa glared at him.

"Anyway," Viktor said, clearing his throat and throwing an arm around Kim's shoulders. "I'd like you to meet my wife Saavitri."

"Saavitri!" Richa threw a cushion at him. "You still need to learn how to lie."

She walked over to Kim and hugged her. "I don't know how he *patao* a sweet girl like you, Kim."

"Hey, how did you know my name?" she asked, returning the hug.

"Sweetie!" Richa said. "*Good friends see each other all the time. Best friends don't need to, but they still know everything.*"

"Aw!" Viktor chimed in, reaching out to join in the hug. "My baby Rix! You have no idea how much..."

"You just shut up, ok," Richa interrupted. "You guys are not yet married. Your mom would kill you if you got a baby before that. Chintu, huh." She turned to her husband. "And you Mr Rahul Sharma! You were a part of this surprise, weren't you?"

"Ooh, full name," Viktor winced. "You are gone, dude. Nice meeting you. Bye."

Rahul pulled him by the collar. "Shut up or I'll let her cook you alive."

"Okay, okay," Viktor laughed, putting his hands up. "I really did miss you guys a lot. Remember our tequila shots? Here is one." He pulled up the bottle from his trousers.

Richa's face softened. Viktor continued, "And that road trip when one of the tyres blew in the middle of the highway and we all thought we were going to die? Doing silly dares at the mall and running around the streets at three in the morning? I miss that."

Silence swept in. Viktor continued, "And that deadly accident of jet-ski on Goa trip when I took a steep turn. God I was almost dead."

She was crying now, and Viktor wrapped her up in a hug. "And you *kaminas* never tried to get in touch with me."

"Saale, it was you who never called back," said Rahul.

Viktor hugged him as well. *"Friends understand the unsaid words, no matter if they are silent for years."*

Rahul punched him, "You wrote this quote? Third class, huh."

"Sorry, yaaaar." Viktor said, "I know that was my mistake too. I was too caught up in my so-called fancy world of immaterial success."

Richa hugged them back, apologising in between sobs. Even Kim was wiping her eyes.

"Well, I think this calls for a celebration," Viktor said, opening the champagne and raising a toast. "It has been more than ten years now, so I think it's only appropriate to drink to that. To our *Basmati* friendship."

They eventually took the party to a nearby club, calling up two more of their friends to join the fun at around 2.00 a.m.

∞

Friday Night

Thank God it's Friday night! Bande bandiyaan honge tight!
Disco ka mera mood nai hai... karu ghar pe open... invite.

Fa fa fa... Friday night... This is the Friday night
O O O Friday night... Friday niiiight

Hai bottle shottle kiske pass Chatt pe aa jao bindass!
Antiquity ka stock nikalo! Chakhna khatam to Maggie banalo!
Office wali ko maaro ghanti... room-mate jo na ho auntie

Nai chahiye koi chain-chain karti... Breezer peene se jo darti
LIT ke level wali... Bottoms up pe shot ho khali.
Workoholic ghar hi baithe... Vadde wale cute jo kehte...
Cheeee! You are so dirty! But I am right...

Challan de Friday night... Fa fa fa Friday night
Na na na Friday night... Friiiiiiiday night.

Make-up shake-up rehn de chhori... Flash maarke lagegi gori
Carlton ki chappal pa ke... lift nahi lechalun uthake.
Gat gat peegi kone mein khadi... Happy-high deewar te chadi
Bahaan kholke hunn chillawe... Titanic de pose bnaawe
Siyappa thalle gir na jaawe... Kehndi kass ke pakdo mainu
O my sweetu shona jaanu!
Ni aaja thalle baith ja ethhe... Hone de thodi booty dirty...
and life bright...
Kyonki hai Friday night... Fa fa fa Friday night
Na na na Friday night... Friday night
Gang hoeya sadda poora talli... Chipak ke baithe koi ni kalli
Ab vo main bajaunga... What?
Guitar main bajaunga... Tujhe Salsa karwaunga
Har pose bhi sikhaunga
Bhai! Gaadi main chalaunga...

Okhay! Short & sweet I will play. On the rocks, then highway
Limit te signal karenge cross... Bean bag with choco sauce
Meetha karega double... Gandawala headache kal
Hangover ka hai jugaad... Yaar tera ik dum faad
Char AM pe chalenge dhabe... Desi ghee ke allu pranthe
Monday blues ki tension karti... bole mujhko nai hai chadti
Baby chill, take it light.
What the... Fa... Friday night... Fa fa fa... Friday night
Na na na... Friday night... Friday night!!

∞

After the party, when other friends had gone home, the four of them decided to go to Murthal Dhaba, a famous eating joint on Delhi highway.

"I want to drive," said Rahul in his drunken state.

"Yeah," replied Viktor. "Let's sit in the back seat and drive."

Richa drove the car with Kim riding shotgun. Viktor managed to haul Rahul into the backseat, where they immediately started an imaginary racing game, mimicking engine noises and pretending to steer aggressively.

"You took a good decision of settling abroad man," said Rahul.

"Yup, but that was not my dreaming," Viktor nodded.

"Dreaming? Driving? You are driving right hand side car there and here you are sitting on left side?" giggled Rahul and started shouting. "Challan, fine, traffic police, any body? Fine him."

"No one can stop me now," said Viktor burping. "I'll fly, towards the sky, Grrrrrrr," he accelerated his imaginary machine.

"Good! Go go!" yelled Rahul.

Viktor looked him and said, "I am flying, but still not living my dreams."

"*Arrey dreams ko poora nai kiya to life kya ghanta jiya?* Life without living your dreams is like a bell without pendulum," replied Rahul. "Start living now, live now, look at me," he inhaled and paused and then exhaked. "See I am living my dreams." And they laughed uncontrollably.

Richa and Kim looked at them and then smiled at each other. They took the opportunity to share stories about their lives. By the time they reached Murthal, they seemed to be the best of friends. Viktor and Rahul, meanwhile, were fast asleep in the backseat.

Kim tried to wake Viktor, but he wouldn't budge.

"I know what to do," said Richa with a little smirk. She grabbed a chilled water bottle from the glove compartment and poured its contents on the sleeping buddies.

They got up with a jerk. "Welcome back!" she said gleefully, ignoring their sputters of protest.

Inside, they ordered tea and *paneer pakoras* and began reminiscing their childhood days.

"You know, Kim," said Rahul, "Mr Viktor here is good at many things, be it programming or balance sheets or even guitar, but he is dumb at playing cards."

Kim laughed. "I know, he can't even play the simplest card game."

"He was so shy and dumb at even talking to girls," added Richa. "He shivered while even touching the back of his salsa trainer. It took us days to make him comfortable with her."

"I know," said Kim. "He told me."

Rahul pulled his cheek, "Naughty boy! You told her everything, haan?"

Then he said stuffing a big paneer slice in his mouth, "I can write an entire novel on all your silly attempts to win at poker, my dear friend."

Viktor laughed replying, "And I can make an embarrassing three-hour movie about you, complete with jingles and dirty animation."

He turned to Richa and Kim. "One time, for example, he was about to give a presentation on shares and debentures. When he plugged in his pen-drive there were images that popped up on the screen for the whole class to see. The problem was these images had nothing to do with shares and debentures; they were pictures of his dirty booty dancing at a birthday party." Richa and Kim couldn't help laughing.

"Yeah, I'll never live that down," Rahul said glumly. "Someone had stolen my pen-drive that contained the actual slides."

Viktor nodded. "And then slipped the birthday photo pen-drive in the second pocket of your bag right before the presentation."

"Saale!" said Rahul with surprise. "How did you know about that?"

Soon enough, Rahul was running with a bottle in his hand and Viktor was running for his life. Richa was a few steps behind, trying to stop them both.

Kim sat back, enjoying the show. She was happy to see Viktor with a mischievous and carefree look on his face, laughing with his oldest friends. It was her first time seeing this side of him, a version of her future partner that was not pre-occupied with book sales and spreadsheets. He was simply himself, free of worries about the future, basking in the moment and reliving his youth.

Viktor and Kim were in Chandigarh with Viktor's mother, attending his cousin's wedding ceremony. Viktor and his mother were dressed in traditional attire and were talking to relatives. The pandals were decorated with flowers and the chandeliers with colored bulbs. The ladies and little girls, who gathered near the chaat and golgappa stalls, were dressed in saris and kurtis and patiala salwars, necks laden with jewellery.

Meanwhile, the gents were in golden kurtas, some in their Indo-Western suits. Most of them were gathered near the bar, where occasionally someone would yell, "*Darru di peti khol bai. Soda thoda pa.*"

Viktor was searching for Kim when someone yelled, "The bride is here!"

Viktor turned back. It wasn't the bride, though. It was Kim, dressed up in an elegant red sari, entering the room with Viktor's cousins. She was so beautiful, he couldn't help but stare.

"She's not the bride!" someone yelled, but all eyes remained on her.

"Congratulations, bro! Bhabhi very *handsome,*" said a drunken relative, reaching over to shake Viktor's hand.

"Hmm?" Viktor said distractedly, still looking at Kim. For some reason, his relatives started congratulating him and his mother.

Just then, a group of girls and boys entered the venue, finally followed by the bride. The boys carried a long dupatta decorated with roses, holding it up from all corners, high with their hands straight in the air, above the bride who was in a red sari that was decorated with golden embroidery.

Kim was amazed to see all this. She was curiously watching the bride when Viktor walked up to her. "Hey, what's that around her wrists? Can you buy me that."

"That's chura," Viktor replied. "These are eighteen to twenty bangles per wrist, indicating that the girl is married. She has to wear them until one year after her wedding."

"And that thing hanging from her fingers?"

"*Kaleere,*" Viktor answered. "Hey, let's go to the rooftop. I'll explain everything in detail."

"We can't leave now, everyone will see us," she whispered.

"Trust me, no one will notice," Viktor said, pulling her towards the stage.

The groom got up from his seat onstage and came to receive the bride near the steps. The sisters of the groom welcomed the bride on stage, and the photo session started.

Viktor rushed towards the exit, motioning for Kim to follow him. After a while, escaping all the attention from Viktor's relatives, Kim finally managed to reach the staircase.

Finding her way to the rooftop, she leaned against the boundary grills to check if Viktor was there.

"Ah!" she yelped in surprise as Viktor hugged her from behind.

"My junglee queen!" he whispered in her ear. "You look drop-dead gorgeous in this sari."

"Stay away, you loafer," she smirked.

Viktor pulled her closer, breathing, "I have revenge to take."

Viktor tightened his grip on her waist and leaned forward. Kim closed her eyes.

"Bhaiya!" a group of girls suddenly came yelling. The couple jumped and immediately let go of each other. They ran up to them and said in unison, "Didi! Let's go."

Viktor remained frozen in place as one of his cousins chuckled, commenting, "Aw! Bhaiya looks like a thirsty crow." She grabbed Kim's hands and pulled her away.

"Stay there, you!" Viktor ran after them, yelling, "And she is not your didi, she is your bhabhi! Sister-in-law!"

His cousins led them back downstairs, where the bhangra bash had just started. Not missing a beat, Viktor began to dance, pulling Kim and his mother to the dance floor.

∞

Kick lick leer di...

Kick lick... Kick lick... Kick lick...
Kikli kaleer di... Jugni sohni heer jaee.
Mahi labdi Ranjhe varga... pyaar kare jo beparwah.

Kikli kaleer di... Sohna sunakkha ranjha vee.
Heer heer karda rehnda... wait kare love story da.

Jugni chad gai banere... sadke jawaan channa tere.
Je mahi nu aaj miladen... poori mannataan karaden.
Mahi de dil vich khich barabar...
Rab sunle taan main jawaan mar.
Akhaan tarsan tarsan tarsan...
Kraade setting chal hun chal hun!!
Kick lick... Kick lick... Kick lick...
Kikli kaleer di... Jugni sohni heer jaee...
Mahi labdi Ranjhe varga... pyaar kare jo be parwah.

Kismat naal doven jad takkre...
Akkhaan'ch gallan hon befikre.
Miliyaan hathaan di lakeeraan...
Fasgaye sentimental janzeeraan.

Zindadi pyaar bina hai kujh ni...
Fer lagge duniya jannat wargi!!
Kikli kaleer di... Peengh paalo pyaar di...
Heer te Ranjha milde rehange...
Sab fair in love & waar ji...
Kikli kaleer di... Kikli kaleer di...

∞

The wedding was one of the best opportunities for Viktor to introduce Kim to all of his relatives. His family seemed to take an instant liking to her. Everyone was already treating her as a member of the family. Kim, though it was her first time to attend one, enjoyed witnessing all of the rituals of an Indian wedding. After all, singing and dancing was always her thing.

As the rituals progressed, Viktor explained them to Kim.

"Hey, Viktor," she said, "When are they going to do that thing, where the bride and the groom walk in circles around the holy fire?"

"You mean the *phere?*" replied Viktor.

"Yeah, *saat-phere.*"

"That's not until four in the morning. We'll be back at the hotel by then."

"No! Please! I want to see it."

"Mom will be there. We don't need to go."

"Come on, it's not every day that I get to be at an Indian wedding."

"Oh, fine." He smiled mischievously. "But you'll have to give me something in return," he whispered in her ear.

Suddenly someone pulled his ear from behind. "Ow!" he cried, turning to see who it was and immediately recognized his aunt.

He quickly bowed in greeting. "*Masi Ji! Pairi-paina!*"

"*Viaah tak rukk jaa kake?* Wait till you get married," said the lady.

Viktor rubbed his ear, mumbling sheepishly," Masi! We were just talking."

Kim quickly bowed as well. "Masi Ji! Pairi-paina!"

"My sweetheart," said Masi in English, pulling her in a warm embrace. "I'm so glad that you're learning about Indian culture."

Kim smiled, blushing.

Masi pulled her cheeks. "Spread some Indian culture in America as well, and give us four or five cute babies as soon as possible, yes?"

Now it was Viktor's turn to blush.

"So what are your plans this evening?" she asked.

"We are attending phere," he replied quickly.

"I thought you said Mom will attend in our place," Kim said with a little smirk.

"No, no. Mom wants you to see the rituals." He scratched the back of his head, avoiding her eyes.

Masi replied quickly, "Go and watch the pheras, then. I'm sure you will enjoy it."

Kim nodded. "Hanji!"

Viktor raised his eyebrows, surprised to hear her speaking in Punjabi.

"See, Laddu," Masi said to him. "Soon she'll be speaking Punjabi better than you."

Kim laughed and added, "I also want to attend the… what do you call it?"

"Which one, dear? Shagun?" Masi asked.

"No, I think it's… something… *Rahat…*"

"Rahat?" Masi looked at Viktor.

"Um, Suhag-Rahat?" Kim said.

Masi's jaw dropped. *"Hayeni main marjawan?"*

"Wow, again Punjabi words? What does this mean?" Kim asked.

"Sorry, masi ji!" Viktor said, blushing. "Catch you later!" He pulled Kim away and asked, "Who is teaching you all these Punjabi words?"

"Your sisters." She shrugged.

"Silly! Suhag-raat is the couple's first night after the wedding," he laughed, leading her towards the dinner arrangements.

"Oh, no!" she whispered, covering her face and cracking up in spite of her embarrassment. "And what did masi ji say? *Haye Haye* something?"

"What do you think? She was shocked."

"Well, it's still a cool word. No?"

"No!" Viktor laughed again. "Come on, let's have dinner and get some rest. We need to be ready by four."

"Aw, baby. Come here, let me give you a good kiss," she said, reaching for his cheek.

"No," Viktor whispered, imitating his aunt. "We should wait till our wedding." Then he started running, beckoning her to follow. As she entered a hall room, he pulled her into an empty room, and without uttering a word, kissed her.

They looked into each other's eyes.

"I love you, Viktor."

"You look awesome," he held her hand above her head and kissed her neck, "Austerity, if I were to define, I'll say, It's YOU." He planted another kiss on her forehead, "I love you too, my junglee queen."

∞

At 4.00 a.m., a few of their close relatives gathered for the ceremony. The pandit started the rituals by chanting Sanskrit mantras. He asked the groom to put his hand forward, and then asked the bride to rest her hand on the groom's palm.

He poured holy water on their palms and handed them a long-tailed spoon, instructing to put ghee in the holy fire. Then the priest asked the groom to recite his vows after him, followed by the bride.

"What are they saying?" Kim asked.

"It symbolizes the seven sacred promises," Viktor's mother replied. "They are promising each other that they will be together throughout their lifetime, and for seven births."

"You know what pheras mean?" Viktor asked Kim.

Kim looked into Viktor's eyes and replied, "A bond between the couple that will last for seven births of reincarnation."

Viktor raised his eyebrows in appreciation.

She smiled back, blowing him a kiss. Viktor pressed his fingers to his lips and was about to return the gesture when he suddenly dropped his hands to his sides.

She raised her eyebrows. He tilted his head slightly by way of explanation. She looked behind him, and sure enough, there was Masi, hawk-eyed and watching the two of them.

Kim covered her mouth, trying desperately to control her laughter.

The pandit asked the bride and groom to stand and start the pheras. Along with them, the relatives also stood. As the pheras started, everyone showered the newly-weds with flowers.

With every progressing phera Kim was enthralled, dreaming of her own wedding.

∞

Early the next day, they caught the Shatabdi Express train and went back to Delhi. In the train, the three enjoyed the photos of wedding and while scrolling through, by chance Viktor's mother saw Viktor and Kim's photos kissing each other. Kim quickly pulled the phone.

∞

Viktor's novel was scheduled for release in another two days, and he was busy making some last-minute arrangements in preparation for the event. Kim helped by interacting with the media personnel for the press release. Without fail, he dedicated his days and nights to the book launch.

His friends, Rahul, Richa and others were excited about it as well; sometimes even more than he was, it seemed, that every time they would introduce Viktor to their other friends they would chuckle, "He is an author, because he is my friend!"

The big day finally came. Viktor found himself standing in front of more than five hundred people. *"They say that well begun is half done,"* he said to them by way of introduction. *"But I think it's perseverance all throughout that takes you through a great journey towards a great end of a milestone and then another trip."*

The hall resonated with deafening applause.

"Mr. Viktor! What's the success mantra you follow?" asked a reporter.

He quoted smiling, with open hands, *"Dream high, beyond the sky; no matter wings so small, keep the vision bright; just dare to learn, for you are born to fly."*

"Sir! Are you an author by chance or by choice?" asked another reporter.

"It was an indication by chance; pursuing it was my choice." He said but audience seemed confused.

He continued, *"There are always enough indications from the universe to us, telling us the sole purpose of our life. You ignore it. The day you find it, you find yourself."*

He showed the pen case to the audience, "I was indicated by the universe with this pen-set case marked *Writer's Dream* and it took me five years to realize the purpose of my life that I have to be an author, so I chose to be one."

"Why did you take so long to realise?" asked a girl.

He replied with a pause, *"When you say, SOMEDAY I'll live my dreams, that is the eighth day of the week and it never comes. Start working for your dreams TODAY.*

"I had so many excuses and kept on cribbing for years, before *I realized that the moment to make your dreams come true is day before tomorrow, same time, called NOW.* That's what I did."

Viktor got a standing ovation as he finished. On stage he had a contended smile seeing such a good response from the audience.

The very next day, a few newspapers flashed about his book release. Viktor's mother got many compliments over phone calls and from neighbors too.

A few local newspapers covered the event. Seeing the way people responded to his efforts, Viktor was able to realize the power of his perseverance. His hard work was paying off, and this day had shown the results.

To pay obeisance for his success, Viktor took his mother to the Lord Krishna Temple as she wished.

"I come here often," said the mother to Kim. "Not only because I am a believer in the deity, but also because of the spiritual lectures that are delivered here."

She always went to visit the same sage, who, though now in his nineties and seemingly very frail, was always happy to have visitors.

"Who is he?" Kim asked.

"Guru Ji," she replied. "He would sit for hours and talk to his followers, just listening to their problems and helping them figure out the solutions."

The hall was full of devotees who were chanting hymns. The guru stood on a platform, addressing his followers, his voice deep and enthralling. "Lord Krishna said," the guru spoke…

"You forgive everyone before you go to sleep, and I would forgive you before you wake up." The words reverberated in Viktor's ears.

"Here 'I' refers to God," the guru added. "God doesn't want you to go to him for finding the path. He is already with you, in your heart. So follow your heart with full devotion. All God wants in return is for you to serve the needy, and beyond that, to make them capable of helping themselves."

Viktor felt chills hearing Guru Ji's wisdom. He was amazed to hear the most important lesson of his life told in such a simple way.

Kim noticed the sudden change in Viktor's demeanour. He seemed peaceful, almost as if he could preach the philosophy of Karma itself, as though he had just reached a state above all good and bad, where there was nothing but silence within his heart.

For the rest of the day, Viktor was wrapped with a sense of calmness. At the dinner table, he spoke very little, still reflecting on the guru's words of wisdom. That night he had the most soothing sleep of his life.

∞

Early morning the next day, Viktor and Kim took a taxi and left for McLeod Ganj.

"I'm sleepy," said Kim, stuffing headphones in her ears and leaning back in her seat.

"Me too," said Viktor, resting his head on her lap and closing his eyes.

The continuous honking of car horns woke him up from his deep slumber.

"Oh! One hour has passed?" murmured Viktor, checking his mobile. "Why so slow?" he asked the driver.

"Yes, sarr! Tiraffic."

"Delhi traffic kills," he said, looking at Kim who was still sleeping with headphones in her ear.

Viktor yawned, stretching his legs. Suddenly someone started tapping the window on Kim's side of the car, rousing her from her sleep.

"Oh my God!" she yelped, startled to find an old woman holding a kid, peeping in and asking for alms.

"O! Hatt hatt," yelled the driver. Viktor took out a couple of oranges from his bag and offered them to the woman. She refused and left.

"They no eat frroot, sarr," said the driver. "They throw, ask paise only."

Then there was another knock, this time on Viktor's side, causing him to jump in apprehension.

"Oye!" the driver yelled. "Hatt!"

It was a young man with rugged hair, carrying a stack of books and holding them up against the window.

"Oye!" driver yelled again.

A memory stirred in Viktor's mind as he sat there, trying to place the man's face. He carefully raised his index finger as recognition began to dawn on him.

"Hatt!" driver yelled again.

"Wait," Kim said to the driver seeing expressions on Viktor's face.

"Hey! You are…" Viktor exclaimed with joy.

The young man smiled back as if he had recognized Viktor as well.

Viktor rolled down his window.

"No Sarr!" the driver said, moving the vehicle, "Not good!"

Viktor interrupted, "One sec. Stop the car."

Viktor held out his hand and offered a handshake. "Hi!"

The young man took his hand and held it tightly. Then he kissed it and, closing his eyes, pressed Viktor's hand to his forehead. Then he looked around, and as he located an old person standing near another car, he started motioning for that person to come to him.

"Oh! He is deaf and mute," Kim said.

"You remember?" Viktor told Kim with joy, "Writer's Dream?"

"My Goddness! He's that guy?" Kim said, surprised, "The one who gave you that pen set?"

Viktor beamed.

The old person came towards Viktor's taxi. He was in his sixties, with a long white beard and a white cap over his head. He was holding a bag full of novels, and Viktor gathered that he was probably the main supplier of the books his young friend was offering to the passengers of vehicles passing nearby.

The boy conversed with excitement, with the older man using his hands and facial expressions. With his every gesture the old man's smile grew wider. As the boy finished telling him something, the old man turned to Viktor.

"Sir!" he said, holding Viktor's hand. "Myself Karim, father of him. I Happy… I meet you."

Viktor stepped out of the car. The old man continued, "Sir you change my son life."

Viktor shook his head. "Your son is a brilliant and smart worker, very intelligent."

"He like books," the old man said happily. "He always want make book business. But no money."

"Five hundred note you give that day, he only buy novel and sell. Earn profit, then buy more, sell more, buy more, sell more. See," he indicated towards a roadside bookstore.

"Coooool! That's amazing," Viktor said with a big smile, patting the boy.

"Today, we get own bookshop, sell novel, story, magazine. Come to shop, please," he invited.

"Thank you, I would really love to, but it's getting a little late," Viktor apologized. "But I will come and visit some other time. Your son is blessed by Almighty Allah. The great Allah stays in his heart, your son will succeed even more." Then he turned to the boy and saluted him, then held his hand towards the sky and placed it over his heart. "I liked your work."

In return, the boy gave Viktor a hug.

"One sec," Viktor quickly turned and said to Kim, "It's in my laptop bag."

Knowing exactly what he was referring to, she located the item and gave it to him. As he turned towards the boy and showed it to him, the boy's eyes widened, seeing the pen case he had sold Viktor all those years ago.

With tears rolling down his cheeks, he showed the pen-set to his father and fellows. Seeing his joy, the old man and his other young fellows too were in tears.

"*Ya Allah!*" the old man exclaimed.

"Vik, show him the book," said Kim from inside the car, handing him a copy of his novel.

He gave it to the old man. "God sent your son to make me realize my dreams."

The old man took the book with a curious look on his face, which was quickly replaced with awe the moment he turned it over and saw Viktor's photo on the back cover. The boy raised his eyebrows in astonishment and pointed at the photo, then at Viktor.

As Viktor nodded, the boy quickly took out his pen from the pen case and asked Viktor to sign the book. The old man put a hand inside his pocket and retrieved a few bills, which Viktor refused.

The man insisted and pressed a hundred and fifty-one rupees into Viktor's palm, saying, "*Shagun hai*. It's an auspicious amount, with blessings for your success."

Viktor took the money with a smile. "Thank you."

"Sarr, going late!" the driver reminded.

"Okay! Khuda hafiz, friends. May Allah bless you with success," Viktor said, hugging them both.

"Allah hafiz!" replied the old man, returning the gesture.

As they got on to National Highway, Kim said, "The world is so small. I feel so lucky that I saw that. Happy for you Viktor."

"It all came full circle," Viktor said, still smiling.

∞

The hotel that they checked in at McLeod Ganj had an exceedingly pleasing view of the Himalayas. But it was already dark, so Viktor and Kim decided to rest and get an early start the next day.

As they left for the outing the next morning, Kim saw a newlywed couple coming out from the next room. Recognizing

Viktor, they asked if they could get a photo taken with them. Kim, not used to being approached by complete strangers, enjoyed the brief moment of being a celebrity. The couple then recommended all of the surrounding Buddhist temples for Viktor and Kim to visit.

They left for their destinations, and Viktor was amazed to see so many foreigners there.

"Bhaiya! St. John Church," he said to their driver.

When they reached the destination, both were amazed to see a breathtaking view of snow-covered peaks. They went inside the church.

"It was built in 1852," said Kim.

Viktor looked at her, astonished. "How do you know?"

She gave him a little smile, saying, "My dad used to tell me all about this place when he was still alive."

"Wow," said Viktor, studying the wooden floor and the pillars that were still intact, as though frozen in time.

"See these windows?" said Kim, pointing at the vibrant stained glass windows. "This is Belgian glass donated by Lady Elgin, the wife of Lord Elgin who was—"

"—the Viceroy of India and the Governor General of the Country of Canada."

She looked at him. "How did you know that?'

Viktor shrugged. "I googled it." They burst into laughter. Viktor was glad to get a laugh out of her. He'd been a little worried that this trip would upset her; it was one of the places where she felt most connected to her late parents.

He was amazed to see the colorful light that shone through the windows, falling on them as if they were being blessed by the Gods.

They lit candles and stood there for a moment, closing their eyes.

"What did you ask God for?" asked Kim.

"Nothing," replied Viktor. Kim smiled.

He added, "I just thanked him for sending someone in my life who helped me find my dreams and changed my life."

He held her hands. Kim smiled but remained still.

"And you?" he asked.

She sighed deeply and said, "I said… hi… to my mom and dad."

Tears started rolling down her face. He held her hands tight as she continued, "And then I said, 'Meet Viktor, the love of my life.'" She raised her eyes to meet his.

"Oh, honey," said Viktor, brushing a hand against her wet cheek. "I am always there for you," he whispered in her hair as he wrapped her up in a hug.

Later they left to visit the nearby forts and temples. They were mesmerised by the mountains, white and glinting in the distance. After roaming around for a while longer they went to the famous water fall and then decided to return to the hotel.

On the way back, they asked the driver to pull over by the local market, where they bought Tibetan artifacts, metal prayer wheels, and prayer thangkas.

The weather was getting pleasant. Kim was enjoying it so said to Viktor, "I want to stay a little longer."

"Ohkhay!" said Viktor asking the driver to go to the hotel as that was nearby.

"See that cave, let's sit there," she said, pointing.

As they entered they saw a small tea stall inside that was run by a boy.

"Tea?" Kim asked Viktor. They sat down and placed their orders. Viktor seemed much more relaxed after their visit to the religious places.

"All those bells ringing at the temples have certainly pushed away all that silly noise in my head."

Kim nodded. "So you're defragged now?"

Viktor grinned. "Yup! And I can see you're enjoying your time off, too."

"Let's go to the Buddhist monasteries tomorrow," said Viktor as they'd had their tea,

Viktor went to the boy and took out his credit card.

"Hon, I think they only accept cash," Kim said.

It was starting to rain and Viktor looked at her, alarmed. "I don't have any cash on me for this travel other than this card!"

Laughing softly, she quickly took out a hundred-rupee note from her purse, gave it to the boy, and pulled Viktor along in the rain.

"Sir! No change!" said the boy to which Kim asked him to keep the change and ran towards the roadside.

"I want to feel it," she said, standing at the corner of the road facing towards the valley with her arms wide open.

Viktor held her from behind and kissed her neck. He rested his chin on her shoulder. For a brief moment, they allowed themselves to escape reality, lost in the beauty of the sight in front of them.

Soon, thundering started, and heavy rains poured. Laughing, they both started running down towards their hotel, which was fortunately not too far away.

Back inside their room, Viktor unpacked his camera and wallet from his waterproof bag. "That was pretty awesome, wasn't it?"

"I loved it," she replied, collapsing on the bed, "Now I know why Mom and Dad were so in love with this place."

"Oh, hell!" Viktor suddenly exclaimed, searching his jacket pockets.

"What's wrong?"

"Where did I put my credit card?" he said.

"You showed it to the kid at the tea stall."

His eyes widened, trying to remember if that was where he could have left it. "I'll be back," he said, scrambling to the door. "You order something, I'll join you in a bit."

"Wait!" said Kim running after him and gave his a five hundred rupee note, "Take this."

Viktor reached the stall, dripping wet in the heavy rain. He entered the cave. An old, bald man was sitting there, dressed in a maroon-colored robe, sipping tea. Viktor guessed he was a monk.

To Viktor's surprise, no other person was there in the cave-like tea stall, not even the tea vendor.

"Excuse me!" he said to the monk. The old man didn't reply and continued drinking his tea. Viktor looked inside the small cave, but found no one.

Outside, there was only one passerby who was running from the rain that was getting worse. Viktor stood looking out, trying and failing to cover his head with his hands.

"Are you searching for something?" asked the monk.

Viktor turned, a bit surprised to hear him speaking in English. He replied quickly, "Yeah! I think I left my credit card here."

"Hmm!" the monk nodded, taking another sip of tea.

"Have you seen it, by any chance?" Viktor asked.

The monk didn't bother to reply and took another sip. Viktor tried looking around outside again.

"I thought you came here searching for peace," said the monk.

Viktor, slightly taken aback by what the man had just said, chose to ignore his strange reply, assuming it to be a technique for somehow swindling money from the foreign nationals.

He bent down onto his hands and knees to look for his card under the table made of stone.

"It's neither under this table…" the monk was saying.

Viktor ignored him.

"… nor under your office table."

Viktor looked up, bewildered, and stared at him. He was a very old man, and yet his face was bright. His eyes seemed to contain a deep sense of calmness.

The monk smiled, pressed his palm against his chest, and said, "It's in your heart, my boy."

Now completely distracted, Viktor gave up on his search and asked, "What is in my heart?"

The monk smiled, taking another sip of his tea.

Viktor turned towards him, his missing credit card now completely forgotten. "Tell me. What am I searching for?"

"Of course, happiness!" the Monk replied.

Viktor took a small step back. "What are you talking about? You've never met me before."

"Peace of mind, dreams of life… " the monk continued.

"Well, sure," Viktor concurred. "Everybody does; so do I. Yes, I want happiness."

"Really?" asked the monk, lifting an eyebrow. "Think about it carefully. *I want happiness*," he said, stressing each word.

Viktor nodded slowly. "Yeah, I want happiness." He sat at the table in front of the monk, now eager to hear more. "Tell me, where would I get that?"

The old man smiled and said, "*Those thinking about the Why, When, Where, and Who are merely the providers of information; the one asking the HOW is the true leader in solving the problem.*"

"Okay, then" Viktor said, nodding. "*How* would I get that?"

The monk smiled and said, "*The knowledgeable has the intelligent answer; but only the intelligent one asks for a knowledgeable question."*

Viktor sat up straight, waiting with rapt attention,when the monk took another sip.

"*I. Want. Happiness,*" he joyfully repeated, laughing to himself.

Viktor calmly waited for his answer.

"First remove the *I*," said the monk.

Viktor furrowed his brows.

The monk didn't bother to explain him and simply continued, "Then remove *Want*."

As Viktor slowly began to make the connection, the old man finally asked, "What are you left with?"

Viktor felt goosebumps all over his skin.

"What are you left with?" the monk asked again.

"*Happiness*," Viktor whispered with reverence. He shook his head, unable to comprehend how something so seemingly complicated could suddenly make the simplest sense.

He leaned forward and grabbed the old man's hand, holding it tightly. "Thank you. Thanks a lot."

The monk smiled and took his last sip of tea. "My tea is over. I must go now." He stood, taking his time.

Viktor stood up in haste. "Please bless me by joining me for dinner tonight."

The monk smiled again. "But I am always with you, my boy."

Viktor thought he felt a jolt of energy from the man's hands, and once more he felt his skin prickle.

"Sir!" a boy suddenly yelled from behind him. "Your card!"

Viktor turned, letting go of the monk's hand, and saw that it was same tea stall boy who was waving his missing credit card.

Viktor was surprised to see that he hadn't noticed there were two other caves on the same side of the road.

"Hey, look at that," Viktor said to the monk, but quickly realized that the old man was gone.

He saw him walking away, down the road, and soon he disappeared in the heavy rain. Viktor stood there for a moment, thinking about what had just happened.

"Sir, your card!" the boy said again, pulling Viktor's T-shirt.

Viktor was lost in his thoughts, a million questions in his mind – except for one, to which he had just received an answer. *How to be happy.*

Viktor thanked the boy and he replied, "No welcome sir. Thank. Thank. Bye."

The boy turned around to leave and Viktor called him, "Hey!"

As he stopped, Viktor reached out and gave five hundred rupees, "Good boy!"

He resisted to it but Viktor gave it to him forcefully and went running back to the hotel, where he narrated the incident to Kim.

She looked at him, wide-eyed. "You know, Gautama Buddha once said the same words to one of his pupils who asked for happiness."

"Really?"

She smiled softly, saying, "Yeah! Dad told me."

Viktor was lost in his imaginations.

"*Everything happens for a reason*," said Kim, who believed it to be a miracle. "It will change your life, Viktor."

That night Viktor played the afternoon's events over and over in his head, trying to make sense of it. He couldn't believe that, completely by chance, he had just had one of the best experiences of his life.

The next day, they covered the Buddhist monasteries, where he kept an eye out for the monk. But the old man was nowhere to be found.

The day after that they went to Ladakh, where the mesmerizing sight of snow-covered mountains and deep green valleys took their breaths away.

Hovering in a helicopter over the valley, suddenly Viktor could see how everything he laid his eyes upon was connected to one another, as though the whole world was opening itself up to him. He felt as though he had finally found the truth of all things, and all he had learned and practiced so far in life seemed meaningless in front of his experiences from this trip. It was a bit unsettling for him and he had tears in his eyes.

"Hey!" said Kim touching his cheeks, "What happened?"

He couldn't speak and nodded everything to be ok. Kim hugged him, "Oh Viktor. Control yourself, I know you are experiencing something beyond your imaginations and emotions."

She looked at Viktor and whispered, "Don't worry, I am with you."

Viktor kissed her and they enjoyed the scenic view. Viktor allowed himself to be embraced by this vastness. He seemed to be at peace in that moment.

∞

After their expedition, they returned to Delhi and caught a flight back to the United States.

"This trip to India was the best journey ever," said Viktor to Kim during the flight.

"Yeah!" Kim nodded.

"And I am happy I experienced it with you. After all, it's because of your tea craving that I met that monk."

They recounted all the events of their trip, from the launch that had gone well, to how quickly Kim had been accepted and welcomed into Viktor's family, to the detour to McLeod Ganj and Leh which had been a life-changing experience. What more could they have asked for?

"But what exactly did you learn from the '*I want happiness*' incident?" asked Kim.

"Removing the *I*," Viktor replied, "means removing your ego. Removing the *Want* means removing your wishes and expectations."

Kim nodded. "And you are left with *happiness*."

They both laughed softly, still unable to believe the simplicity of it. Then Viktor noticed that an Indian man had been staring at them for some time.

Immediately the man got up from his seat and walked over to them. "Are you the author of *10 Alone*?"

Viktor smiled. "Yes. Yes, I am."

Next moment, Viktor was giving out autographs to the passengers who got to know one by one. Kim was feeling happy to see Viktor amidst all this *happiness*.

Sadness is...

When somebody you love...
becomes someone you loved

At 10.00 a.m. the following day, Viktor was back behind his desk, sorting out the clutter of mails.

"Welcome back, buddy!" greeted one of his colleagues, patting him on the shoulder. "You're all smiles today, ahem! You seem to have enjoyed your vacation a lot. So where are the pics?"

"I'll share them soon," Viktor nodded.

He resumed working through the backlog, still smiling. The whole day he received many welcome back notes and in return, he wrote back some witty one-liners, as thanks.

In the evening, Viktor, Kim and Christine went to Café Circle and Kim shared images from her mobile. They enjoyed a one hour break where Christine teased Viktor and Kim for cosy photos they shared with her.

In the late evening, he picked up Kim from the client site to drop her home.

"Hey there, happy head," said Kim, noting the smile still on his face. "It seems like you had a great day."

"Her highness!" Viktor made a sweeping bow, his smile widening to a grin. "From this moment on, every day is gonna be great and different from the one before it."

"Well, I am happy for you," Kim said, wrapping him up in an embrace.

"You know," he said, pulling back a little to look at Kim. "I've been thinking if I should leave my job and focus on writing full-time."

Kim was surprised by his train of thought, especially since he'd been worrying about the declining sales of his first novel. She waited for him to continue.

"But then I realized," Viktor added, "*Life is not about running from the things that you don't like and just doing what you want; it's about keeping the balance between urgent things and the important ones.*"

Kim looked into his eyes and nodded her head in agreement. She leaned forward, her lips meeting his in a gentle kiss.

∞

For the rest of the week, both Kim and Viktor had a very busy schedule. Viktor couldn't even squeeze in a minute to talk to Kim at the office.

One morning Viktor dropped Kim a text, "Dinner?"

"Nop! Tight timelinez."

"Nxt week?"

"K!"

"May be with family."

"Wll see."

Viktor was surprised to see her quick and short text but thought her to be busy, so didn't disturb her.

Things were so hectic that they hardly saw each other at all.

Next week, Kim forced him to cancel the dinner and they agreed to meet over the weekend instead.

One day Viktor was able to snatch a moment, so he went over to the client site to see Kim, only to be told that she had left early.

He tried calling her number when things slackened a bit in his busy schedule, but all he heard was her saying, "I'm a bit busy right now; I'll talk to you later."

Concerned, he asked Amber if everything was all right and if she could get her cousin to talk to him.

It was already Friday, but even then, they still couldn't catch a moment to talk. Viktor sent her a message, setting up a date. "Dinner tom @ Chinese Downtown?"

She replied with a single letter in confirmation, "K."

When he received her text, he tried calling her back, but she didn't pick up. She sent him another text that simply said, "Busy, TTYL."

∞

That Saturday evening, they met up at the Chinese restaurant. Viktor couldn't stop himself as he put his arms around Kim, holding her close.

"At last," said Viktor, breathing in her scent. After a while, he drew back. "How are you busy bee?"

"Good!" she replied. He pulled a chair for her.

"And how's Amber?"

"She is preparing for her exams."

He took a seat, rested his elbows on the table and stared at her for a while.

"What?" asked Kim.

"Let me enjoy the sight of the junglee queen I had missed so much." He quipped but he noticed something that made him furrow his brows in alarm. "Hey! What happened to your eyes?" He reached out to touch them gently with the tips of his fingers. "Why are they so puffy?"

She shook her head. "I just haven't been getting enough sleep." She started sipping her soup, keeping her face turned away from him.

"Night shifts, haan?" asked Viktor.

"Yes. And I'll probably be busy the whole of next week with my client work, and I also promised Amber I'd help her study." She picked up the menu and started scanning its contents.

The rest of the dinner passed in silence, and Viktor couldn't help but notice that it was the most silent meal he had ever shared with Kim.

After dinner, Viktor went to drop her. On the way he bought White Mischief ice-cream for Amber.

As she got down from the car upon reaching home, Viktor said, "Call Amber down."

"No, she might be studying."

"Okay," Viktor grinned. "Let me call her up, then."

"Viktor!" A stern look crossed Kim's face. "I told you she's studying; please don't disturb her."

He was surprised at her addressing him with full name, but he ignored and said peeping in, "But her room light is off."

"Please Viktor."

"All right." He put his hands on her shoulders in an attempt to placate her. "Calm down, I'm sorry."

When she didn't respond, he withdrew his hands and instead, gave the ice-cream brick to her.

After a moment's hesitation, he made a move to hug her. "And you need to take better care of yourself to make this puffiness go away," he whispered.

He felt Kim nod against his neck but still didn't say anything else. Viktor waited for her to hold him close, but instead of a tight hug, all he got were her arms wrapped light and loose around him. In spite of this, he tightened his hold on her, pressing kisses on her forehead and then on her nose.

He pulled back in order to look into her eyes. "I love you, Kim."

Kim's eyelids were already drooping, her face looking so drawn and tired but showing no other emotion.

"Good night," she said, giving him a quick kiss. Then she turned around and walked back inside without a second glance.

Viktor stood there, watched her, waiting to get a glance of her face if she would turn back. Alas, she didn't. She closed the door and Viktor heard her stepping up to the room.

He came back home. Texted her, "I've reached." and waited for her text, but didn't get any. He dosed off hoping for a better tomorrow, for her.

∞

Another week of tight schedules had started. Viktor's workdays ended so late that he had been leaving the office at 2.00 a.m., but this time, his approach towards life had changed.

In spite of the cramped office schedules with barely any breaks in between, he started writing a draft for another novel. He made sure to spend at least ten minutes daily, building up the plot and developing the characters.

His workdays also extended to the weekend, which he spent working on presentations and spreadsheets. Despite missing them, he didn't disturb Kim and Amber, thinking that they were probably also busy with their work and studies.

He did have the chance to talk to Kim over the phone during that weekend. Viktor shared his idea of writing another novel, to which Kim expressed her happiness.

But for some reason, she didn't seem to respond with the same level of enthusiasm as she always had in the past. He brushed it off, thinking that Kim was probably just busy helping Amber with her studies, on top of her own office work.

∞

Another week went by, no different from the first two preceding it. Despite the busyness of workdays that stretched way into the early hours of the morning, Viktor still managed to set aside time to work on his second novel.

He still called up his mother every day, and he would explain his schedule to her while she told him about the latest goings-on at home.

He felt as though he was experiencing and handling his life much differently now. He knew that all his old friends were busy, but somehow he still felt connected to everyone. He still had time for them, and for himself.

This was the life he had always wanted to live, being satisfied with what he did every single day.

"Hey, how are you, baby?" he asked Kim over the phone. It was Saturday night, and he was finally able to leave the office earlier than usual.

"Viktor! It's almost midnight," she replied groggily.

"Oh! I'm sorry! I didn't know you slept early."

"I'll talk to you tomorrow, okay?" she said, and abruptly ended the call.

Viktor was a bit surprised and tried not to feel hurt, "Maybe she was just exhausted," he thought.

The next day, Viktor tried reaching her again.

"Hey," he said tentatively.

"Viktor, listen! I'm busy! Ok! I'll talk to you later."

Something was not right. He knew they were both busy, and he respected her time, but they couldn't let their schedules take over. They'd have to make time for each other eventually. Already expecting an angry response, he dialled her number again.

"Kim, I know you're busy, but…"

"Why are you being so casual about everything, Viktor?" she interrupted.

Now Viktor was utterly confused. They hadn't had a proper conversation for a long time, but he never expected this kind of a response. "Hey, honey, wait a second. Is everything okay?"

"Yes, everything is fine," she said tersely. "It's just…" She paused, and then sighed. "We need to talk."

Viktor felt the colour drain from his face. He continued, as calmly as he could, "Yes, that's what I want, too. I want to talk to you."

"Okay. Let's meet in the evening."

"I'll be there to pick you up."

"No, I have some relatives coming over. I'll text you the place."

Later that evening, Viktor drove to their meeting place and waited for her. After ten minutes, he saw Kim entering. Happy to see her, he got up from his seat to give her a quick kiss. He was shocked to see dark circles under her eyes.

"Hey," he said softly. "All well?"

"Wow," she said sardonically. "Thank God you've got time to ask."

Viktor frowned. "Kim, what's going on?"

"Let's just sit and talk," she muttered, taking her seat.

Viktor calmly waited for her to settle and handed her the menu.

She returned it, saying, "Order whatever you want."

"You know that I am bad at ordering."

She didn't reply but started at Viktor and then looked away.

"Sorry, I'll order," he said raising his hand to call the waiter's attention. "One cappuccino, please."

"Okay, sir! And for you, ma'am?" the waiter asked.

"Just one, please, for both of us," Viktor replied, glancing at Kim.

"No, make it two, please," she said. "I'd like to have a full cup tonight."

Viktor shrugged apologetically. "Okay, then. Two, please."

The waiter smiled and walked away.

Viktor looked at Kim, but she seemed determined to avoid his eyes. He wanted to give her time to say whatever she wanted to, so he waited for her to start the conversation.

Kim's phone rang, so she stepped outside to take the call. In the meanwhile, their coffee was ready, but Viktor didn't want to start without her.

She came back after ten minutes. By then, it was Viktor who was busy with his phone. She stood for a minute, waiting for him to notice her presence.

"Now you're busy with your phone," she said, finally taking her seat.

"Oh, you're back! Done with your phone call?"

"Why do you keep texting when I tell you that I am busy?" she asked bluntly.

"One sec!" he asked, raising his hands and offering a smile. "First tell me what's going on with you."

"Oh, really?" said Kim, throwing her arms up in exasperation. "Shouldn't I be the one asking you that?"

"Oh, God. Kim," Viktor said as gently as he could, trying to calm her down. "Please tell me what's wrong. If I did anything wrong, I'm sorry. Just let me know what…"

"You did do something wrong," she interrupted. "In fact, not just one thing, but many."

"But I don't…"

"I haven't had any proper sleep since who knows when, because of work and helping Amber with her studies," she hissed. "And here you are, just…just…my goodness!" She shook in anger.

Viktor moved the coffee cups aside and held her hand. "What did I do? Please, just tell me so I can understand."

She brushed away his hand. "It's so easy for you, isn't it?"

"Honey, please calm down." Viktor was growing tense now. "What's bothering you?"

"You didn't try to see me for two whole weeks!" she finally snapped.

"I *did* try, but I thought you were busy," he replied.

"No, not me," she said angrily. "You. You are so self-obsessed, so busy with your so-called life goals that you forget the people in your life."

Viktor stared at her, trying to understand her behaviour.

"You only want your own success," she continued. "You don't have any concern about the success or failure of anyone around you."

"Wait, did you just have your appraisal discussion?" Viktor joked. "This is a prank, right? Are you getting that raise?"

"Oh, shut up, Viktor!" she spat. "I'm trying to have a serious conversation about *our relationship*, and you're actually making fun of me? In public?"

"Hey, wait!" The smile fell from his face. "I'm not making fun of you."

"What the hell do you think of yourself?" she said, loudly now.

Everyone in the restaurant turned to see what the commotion was about, but without bother, she continued, "You are lost in your own imaginary world. You have no idea what everyone in the real world is saying behind your back."

Viktor was at a loss for words.

"You started your second novel," she continued. "You didn't even try to ask how I was. You just assumed that I was busy and didn't give it a second thought."

He stared at his lap quietly, overcome with guilt and humiliation.

"If we're going to make this work – if this is even going to work – we'll be sharing our lives one day, our *future*. And that includes *my* life, Viktor, *my* future. Not just yours." She let out a shaky breath, her eyes tearing up. "I don't know if you even understand any of that."

"Hey, hey, wait," Viktor said, "Maybe we should talk about this at home so I can—"

"No, we're doing this here. And let me tell you, Viktor. Your first novel is a big flop, and people are making fun of you... and me too. You're just too blind to see it."

Viktor couldn't believe what he was hearing.

"This is all you do, Viktor," she continued. "You spend all your time fantasizing about whatever success the future holds for you. You just sit there and imagine, and you have no idea what is going on with the rest of us."

There was a heavy silence between them. Kim's fists were shaking, and there were tears in her eyes.

But Viktor suddenly didn't feel like wiping them away this time. Everything she said was hurtful. He barely understood any of it, but it hurt anyway.

"Are you done?" he dared to say. "Is there anything else that you want to say?"

"Well!" she began collecting her things. "I don't have the time to say anything more. There's someone else I need to meet up with. I'll see if I could talk to you later."

And with that, she left the table and walked quickly towards the exit.

Viktor sank into his chair, not knowing how to react to what had just transpired. His chest tightened as her hurtful words swam in his head.

"I was a failure? I was selfish? But didn't I always tell her I loved her? Didn't I show her I cared? I always tried, didn't I? Wasn't that enough?" he thought.

He realized that everyone in the restaurant was looking at him, and as he lifted his gaze to look at them they started behaving normally as though they hadn't just witnessed the worst moment of his life.

He tried Amber's mobile number. She disconnected his call. He tried again when he returned to the privacy of his car.

This time the call was answered.

"And don't you try to reach out to her," Kim said, not bothering to say hello. "Call me on my cell if you have anything to say."

She hung up before he could respond.

When Viktor reached home, he switched on his laptop to check her profile in case she had posted any status updates, but nothing was there.

Amber didn't answer his messages, either. Despair threatened to overwhelm him more and more.

He tried calling Christine who could only confirm that everything seemed to be normal at work.

Finally, he called Rahul and told him everything.

"Dude, give her some time," Rahul advised.

"I have never seen her in this mood," Viktor said. "Ever. I didn't know what to say to calm her down."

"You know, many times even I don't know what Richa wants," Rahul said. "Actually, sometimes I'm pretty sure she doesn't know what she wants either." He chuckled.

But Viktor couldn't bring himself to even smile at his friend's quips. "Okay, I'll try not to disturb her. But I really want to talk to her, yaar."

"Do it tomorrow after dropping a text."

"You know, I feel," Viktor exclaimed, "*Sometime, life is like a vacuum cleaner. You know what it does.*"

"*All you need to do is to kick the power plug and take the charge,*" Rahul completed.

"Yeah, anyhow, I'll try to talk to her tomorrow. Thanks, buddy, thanks for your time."

"Saale! Learning etiquette, haan? Good night, or else Richa will kill me for talking to you at night. I used to tease her that I had an affair with you, now she might think it's actually true." He laughed.

"All right. Good night, Rahu."

∞

The next day, Viktor continued to wait for her call but didn't receive any until noon. He was surprised to see her message, which read: "Let's get married this month."

He immediately called her, but she didn't pick up. What was going on? They had been planning their wedding for months, but it wasn't supposed to happen until next year. Was this some kind of game that she was trying to play? They'd just had their biggest fight, and now she wanted to get married? How did she expect him to respond? Viktor had certainly not prepared himself to face this kind of situation.

"Can we talk?" he texted Kim, and waited for her reply. After ten minutes, he tried to call her up, but she still wouldn't answer.

Viktor's work schedule was very busy that day, and with his back-to-back conference calls with clients, he couldn't spare any time at all to try Kim again.

Soon enough, it was past midnight, and as he left for home, he realized that he would only disturb her if he tried to call. And so he hoped that it wouldn't be too late if he tried to catch her the next day instead.

He came home far too distracted and upset to check his e-mail as he usually did, even though he was sure he now had at least a dozen messages from his publisher and agent in India that needed urgent response. He'd already missed so many long-distance calls from the distributor.

Viktor was too circumspect, and Kim too tired, for further arguments. But he couldn't keep himself from replaying the scene over and over, wondering why Kim had reacted in such a manner.

As the night passed by in the soft cradle of the clouds, Viktor decided to try to forget that the whole thing even happened.

He hoped for a better beginning the next day, for her.

When he woke up, he saw a message on his cell and immediately sat bolt upright.

It simply read, "I got my reply."

He tried to call her up but got no response. After the hustle and bustle of preparing for work, he continued waiting for her call and trying her number, to no avail.

At the office, he went to the breakout zone to check his personal inbox. He also checked Kim's online profile in case she posted any updates, but she seemed to have deleted her account.

He quickly went to Christine and asked about Kim.

"She left early for the client site," said Christine.

"Have you noticed her acting strangely these days?" he asked.

"Hardly seen her lately, actually," she replied. "I've been busy, too."

"I can't find her profile from my login. It won't show up on my phone," he said, fumbling with his mobile.

"Well, I saw her updates this morning," she shrugged.

"Where?" Viktor asked immediately.

She showed him her mobile. As Kim's profile page loaded Viktor was horrified to see her photographs from the previous day.

"She seems to have gone partying," said Christine, pointing at a photo of Kim with another man. "I thought that's you."

They were standing close to each other and seemed very cozy. Too cozy, Viktor thought. Now upset, he immediately scrolled and minimised the photo, afraid that others might catch a glimpse of the photo.

He scrolled through the rest of the images and tried to zoom in to know who the man was, but couldn't recognize him.

He gave the mobile back to Christine. "Thanks. Any idea which client she met with today?"

"Universal," she replied.

"Okay, thanks," he said, and quickly returned to his seat. He looked for the mobile number of the client and dialled them. "Could I talk to Kim please? I believe she's in the audit room."

"Please wait for a moment, sir." There was a brief pause and the faint sound of typing in the background. "Sir, it says here that she is on leave today."

Shaking his head in disappointment, Viktor hung up and immediately dialled Kim's number.

As expected, Kim ignored his call. He went back to Christine and asked to borrow her mobile phone. He went to a corner and dialled Kim again.

As soon as she answered the phone, he asked, trying to keep his voice even, "Who was that person with you at the party?"

"Oh, you are unbelievable," she hissed. "Now you start doubting me *and* involve my friends and colleagues in our problem."

Viktor was speechless for a moment, but his anger won out. "You had the time to go to some party but you couldn't be bothered to pick up your phone and talk to me?"

"Look, Viktor," she said harshly. "I am not your secretary. I can go anywhere I want and with anyone I wish."

"Kim!" Viktor held his head in frustration. "I'm sorry, but I just really need to know what's wrong with you, okay?"

"Wrong is with you, not me."

"Kim, can't we just…let's…let's sit and talk. For God's sake, please."

"I don't have time," she replied curtly.

"Then *make* time," Viktor insisted, now unable to keep his voice down. "Tell me where you are. I want to see you, *now*."

"How dare you yell at me," she shouted. "You think you're such a hotshot, telling people what to do. Well, let me tell you, Viktor. Today you are nothing but a failure."

There was a silence on the other end, but he thought he heard her sigh. Then, her voice now tired, she finally said, "Look, I can't take this anymore. Just stop calling me." She hung up.

Viktor stared at the phone in his hand, unable to grasp what had just happened.

Only two days had passed, and here he was, completely shattered. How could so much happen in so little time?

Just then, his own phone rang. He picked up immediately without checking the number, hoping that Kim had somehow suddenly changed her mind.

"Viktor, where are you? We have a video conference with CEO Japan in five minutes. We're waiting for you."

He returned Christine's mobile and left for the conference room. On his way he passed by Kim's desk and recognized his handwriting on one of the notes pinned to her corkboard.

It read, "*Irony of the world is that it wants to simplify the complexity and complicate the simplicity.*"

He tore off the piece of paper, put it in his pocket, and went to his meeting.

He spent the entire conference distracted, thinking about Kim who had left him alone in the middle of this mess with nothing to hold on to. He felt like a piece of his heart had been cut out, and the pain was intolerable. He had been so sure that this would be it, that she was the one.

He had been so careful, so determined that he wouldn't go through another breakup again...and yet here he was, right in the middle of one.

In the evening, he tried Amber's number, but received no reply. He took time off and dropped by their house.

"She told us to stay away and let Kim handle her own personal matters," said her mother.

They seemed helpless. Her father added, "Sometimes we believe you have put her in this situation." Silence hung around.

Viktor came home. It was the most dreadful night of his life. He spent the whole night at the rooftop, dialling Kim's number, and after several failed attempts, an automated voice conveyed that number was busy.

Defeated, Viktor went back to his room and slept.

The next day, he woke up still hoping to receive a call from her, but he didn't even get an SMS. He ignored the urge to contact Christine, wanting to avoid accidentally sparking rumours at the office and giving Kim any more problems. He might be hurt, but he deep down knew that he still cared.

∞

He did his best to keep himself busy with work, and soon enough, a week had passed. It was Tuesday, and Viktor was in the meeting room, preoccupied with presentations. His cell vibrated in his pocket, but his boss was in the room, so he ignored it.

After the meeting he checked his cell and saw that he had received a new text message:

"Move on, as I did. He is amazing."

He took a deep breath and dialled Kim's number for the millionth time that week. The call didn't go through. She seemed to have blocked his mobile number.

He checked her status that read, *"Forget the pain and the one who caused it, but not the lesson you learnt."*

He took the rest of the day off and drove to Kim's house, if only to at least speak with Amber. It was her parents who answered the door.

He knew that they could see the desperation on his face; he no longer had the energy to hide it. He knew that they heard his voice breaking slightly when he asked if he could talk to Amber. He knew that they sympathized with him, even as they replied, "We can't help you, Viktor. Please talk to Kim instead. It's her decision."

Another day passed, and Viktor realized that he no longer knew anything about Kim's life.

He updated his status, *"From the balance sheet of humanity, to the profit & loss account of emotions, I am all in good books."*

He had no clue when she came to the office and when she left for the client site. He had no clue who she spent her time with. It had only been a week, and he felt as though he no longer knew a single thing about her.

"It hurts deeper when somebody you love becomes someone you loved." He wrote on a sticky note and pasted on his wall.

∾

Aadhi aadhi kyu baant di

Jo tha tera kabhi, vo ab tera nahi;
Jahaan thi manzilen, na rahi vo zamee;
Akele raaste hue, aasmaa baadlon se ghire;
Khali khali dil kyu tatolta, kyu banjaara hua phire.
Baarishein ye gamon ki; har dum saansein naapti;
Ik thi jo zindagi hamaari; Aadhi aadhi... aadhi aadhi...
Aadhi aadhi... kyu baant di? Aadhi aadhi kyu baant di?

*Haule haule pal pal ki ye ghutan; na jaane thamein kis
lamhe.*
Ik thi jo har khushi; SMS aur tring tring karti;
Jo connection strong tha; vo taarein kyu kaat di?
Ik thi jo zindagi hamaari; aadhi aadhi... aadhi aadhi...
Aadhi aadhi kyu baant di? Aadhi aadhi kyu baant di?

∞

A month passed. Viktor tried several times to get her back, but
she refused to even consider spending a few minutes on the
phone with him, much less the rest of her life.

It was almost funny, now that he thought about it. They used
to be engaged, and now he had to resort to checking her online
profile for the smallest update on her life. All he learned was that
she posted about her new friend almost on a daily basis. It was
disturbing for him, but most days, it only filled him with bitter
emptiness.

Suddenly a call came from outside the house.

"Courier!"

He dragged his feet towards the front door and collected his
package. It was from an anonymous sender, and there was no
return address. He closed the door and started unwrapping the
package.

Once he reached his bedroom he had a small velvet box in
his hand. Trembling, he opened it, knowing full well what was
inside.

Kim's engagement ring – or at least, what used to be –
glistened, light reflecting from the stones.

Frustration ran through his head. He threw the box across
the room where it hit his guitar with a loud twang. He was now

on his knees, trying to fight back his tears and failing. He felt a pressure in his temples and inside his chest. His heart pounded ruthlessly.

His eyes landed on the ring on his own finger, and he slowly took it off. He supposed he didn't need it anymore. He wiped his eyes and went crawling towards his guitar, picking up the velvet box and opening it once more. There was a note tucked inside, written in Kim's familiar handwriting. *I'm sorry,* it said.

Shaking his head, he freed the ring from the box and, together with his own ring, slipped it into the guitar's sound hole. Then he picked up the instrument.

He remembered the time he had spent with her on the roller coaster, in the hill top restaurant, sitting on the car bumper and roof tops watching the moon.

He picked up the guitar, tuned it, and started singing.

∞

Laut Aa

Teri yaadon se judke… Kab lamhe hue mere juda…
Karwatein ye khaamosh si… Safar pal pal hua tanha…
Haasil kiya jo tere liye sab… Fir bhi… tuuu…. kyuuuu…
Mujhse hai khafa?
Jaane kyu… tere bin… Main vo main na raha…
Tu meri thi dhadknein… Tu meri thi saansein…
Tu meri ibaadtein… Laut aa…

Teri bahon mein simat ke… Zindgi main jiya is kadar…
Din jo raaton ki silvaton se… Khuda ne khud kiya tha nazar…

Haqeeqat se pare tha sama vo... Shiddatt se tha khwaab buna jo...
Fir aaj tu... kaise kyun... mujhe hai juda?
Tu meri thi dhadknein... Tu meri thi saansein...
Tu meri ibaadtein... Laut aa...

Happiness is...

Loving what you do and doing what you love

For days to come, Viktor was depressed. So much so that he could not contain his anger. Every moment he would sit down to write his second novel, he ended up throwing things across the room and tearing up his drafts. Most days he hardly had any appetite for even a single meal, and he didn't bother leaving his house during the weekends. He continued to wait every day for Kim to return any one of his messages, but it was all in vain.

In all this mess, he found himself troubled by another mysterious problem. He had been having disturbing dreams, and in them he was always faced with some insurmountable obstacle. Even in his dreams he was a failure, and it always felt as though everything was moving away from him.

Occasionally, the main character of his novel would appear in his dreams, equally distressed by his own similar circumstances. Just as Viktor wanted Kim back, so did his protagonist yearn for his own lady luck.

He missed going to work for three days, until he finally got a call from his boss, confronting him about his absence and ordering him to show up for an urgent meeting.

Now here he was, in the office washroom, absently staring at his reflection while drying his hands below the hand dryer.

"Hey, Viktor, all well?" asked one of his colleagues.

"Yeah," he said, still lost in his thoughts.

"You forgot to rinse your hands."

"Huh?" He looked at his soapy hands. "Oh. Thanks." He smiled weakly and returned to the sink.

He remembered the first time he had run into Kim outside the ladies' room.

As he walked out the door, Viktor could almost see the past versions of the two of them, standing right where they had met for the first time. For the rest of the day, he remained distracted, silently re-living everything that happened over the past few years.

That night as he was getting ready for bed, he found himself once again staring at his reflection in the bathroom mirror.

The image suddenly began to speak. "What's wrong with you, Viktor?" he said.

Viktor blinked. He really must be starting to lose it.

"You always wanted happiness?" his reflection continued.

"But I never got it," Viktor replied, in spite of himself.

"I never dreamed of it," the image said.

"Dreams you sow, Happiness shall you reap," the image said. "I was a failure not when the world won against me, but when I gave up on myself."

Viktor realized he might as well have been conversing with the protagonist of his next novel.

"When Jess, my lady luck, left me, I thought it was the end of the world," the image continued. "I had forgotten how to live a life without her around. It is amusing to think about it this way, since I grew up alone and only met her when I was twenty-three. I spent the past four years dependent on her for practically everything. And here I am, feeling helpless and miserable, now that she has left me forever. When a person commits to loving somebody, they don't really anticipate that these things would happen."

And with that, the image ended their brief conversation. Viktor stared into the mirror a little while longer, but nothing more came. And so he quietly went to bed and stared at the ceiling until he finally fell asleep after writing a quote on his social profile wall.

"When the wind is against you, like a kite, have your chord of faith rooted and you would fly highest ever."

∞

While driving to the office the next day, he opened the voice recording application on his mobile and dictated, *"Today is yesterday's tomorrow...a better day...to start with."*

Then he narrated the storyline that he had imagined the night before. It was going to be an intense romantic drama this time, not so different from what he had been experiencing. Strangely enough, he actually looked forward to writing it. He was filled with renewed vigour and an inspiration so strong that he could not resist it flowing out of him and onto the page.

That night after reaching home, he gave Rahul a call.

"Dude! How are you?" asked Rahul.

"Smart as ever."

"Smart-*ass*, you mean." His friend laughed."But, hey, you sound happy."

"Happy? Do you know what happiness is?"

"No, I'm married," Rahul smirked.

"I think happiness is… doing what you love and loving what you do."

"*Eggzactlee*," nodded Rahul, "I also think that *happiness is knocking on the door of opportunity, and if no one opens, then bolting them from outside and fleeing.*"

"Happiness is… talking to a friend like you," Viktor said.

He heard Rahul snort on the other end. "You sentimental sap," Rahul said. "Actually, the biggest happiness for me is making my wife happy, and if she saw me talking to you this late, then she will be very unhappy and I, very dead."

Viktor was contented. He went back to writing his novel. He started from the middle, wanting to construct his story from the point where his protagonist had broken up with the person he loved.

"*The road to success is built up as you travel, its blue print never exists,*" he wrote on his computer.

Unlike most love stories that began on a happy note, Viktor wanted to probe into the riddles of life.

"To say *I love you* is always a commitment for life," he recorded in his mobile, the next day on his way to work. "But it is in pressing times that we forget the commitments we make during our happier moments. And then we decide to part ways, sometimes amicably, other times with more bitterness. So when Kim, sorry, *Jess*, Jessica and I lost sight of our commitment and decided to part ways, it was like an avalanche of emotions tearing through my heart in ways that I couldn't explain. Though my breakup was sort of… simple… amicable… amicable? Whatever… I still cannot get myself to believe that it has happened. And that my time with Jess has finally come to an end."

"When I spent all those hours lazing around in bed," he continued, "Unable to decide how to take it from here, I wasted many important hours of my life. It is an amusing concept, to be honest. Time passes by, but it is we who get spent. And if we wait for longer than we are supposed to, then we get spent completely, to such an extent that the loss is not recoverable. One can't wish to go back in time to enjoy the fancies of life. When I realized this, I decided to return to work. After all, I had to work to earn and keep myself afloat."

He did his best to recall every detail of the dreams in which his protagonist made an appearance. In them, he looked for wisdom that he could share with the world through his writing. He sat late nights, writing exactly what he saw in his dreams, and a week later he had a full-fledged plot ready.

"Best quote of the day," he wrote, *"Don't just sit and read the quote of the day; implement it."* And with that, he ended another chapter. This, he thought, was his new revelation about life. He had decided to turn the tables.

∞

Two more months had passed. He edited and re-edited his new manuscript, something that he connected with a lot more. He was, after all, going through the pain himself. But rather than working on how to do things, Viktor was now working on why it was he did them.

Viktor realized that his characters were essentially a part of himself.

The protagonist of his second novel, a romantic drama, was a rather striking image of Viktor himself. He wrote in first person because he felt compelled to do justice to the emotions faced by his character. It felt more personal this way, as though the character himself spoke directly to the reader, telling his story exactly as he experienced them. This also meant that the development of the plot was constrained by his protagonist's opinions, but Viktor found that he enjoyed the challenge. It was the very thing that drew him to his writing desk each day.

"Success is like an umbrella. It has wires in it called faith. It has no meaning if there is no rain and storm called ebbs and flows of life." He wrote on his mobile and saved as ending for one of the chapter. *"So.. Challenge yourself today, to improve for a better tomorrow than yesterday."*

∞

One Sunday morning his phone woke him up from a deep slumber and found himself on the rocking chair with his laptop still on his knees and his earphones tucked in. Several sheets of paper and his pen lay on the desk in front of him. He searched for the phone under the pile.

He was surprised to see Amber's name on the screen. He wondered whether it would be wise to take the call. In his sudden nervousness his fingers slipped, causing him to cancel the call by accident.

He thought of calling back but, wary of the possible consequences, he chose to wait.

"Viks, I need 2 talk 2 u," an SMS flashed on his mobile screen.

"It's urgent." Another text.

He quickly returned her call. Amber picked up after the first ring, but he quietly held the phone against his ear without speaking.

"Viks!" she said without greeting. "I need to talk to you," she sounded worried.

"What now? Is she getting married?" he scoffed.

"I see you haven't changed."

"Not at all, I'm the same as before."

"Good," she replied.

"You know!" he got up from his chair, *"Good people won't do bad to you if you hurt them. They'll just be neutral and walk away, with experience and a lesson; and you'll be left with well-wishers less one."*

"Viks! I know what you went through."

"No! You don't know what I went through."

"Viks! It's learning."

"Yup!" he nodded, *"Either you learn from or you are taught by the people."*

"Ok! Listen to me carefully, and don't ask any questions," she said.

Viktor listened to her in silence, but from that minute onward, his eyebrows furrowed deeper with every word she said.

By the time he put the phone down, his face was red with anger. Hot blood rushed through his veins as if searching for a way out.

He glared at an old photo of Kim that was still hanging on his wall. He picked up his car keys and stormed out of the house, slamming the door behind him.

∞

"I am sorry, sir, but you're not allowed to go inside without permission." The security guard tried to stop Viktor as he tried to barge through the main gate.

"See, this is something urgent," said Viktor. "I need to go upstairs."

"Sir, please calm down. You are speaking to a special security officer. Entering the premises without permission is considered a crime, and—"

Viktor pushed him and marched inside. He climbed the stairs, two steps at a time. When he finally reached Kim's room, he pushed the door wide open.

Suddenly he was in the same room as Kim, who stared at him with a startled look on her face. Viktor looked tired and weak himself. He had not shaven and had been wearing the same T-shirt for a few days now.

Kim put down the book that she had been reading but remained seated in her chair. Viktor took a step towards her, quickly noticing that it was his book she held in her hands.

The security guard was not far behind Viktor and grabbed his arms. "I tried to stop him, ma'am. But he refused to listen. I will file…"

"Thank you," Kim interrupted. "I will take it from here. I apologize for his behaviour."

"Are you sure, madam?" asked the guard, still gripping Viktor's arm.

"Yes, I am," she replied with a smile. "Thank you."

The guard lingered for a moment, eyeing Viktor as if to give him a warning. As he left, neither Viktor nor Kim spoke. They quietly glared at each other until Viktor finally cracked.

"How could you do this to me, Kim?" he asked, his voice trembling with anger and sorrow.

"What did I do now?" she replied getting up from chair, leaning against the table for support.

"Stop pretending that you don't know what I'm talking about. I already know."

"What are you—" Her voice trailed away as someone opened the door behind Viktor. He turned his head and saw Amber, who trudged forward, avoiding her cousin's disappointed eyes.

∞

"You are nothing but a failure."

Amber tried to meet her cousin's eyes as Kim spoke into the phone, mustering all of her strength to sound firm. Kim paused, letting out a soft sigh. "Look, I can't take this anymore. Just stop calling me."

She ended the call, sat down, and broke down in tears. Amber ran to her side and tried to console her.

Amber's mother entered the room. "They need to scan you," she said gravely.

They went to the scanning room where an enormous machine waited for Kim. A nurse assisted her as she lay down on top the patient table. Then she was slid into the machine for scanning.

Amber waited outside, crying. For a moment she gathered some courage to call Viktor and tell him what was going on, but she hung up as soon as Kim's request echoed in her ears.

After a few days, they returned to the hospital for the test results. Kim sobbed, unable to contain the pangs of grief and frustration that seemed to erupt from the very center of her existence.

"Malignant mesothelioma" was what the doctor said. There was no drug that would kill the cancer cells without affecting the healthy ones. Treatment would leave the body weak and vulnerable to any kind of infection or disease. Chances of survival seemed bleak.

The last thing Kim wanted was to let Viktor suffer with her.

"You'll need to tell him sooner or later," Amber said. *"Viks has to know the truth."*

"No. This would kill his hopes. He'd leave all his dreams behind. He'd stop living his life. He can't find out about this." She held Amber's hand.

"Amber, I need your help."

∞

Back to the room where Viktor was standing still.

Kim looked up with surprise, with happiness in her heart. But she realised that she had decided to ignore him so she replied blankly, "What?"

"I'm just a failure, right?" Viktor said, looking at her steadily. "That's what you said that day."

"Yes, you are," she replied, not meeting his gaze.

"Look me in the eye and say it," he challenged, clenching his jaw.

She got up, took a step forward, saying, "You don't know where you are headed in life, and I can't spend *my* life with a failure like you." With that, she brushed past him, towards the door.

Viktor grabbed her hand firmly. "You can't go like this," he asked again.

"Leave me," she snapped, yanking back her hand, walking towards the door. "Why won't you just let me go?"

"Because I love you," he said firmly. He took a step towards her.

∞

A tear rolled down her cheek. Her chin trembled as she moved closer towards him. Her face, usually so radiant and full of life, suddenly went blank. She tried to steady herself, but her legs gave out. She was fainting.

"Kim!" Viktor yelled in panic. He ran towards her, desperate to catch her before she hit the ground.

∞

Kim opened her eyes, disoriented and unable to recall where she was or what had happened. Squinting at the bright light above her head, she realized that she was lying on a hospital bed, with a doctor examining her eyes.

When it was over, another hand brushed her forehead. She knew that touch. "Vik."

"You passed out," he said. "Do you want some water?"

She turned her head to face him, "I am sorry Vik!"

"Shh!"

Tears rolled down her eyes, "No! I am sorry Vik!"

"It's Ok!"

"You know," she sobbed, "I was with Amber that one time you called her. I was the one who hung up the phone that day."

"Shhh." Viktor put his finger on her lips. He leaned in and kissed her forehead whispering, "I know. She told me."

There was a team of doctors standing across the room. They seemed to be discussing something about her. She looked around for a distraction. "The vase has no flowers," she observed.

"Here," Viktor said, leaning down to grab something from the floor. He handed her a colorful bouquet of daisies. "All for you."

"I am sorry Viktor." She held his hand with a tear escaping from the corner of her eye.

"But I haven't missed talking to you," he caressed her cheeks, "Idiot, I was almost dead."

"Shh!" she put her finger on his lips, "Don't you dare to say that."

Just then her primary doctor walked in. "Hi, Kim! I hope you're feeling a little better."

She smiled weakly and gave a slight nod.

"We'll start the rounds of chemotherapy," the doctor said to Viktor. "My team will come and move her to another room."

When the doctor left, Viktor lightly touched her side. "They say it's here, where the book had hit you?"

"Yeah," she croaked.

"I am sorry, Kim," he said, holding her hand. "I feel so terrible…"

"Shh!" she interrupted quickly. "Don't be sorry. It's not the book that gave me cancer," she chuckled. "Besides, if it weren't for that bruise, they wouldn't have made the right diagnosis."

"A week after she came back from India, she found a lump there," Amber added. "It went away for a while, then it started swelling again, so the doctor ordered a blood test." She sighed. "That's when the discovered the can…I mean…that's when they reached their…diagnosis…" Her shoulders shook as she started sobbing.

"Hey, hey," Kim said softly. "Don't. I'll be fine soon, don't worry."

"You have to be," said Viktor, brushing her hair with his fingers. "Okay? You have no other choice." he smiled.

Kim smiled back weakly.

Viktor added, *"Cancer can merely touch your physical existence, but neither your soul nor your thoughts."* He held her hand tightly. "And least of all your heart, because that one is with me, and I won't let anyone take it away."

∞

A month passed. Viktor visited Kim at home or at the hospital every day on his way to work. Though he usually found her asleep, he still made it a point to see her daily, even if only through the glass window as the doctors performed more scans on her frail body.

Signs of improvement were nowhere visible. The chemotherapy had only made her weaker. Nothing seemed to be working.

Viktor knew that she was slipping away, but he couldn't let her go without a fight. He was determined to do everything in his power to keep her from having to face such a fate. And so, in a desperate attempt to find a cure for the disease, he did his research and came across a few possible options in traditional medicine and Eastern philosophies.

Viktor called one of his friends based in China. "Akita, I need your help."

With the help of his friends, he arranged a visitor from Beijing who had the mastery to teach Kim tai chi, a Chinese martial art and form of exercise with health benefits that might help her live a little longer.

"Do you believe these things would help her?" the doctor asked Viktor.

"You know," Viktor replied, "*Science can keep a heart beating with a ventilator, but there is only one power that makes it live, and that is LOVE... purest form of faith.*"

The doctor smiled and put a hand on Viktor's shoulder. "The power of love. Go ahead, then. But she seems to have lost her own faith."

"She has to believe that she can still beat this," Viktor said. "And she *will* win. I'm going to make it happen somehow…" he choked back his tears.

"You have my support, Viktor. We're all counting on you."

∞

Every day Viktor would cut his lunch break short to visit Kim and watch the tai chi master teach her his wonderful techniques.

Once, he found her asleep in her hospital room. He sat by her bed and watched her sleep.

He noticed that the bed next to hers had just been assigned to a new patient. It was a girl of about ten years, and she had already lost all her hair. She was unconscious and seemed almost lifeless, a glucose pipe in her mouth and several tubes attached to her body. Her parents were sitting next to her.

Viktor walked over and stood there for a moment. Unable to refrain himself, he asked, "What's her name?"

Her mother looked at him without a reply. She was digging for something inside her bag, a teddy bear, which she carefully placed by her daughter's arm.

The stuffed animal had a red felt heart stitched onto its chest, where a word was engraved in small letters. "Irene," read Viktor softly.

"Yeah," replied her father.

Viktor didn't know what else to say, how to console them, how to share their grief, how to say that everything would be all right. His heart ached for them.

"Vik!" said Kim.

He turned quickly. Kim was awake and seemed frightened. He returned to her side and held her hand. "What happened? Is everything okay?"

"Yeah," she whispered. "I just had a horrible dream."

He tightened his grip around her hand. "It was only a dream. You're safe. I am always with you. Okay?"

She nodded and smiled.

He began feeling more and more helpless as he realized that there was very little he could do besides try to share in her suffering. But he continued his efforts. He decided not to surrender to circumstances and did everything to cheer her up. He brought her childhood friends to the hospital and showed her old photos of the two of them together and silly videos from the Internet.

Kim saw her reflection in the mobile screen and said, "Vik! My face seems sad and tired, these dark circles are scaring me."

He quickly snatched the mobile from her, "For me, you are as heartbreakingly beautiful as always. I want you to sip wine every night with me, from one glass, as we used to do. You have to support me, don't give up hope. Promise?"

"Yup! I promise." She smiled.

∞

Soon, Viktor's mother visited from India and went to see Kim at the hospital.

The first thing she noticed were the bluish bruises that dotted Kim's arms. She moved to cover her mouth in shock, but Viktor indicated her to hold back her emotions. She gathered courage not to cry in front of Kim, placed a warm hand on her forehead, and asked, "How are you, my daughter?"

Kim managed a small nod and a wispy smile as Viktor's mother did her best to hold back her tears.

Softly, Kim asked about the school's progress, and then asked about Viktor's novel. "How are sales doing in India?"

"Not good," replied his mother.

Kim's face fell. Her weak body slumped against the bed, her face filled with sorrow.

Viktor's mother glanced at Viktor, then at Kim, and added, "Not good, but *superb*."

"What? Oh my God. Like mother, like son" she said, shaking her head as she beamed at Viktor. Then she lifted her hand and held it in front of Viktor's face, "Sir, autograph please!"

Although the cause of her excitement was far from the truth, Viktor and his mother were nevertheless extremely happy to see her renewed energy. Hoping to encourage it, he quickly added, "You know, I'm about to finish my second novel."

"My goodness! That's awesome, Viktor." She reached for him, and he leaned down for a hug. "Why didn't you tell me?"

"I'll bring the manuscript and read it to you every day," he said. "You would be my editor for this novel."

They smiled at each other as the nurse entered the room and announced, "Visiting hours are over."

"Now she has something to look forward to every day," his mother said to him on their way home. Viktor couldn't wait to think of ways to surprise Kim so that she could wait for another dawn with curiosity and a renewed will to live.

Viktor dropped his mother off. He was supposed to leave for the office but just as he was about to open the door, the thought of Kim crossed his mind and suddenly he couldn't bring himself to move. He went back inside and searched for his mother.

"What happened?" she asked sitting on the rocking chair, busy with knitting a sweater. "You forgot something?"

He shook his head tearfully, going down on his knees and wrapping his arms around his mother's legs. "I don't want to lose her, Mumma. I don't want to lose her," he cried.

She placed a warm hand on his head and gently brushed his hair with her fingers.

"I need a miracle, Ma," he sobbed. "I can't watch her die slowly every day. Please bring her back. Please, Mumma. Please. Please do something."

She curled his hair. "You know, when your dad passed away, it happened so fast. I didn't even have the chance to talk to him, that one last time."

Viktor looked up. She had tears in her eyes.

She continued, "She is still here. You still have her. Love has great powers, but you and only you can help her stay. You have to ignite her will to live and tell her to fight the cancer from within."

Viktor's mother leaned and pulled him up. She wiped the tears from his face and held him in a warm embrace. "*The purpose of life is to keep trying to achieve what you dream,*" she said. "Right now, your sole dream is to make her better, and your purpose is to try and achieve that. *When the stream is stagnant and moving nowhere, what all you need to do is keep paddling.*"

∞

That day onwards, he would visit Kim at the hospital and read at least two pages of his novel to her. She seemed extremely happy with his work, and so he started spending late nights at his desk, adding more to his story so that he could complete it and present it to Kim.

He also started taking beginner's lessons from the tai chi master, hoping to bring whatever change he could to Kim's already depleting condition. He knew that his chances were slim, but the knowledge that he was doing it for her made the effort worthwhile.

Every day he would practice the techniques and movements with Kim, and when she was asleep or busy with treatment, he worked on his manuscript. Writing was the only thing that could take his mind off Kim, although that was for her as well. He experienced her pain through the characters of his story.

∞

Two months had passed. One Saturday, he picked up Amber and her friend Greg, the guy who helped them fool Viktor into thinking that Kim had found someone new.

They all went to see Kim, and on the way to the hospital Viktor bought a bouquet of red roses. When they reached the ward, Kim greeted them with a huge smile.

Viktor gave one rose to Greg, who offered it to Amber as he asked her to be his girlfriend.

Kim gasped and clapped her hands in delight.

Then Viktor walked over towards her with bouquet of roses. He got down on one knee, saying, "Lovely lady, will you be my…"

The smile faded from Kim's face. "Stop it, Viktor," she said quietly.

"Please, Kim. Marry me," he pleaded. "What's the point in waiting?"

"Don't pretend that this is about waiting, Viktor. You know that's not what this is about." She shoved the roses in his chest. "There is *no* point in waiting and there is no point in anything, because I'm not getting any better, Viktor. I'm never going to get better!"

Suddenly, Irene, the girl in the bed next to Kim's, the same girl who spent her days and nights lying down and always refused to walk despite her family's requests, got up from her bed.

Viktor was stunned to see her walk, and Kim too.

She walked towards the bouquet, now lying forgotten on the floor, and picked it up. Shooting a pointed look at Kim, the young girl turned to Viktor and said with a bold wink, "Hey, handsome! Will you be my valentine?"

Viktor bent down to her level and accepted the flowers. "Yes, sweetie, of course."

Irene glared at Kim once more, sticking out her tongue. Viktor hugged the child, with tears in his eyes. He kissed Kim on the top of her head and left the ward.

Thereafter, Viktor would always visit the hospital carrying two red roses... one for Kim and another for Irene. Everyone noticed the change in the little girl, whose demeanor grew more positive day by day. She would wait for Viktor and sit with him, telling him about her dreams.

∞

After another month, the doctor asked Viktor to meet him. "We have suggested shaving her head," the doctor said. "She's already experiencing hair loss."

Viktor went to Kim and held her hand. "I need to tell you something."

"I'll go bald today," Kim replied. "I know. I have accepted the fact that I have to live with all these things, however long I still have."

"Shhh." Viktor put a finger on her lips. She smiled weakly and waited for the nurse.

Viktor drove home, struggling with his thoughts. He fought for focus and sat down to write, completing another chapter.

The next day, Viktor picked up Amber and her new boyfriend Greg, and the three of them went to see Kim.

When he entered the medical ward, Kim was surprised to see him wearing a hat and carrying his guitar, which rested on his back, hanging by the strap over his shoulder. He grabbed the instrument by its neck, shifting its position smoothly, and started playing:

"Austerity...
If... I were to define...
It's you... yoo hoo!"

An electric charge seemed to run through the entire room. Even the patients in adjacent wards came to Kim's ward, excited to see the show.

"Happiness is what...
That makes me feel divine...
Smiling you... yoo hoo!!"

But Kim was still angry, knowing what he was up to.

Viktor put a hand in his pocket and a made a show of searching for something inside. He pulled it out, keeping it hidden from Kim but showing it to Irene, who leaned over to take a peek.

The little girl placed her hands on Viktor's cheeks, nodding excitedly with a smile on her face.

Viktor put the guitar on a chair and took a step closer to Kim's bed. He opened his hand, revealing two rings... their old engagement rings. "Marry me," he whispered.

"Why don't you understand, Viktor?" she said loudly. Everyone around them was shocked.

"Please, Kim!" said Viktor.

"No." She turned her face away. "I can't." A tear rolled down her cheek.

Viktor leaned close and wiped the tear with his finger. "I'll die without you."

With a sharp intake of breath, she slapped him across the face.

His hat fell off, rolled on the floor, and settled near Irene's bed. Everyone was stunned to see what Viktor's hat had been hiding, including Kim. In her shock, her hands flew up to her face, covering her mouth.

Viktor was bald. He bit his lower lip to hide that it was trembling, not because he was humiliated, but because he couldn't make her happy. He tasted blood and realized that the slap had cut his lip.

Irene got down from her bed and picked up the hat. Viktor looked at her and faked a smile.

Then he felt a touch on his hand. It was Kim, who held his hand and slid one of the rings on his finger.

A patient started clapping his hands. Viktor put Kim's ring on her finger, and everyone else started clapping, teary-eyed.

Irene came to Viktor, wearing his hat. She kissed his cheek, feigning anger towards Kim, who laughed. The young girl then smiled and kissed her as well.

"You know, I really hated all these treatments at first," said Kim, "but later on I just accepted that I had to live with this, because I didn't have very long anyway."

"Don't say that," said Viktor, pleading with his eyes.

"No, I need to say this." She looked at Irene, and then at Amber, and continued, "Today, I once again felt the desire to keep living... and whatever life I still have," she put her hands on Viktor's face, tears rolling down her cheeks, "I want to spend it with you, every single day, every single hour, in your arms."

"Every single day slapping me, you mean," Viktor couldn't help but joke.

She burst into laughter."It's always my wish to be with you, if not through life..."

"Shhh," Viktor interrupted, placing a finger on her lips.

She gently removed his finger and continued, "If not through life, then through your novels."

Viktor looked at her.

"Make me a part of your novel."

Viktor didn't know what to say.

"I'm joking," she chuckled, seeing the look on his face. "Hey, how come they didn't stop you from playing?"

He looked at her blankly.

"Vik," she jolted him. "Didn't they stop you?"

Viktor smiled quickly. "I asked permission from the admin last week, and they were happy with the idea."

∞

For the rest of the day Kim's words resonated inside his head. *"I want to live through your novels."* The novel was already dedicated to her, he decided moulding it to tell Kim's own story was only logical.

Thereafter, every day, Viktor visited the hospital at noon, carrying bouquets of flowers that he handed to all the patients in her ward. His love for Kim felt too great not to share, and seeing the smiles on the patients' faces was certainly worth it. It was a small gesture, but if it inspired their will to live and continue their fight, then it was Viktor's honour to keep doing it.

The world was his family now. Seeing people like Amber, Greg, Jeff and many others living their dreams made him go across places in the world, and meet and tell people about achieving their dreams.

Before returning to the US, Viktor addressed another conference at a cancer hospital in the same city.

"You know you all are awesome," said Viktor addressing a conference, "You already have what all you need, you just need a reason to believe in yourselves."

∞

Fifteen more years had passed. Kim was down with cancer again. Viktor kept the same schedules of coming home with a few extra bouquets of roses and going to the hospital. There, he would distribute it amongst the people who would wait for him.

"Smoking eats... YOU," he said addressing the audience at a drug rehabilitation centre. *"You are not smoking cigarette, it's cigarette that is smoking you."*

His visits to the cancer hospitals across the world were still on, that also covered maximum places from the Middle East to Far East.

∞

One morning, Kim had severe pain in her ribs again. She was hospitalised. With the quick medication, she felt relieved.

Amber and Greg insisted Viktor go home and have a bath.

Viktor reached back home and realized that loneliness has spilled over in every corner.

A greeting card was lying near the carpet with a thanks in his name. He had tears in his eyes, wanting Kim to be with him.

He opened that and found it to be from Irene.

She asked him to see the link that was a mobile recorded video, shot by her on the day he proposed Kim in hospital.

He picked up the guitar and went to the hospital and showed the video to Kim. Kim was too weak to reply, dark circles around her eyes made her struggle to see the video, but she somehow managed to express her happiness.

He spent that night with Kim. Next morning, the sun rays entered from the window and lighted up Kim's hand.

Viktor woke up and saw her hand. He touched the tip of her ring finger with the tip of his ring finger.

"Hmm!" whispered Kim, "Good morning."

"Good morning," said Viktor with a peck on her forehead and then indicated towards her hand.

She looked at her hand, raised up her hand with a little discomfort but then enjoyed the sunrays.

"You are making the sun shine," he whispered kissing her ear.

She smiled and replied, "Thanks Viktor, for making my life wonderful."

"Shh!" he said, putting his hand on her lips, "That's my dialogue," and slowly bit her lower lip.

"Junglee!" she whispered slowly.

Viktor smiled and kissed her forehead, "How are you feeling now?"

"I still want to sleep. A peaceful sleep, I want to rest deep," she said, smiling, but in a low voice.

"Hey!" he said, holding her hand, "What happened to you today? Why are you talking like that?"

"Can you play that tune for me?" she asked.

"Which one?" he asked.

"Austerity, if I were to define...."

Viktor smiled and the next moment got his guitar from the adjacent room.

"Austerity...," he started singing and playing soulful notes. Kim smiled and struggled to lip-sync along with him.

"If I were to define..."

Though Viktor was playing the guitar slowly, his voice was audible enough for the other patients to make them join Viktor and Kim in their room. Amber, Greg and their child also had just reached the hospital.

Viktor looked at them and smiled. They too joined the chorus, *"It's you... yoo hoo..."*

Viktor increased his guitar strumming.

"Happiness is what..." they sang.

"Yoo hoo..." he sang at high notes with closed eyes.

All were lost singing with him and enjoying.

"That makes us feel divine...

smiling you... yoo hoo!!"

"Kim!!" said Amber loudly.

Viktor opened his eyes and quickly looked at Kim, her eyes were closed, hands loose, no movement.

He ran to her, "Kim!"

He held her wrist to her ear, then touched her throat, no life.

"Kim!" said Amber rubbing her hand, "Greg! Ring the bell."

"Kim! Get up," said Viktor slowly snapping her cheek, "Kim! I said get up."

A nurse came and checked Kim. She was gone.

A team of doctors came and pulled the shockers and started giving electric jolts to Kim, but in vain.

The line on the monitor was straight. Life had kissed Kim goodbye. Viktor pushed everyone aside and held Kim, "Get up Kim! Complete the song. Please. You can't go without completing. Kim, I said get up… please. You can't go like this. Please."

And he broke down in to tears. Greg and Amber hugged him crying.

∞

Why would I

Why would I… Be sad and cry?
If you are not here with me.
Coz I know how much… Had you loved me.

Why would I… Dream my life… Without you?
Coz you know how much… Had I loved you.

But why did… our world and sky…
On this earth fall apart?

So why would I… fly beyond these skies?
You know that… my rainbow is you.
Yoo hoo… Yoo hoo…

∞

"Think again Viktor," said the CEO of the company.
Viktor smiled, "I did," and he signed his resignation letter.
On the way back home, he called up Rahul.

"Are you crazy?" he shouted at Viktor. "Idiot, you left your high profile big pay pack job? Why?"

"For happiness."

"Which happiness?"

∞

"Time spent for temporary happiness like a movie or an outing or a weekend on a beach is all synthetic, with a shelf life of a day or two. Work for your bigger dreams that should last for a whole lifetime," said Viktor to the patient listeners, the cancer fighters.

He started teaching meditation techniques using his guitar. He wrote various motivational novels and roamed around the world. All the revenue he earned went to the NGO he had established for philanthropic purposes called, "Life Beyond Living".

Tune. Play. Repeat.

Every weekend, he used to play guitar in the hospital auditorium where all patients used to gather with their family members.

Kim too had shown signs of improvements. His daily routine was to share their lifelong plans of visiting different places across the world.

Sessions of Chi and Telekinesis and chanting along with flowers, hugs, kisses had shown a positive impact on Kim's health. Above all, it was her will to live and fight with cancer that had a positive impact on her health.

One evening, as Viktor was done with his guitar session, an old lady came forward from the crowd. Struggling with her stick, she held Viktor's hand with shivering hands and said pointing towards a boy, "Son! Can you please help my grandson Ron?"

Viktor looked at her son, he was a 26-27 year old chap, who was in a wheelchair. He was down with a critical stage of cancer. He was so dull that it seemed as if life was already sucked out of him.

The lady added, "My son and daughter-in-law too were cancer patients and passed away a few years back. He had a dream of becoming a reporter, but he has no time left now to do that."

Viktor promised to have a discussion with him. Soon, more and more people started approaching Viktor during his visits to see Kim. They approached him not only for the guidance of their loved ones who were down with cancer, but for their own problems.

Viktor started rendering his motivational sessions to the patients; telling them how they should first make themselves strong enough from within to fight with cancer.

"Rainbow of happiness is the byproduct of your inner sunshine, after the rain of sorrows," he said on a weekly visit to a hospital.

Sometimes, he used to go to the hall room and start playing his guitar.

The hospital had become like an open school where a bell used to ring, indicating the start of his sessions.

He would start his session with a short song of two lines, sometimes on-demand song from joiners, and then would discuss any five concerns of people selected from the audience. With his sessions, doctors also felt that a wish to live and fight with cancer was rising among the patients.

On the personal front, Viktor had finished his second novel, where his protagonist recovered from cancer with his strong will.

One Saturday evening, Viktor and Kim were sitting in the balcony, in front of the setting sun.

Kim read out aloud from the printed sheets she was carrying, *"The only difference between a winner and a loser is that one second when the winner decided not to give up."*

She turned towards Viktor after she finished reading the story and said, "This one seems promising."

"I will be submitting it to publishers today," said Viktor holding her hand.

"So happy to see you happy honey," said Kim.

Viktor quickly kissed her. She was surprised at his quick reaction.

He pulled her closer and bit her lower lip.

"You junglee! What's wrong with you?" she touched her lower lip to check if it was bleeding.

He held her hand and went down on his knees.

She was surprised, "What now?"

"I haven't brought anything today to offer you," he said, as he shifted her hand to his left hand and put his right hand on his heart and added, "My heart is already yours." Kim was still guessing what he was about to say.

He leaned forward on his knees, held her from the cheeks and whispered, "Marry me, Kim."

Kim didn't know what to say. She was spellbound, closed her eyes, and said no by gestering with her head. Next, she started crying. "Make me complete by being with me forever," he added, "I'll take good care of you, I promise."

Kim started sobbing, still moving her head saying no. "Why you are ruining your life? You know, even if I survived I still can't make you a father."

"Please!" he said, holding her cheeks, "You and only you made me realise the purpose of my life. You gave me a bigger family, the ones I'll be crossing my paths with."

"No!" she said and cried uncontrollably.

He further said, "I know I am a failure but I..."

"Shh..." she quickly put her finger on his lips as he was about to complete.

She took a minute to get back to normal and then whispered, "You are not a failure, Viktor. You are a winner; you have already won my heart."

She looked up, behind Viktor and was surprised, but happy too. She squeezed his cheeks and said again, "You have won their respect too," she pointed to the patients standing behind him who were standing there with flowers.

Every single patient, nurse and doctor standing there was in tears. Meanwhile, Ron came forward on his chair with a newspaper in his hand and gave it to Viktor. He seemed happy and energetic too.

Viktor looked at him and opened the newspaper. The guy said, "I always wanted to be a reporter, but cancer ruined all my plans. My mother was the happiest lady on earth to see this in the morning today."

Viktor saw his photo published in that day's local newspapers along with a short story titled, "Crazy for you".

The guy added, "The other day, I had written a fiction about how you had planned to propose Kim and they published it."

His mother came forward and hugged Viktor, "You gave my son a reason to smile after a year-long sickness. You are the winner my son; you are the real winner."

Viktor couldn't hold his tears seeing such respect from everyone. That day he seemed to have understood the meaning of real *happiness*.

He remembered the words of the monk he had met in heavy rains in India, and he could sense that the monk was standing behind the crowd and smiling at him. He was happy for him too.

∞

Next week, Viktor got rejections from almost all publishers. Few of the reply back e-mails read:

"Your first book wasn't as promising in the market and we are rather afraid that the second one would prove as bad. We are sorry."

"Well, we would love to work with you, but not at this stage."

"Your book seems nice, but we would have to invest a lot in the promotions because your earlier book failed badly."

"You could try modifying your story to fit with the mainstream likes of the readers and then we could negotiate again."

All of these statements meant the same thing. They were not willing to invest because his previous book wasn't successful.

They wanted to place their bet only on successful writers. And he was sure that most of them had not even read his manuscript before turning him down.

He smiled and replied to all of them, thanking for replying sooner than expected as they would never reply before three or five months after the submissions.

Viktor's attitude towards failures had changed a lot in the past few months.

"I am experiencing *Life Beyond Living*," he said to his image in the mirror.

He saw the last mail that read an apology letter from his first novel's publisher for not being able to accept his second novel due to financial crisis.

But he altogether suggested himself to get it self-published, and spoke to himself these words, "We believe in you, Viktor, and your writings for sure would be a success one day."

These words made his day and he decided to self-publish his novel. He scrolled a few of the self-publishing houses on the internet and zeroed upon three. He called them up to know how they are different from others.

"Life goes on... no matter you are happy or not... no matter you want someone to be happy or not. So happiness is a choice." He wrote as a reply to someone who had asked him about life problems on his blog.

After comparing services, costs, marketing strategies and checking their websites, he selected one.

The next day, he went to meet Kim and told her about the finalisation of the publisher.

"I am too happy for you Viktor," she said hugging him.

Viktor went near to her ear and whispered, "Let's get married next month."

She blushed, smiled, biting her lower lip, and nodded in a yes.

"Hey! One idea!" she turned her head up with a jerk, "Why don't you share both the news with everyone after today's session?"

Viktor curved his brows wondering, "Second news?"

She added, "One is our marriage and another about your second novel."

"Do they know about my first novel?" asked Viktor.

"Oh! Yeah, actually they don't," she said widening her eyes, "We never thought of sharing, right?"

"Nope!" he shook his head. "I never see them as my prospective customers," he looked outside the window, as all patients were settling in the garden for his guitar session. "They are my family and I have only one relation with them and that's based on unbiased, pure love and respect, nothing else."

"That's why I love you more than myself," she added hugging her tightly.

"Hmm," he cuddled her head saying, "Don't tell them I am an author."

She agreed and they walked down towards the garden.

He settled in the garden on the boundary of a fountain and started his session, "Today's topic is…. The word that connects all of us to all of us. Any guesses?"

"Some sort of adhesive?" said a little girl and everyone started laughing.

"Yes, adhesive does connect things, it can connect people too, but externally. The thing I am talking about connects hearts," he said looking at Kim.

Everyone started hooting and Kim continued blushing.

"Love," said a guy.

"True," said Viktor and started strumming the guitar chords.

"Love…. Love…. Love…. And *Love is deserved, not desired,*" he added playing soulful notes on the guitar.

"I love every girl," said a boy. "But I don't get it back though I deserve it."

All started laughing again.

"Next time, try loving without expectations," replied Viktor.

"Viktor!" a man in the mid-forties raised his hand, "Do you believe in god?"

"Yup," Viktor nodded, smiling, "but…." he strummed a happy note on the chords of guitar and added, "*I have a different god. I see it in the smile of others. My worship is to make people happy. Love is my religion.*"

"Does god love humans?" he asked.

"Of course!"

"Then why did he infect us with cancer?"

Silence spilled over, happy faced turned sad and looked towards him.

"Why did he make us suffer? Why does this little girl have to go through so much pain?" he added.

"It's.... it's.... a kind of.... probability," Viktor fumbled.

"What probability?"

"Happening or non-happening of certain things, like the generation of substances and chemicals in the body."

"And god for sure created it, but doesn't control it's malfunctioning. Like god created opium that has medicinal properties, but has its misuses too. Similarly wind, but without any control over a hurricane."

"God is not responsible for this. Probably god or anyone doesn't have an exact answer to your question. It just happens."

"I'll tell you a story," said Viktor and all had smiles on their faces.

"There was a guy," Viktor added. "He loved a girl more than anything else in the world," Viktor said looking at Kim.

"That girl ditched him." All raised their brows in surprise.

"But a few months later, the guy got to know that she wanted to go away from him because she had cancer."

"It's pure love, the soulful godly love that connected them again."

"Though the guy was not on talking terms with god now," said Viktor and everyone started laughing. "But now, in spite of fighting with god, he concentrated on creating the best ever moments for the girl. In turn, he came to understand the almighty better and his love for humanity also grew by leaps and bounds.

"Love can transform lives; it can make people do wonders, beyond their boundaries."

"Can love make me lucky?" asked a lady.

Viktor replied, *"Being lucky is in your hands as it's an outcome of your deeds."*

"I would declare a good news tomorrow," Viktor said, "and if you all believe in the power of love, I'll see you here again tomorrow."

Everyone went back to their wards eagerly waiting for the next day.

Viktor didn't see any sense of satisfaction on the old man's face. Kim noticed this and went and hugged him. She said, "I believe in you Viktor, and your love for all of them."

∞

Next day, he shared with everyone the date falling in the following month, when he would marry Kim. Everyone was extremely happy not only for this news, but another one that all the rituals would happen in the hospital only.

A week later, he got a mail from another cancer hospital, asking him to have a guitar session for their patients too.

Viktor went there, shared his same session based on the topic love. He got a standing ovation in the hall.

"Viktor," said the chief medical officer, "Thanks for this amazing session. You have done magic on our patients."

Viktor looked at the audience, *"Let's not call cancer patients as patients, they are cancer fighters. They are brave hearts."*

Many in the audience had tears rolling down their cheeks.

Kim saw the live streaming of that event with Amber and Greg's help, and was happy to see him since he was working for humanity now.

"Your cause for life has grown beyond your dreams, Viktor," she said as Viktor met her in the evening.

∞

For subsequent weeks too, he visited three more cancer rehabilitation centers for his sessions.

"Kim is improving astonishingly, Viktor," said her doctor, as they met him with her reports.

"How is Irene?" asked Viktor.

"Last stage," said the doctor. Viktor had tears in his eyes.

"You know Viktor," said the doctor, "You are doing a great service, we had never seen our cancer fighters smiling in the past few years."

Viktor tried to smile, wiping off his tears.

"But you are doing bad to us," added the doctor.

Viktor was surprised.

"You made us emotionally connected to them. It's harder for us, but now the way we get love back from them is amazing."

Viktor just smiled, "I didn't know it would turn into my dream to serve them."

"See this mail," he showed his mobile to Viktor. "This medical college asked us to connect with you to deliver a session on their annual event."

∞

He was on stage, holding his guitar and the audience was waiting for him to share his heart out.

"*Life is like a guitar, Tune. Play. Repeat,*" he said.

"Always tune yourself up before you start your journey to your dreams," he said, strumming each chord separately and started turning the nuts at the end of the chords to tune it.

"Life, like Guitar, has wonderful rhythms," he continued. With this he played the happy notes on the guitar, "Some are happy ones."

The audience seemed so captivated in his talk that they found themselves swaying to his tunes.

"Some are sad."

He placed a hand over the strings to mute them, saying, "It's *you* and only *you* who can decide which tune to play."

He walked down the steps and into the crowd. "You might face some tough moments in your life, but you have to keep on playing, sometimes for yourself, and sometimes, for others."

"Most of the times, you'll learn them by yourself, but sometimes you'll have to learn them from...?" He raised his eyebrows, encouraging the audience members to answer.

"From Lisa, my tutor," the guy replied, instantly relaxing the mood in the auditorium. Everyone laughed in cohesion.

"Correct," he said and started descending stairs, "You would face failures." He put his guitar on a chair, "Stop it, Tune it, Play it. Stop... Tune... Play...".

The eyes in the crowd gazed at his vitality, followed his movements while their ears intently stuck to his eloquence.

"How many of you know how to play guitar?" A few raised their hands. "You there," he said, pointing to a man who didn't raise his hand. "Could you play this for me?"

He shook his head, but Viktor urged him to take the instrument. "Come on, just give it a shot. Play it like you see people doing it in the movies."

The man gingerly held the guitar and then began to strum randomly, banging his head like a rock star. The audience seemed to be amused by his childish antics.

"Thank you! You rocked my friend!" Viktor said, smiling and taking the guitar back.

"This would happen when you expect others to make your dreams come true for you. Public would laugh, the person would enjoy, but you will be screwed.

"Because that's your guitar in someone else's hands. How much will you be able to trust them not to make a mistake with it? What if they break a string? What if they drop it?" Everyone was silent but nodded for understanding the meaning.

Making eye contact with the audience, he continued, "*Never ever let anyone take charge of your Guitar called LIFE. Tune your dreams, for you are the composer of the tracks of your life. Why do you wait? What are you scared of?*" No one dared to answer.

He yelled, "You have to continue in spite of failures because...." he paused for a moment and pin drop silence was spread across the audience.

He plucked a chord with happy note and a line flashed on the projector.

"Come on!! Say with me," he yelled, pointing on the projector, "Thy are the VICTORIOUS..."

All the students repeated in unison. Next came, "Who dare not to GIVE-UP," the celebrated line from his book.

He added, "Take best care of your Guitar... and help others in keeping theirs. That way you'll live the HAPPIEST life ever."

After the session, students rushed to the stage to thank him. They surrounded him and started clicking photos.

Afterwards, when he reached home, he saw his profile flooded with too many friend requests.

∞

Next day, he visited Kim and saw Amber there already as she had reached directly from her college.

"Sweetie pie!" said Viktor giving Kim a gift, "Happy Birthday."

"Thanks honey!" she said happily taking the pack.

As she opened, she was shocked to see her name, embossed on the book cover titled, "Kim."

"God!" she was astonished, "What is this?"

"My second novel, dedicated to you. You said you want to be a part of my novels."

"You are crazy. I was joking that day."

"*Say your heart out… Work that dream out… For the time won't be back again,*" he replied.

"You are my dream, my heart is yours, and I want to be with you every moment to make it beat."

"But Viktor…." said Kim.

Amber interrupted, "Oh, hello Mr. *Guru with Guitar.*"

Viktor was surprised, "What?"

Amber quickly added, "Check this video," and gave him her mobile.

Kim snatched the phone from his hands and started seeing the video online.

Viktor requested, and she shared one headphone speaker with him.

He got goose bumps as he heard, "It's my voice". He pulled the mobile from her hands. It was his video.

"I saw it being shared by one of my friends. It's getting viral," Amber said curiously. "And you know what they call you now?"

Viktor was stunned as he read the title of the video.

Kim added, "*Guru with Guitar?*"

Viktor had never expected to get such a huge response. Too many comments were there. Few people had asked for his help too.

Last comment on the video was, "Hi Viktor! I am Steve. My son is cancer stricken. I have lost all hopes in God. All I want is to make him happy. Can you please guide me on how to support myself."

He replied to that, "Hi Steve, sorry to hear that. Let's connect over a call and I'll be happy to help you in any way I could." As he was done replying to that, his cell rang up.

He was surprised, "It's from India?" He said and went aside to talk.

He came back after five minutes with a tensed face and handed the phone to Kim with his frozen hand.

"What happened?" Kim was stunned to see his expressions, so was Amber.

"Hello! Hello!" someone said aloud on the phone as it was still on call.

Kim took the phone, "Hello! Yes!"

"Who is this?"

"Viktor's fiancé."

"Hello madam. We are trying to reach Viktor for the past one month," said an old guy from the other side. "We are distributors and want to buy overseas distribution rights for his novel *10 A.L.O.N.E.*"

"Oh," Kim was extremely happy, "but…"

"See!" the guy interrupted. "We have talked to his publisher there and we have pending orders for this novel in thousands."

As he said this, she dropped her jaw and looked at Viktor. He smiled and nodded, then she put the phone down and jumped to hug Viktor. "I told you, you'll make it one day."

"Hello! Hello!" yelled the guy on the phone.

Amber picked that up and asked, "Yes?"

"Who is this," the guy asked.

"Umm… Viktor's fiancé's sister."

"See madam," said the guy again explaining the whole story. After two minutes, she too was stunned, her hands were frozen, and looked at Viktor and then Kim and they nodded together smiling.

∞

Next day, he finalised the contract with "AuthorsOwn" and sold the overseas distribution rights to an Indian distributor.

"Could you please write the cheque in some other name that I'd tell you over-mail?" asked Viktor.

"Nope, audit issues," replied the distributors.

"Please see if it is possible," requested Viktor.

"Umm! Okay, but please get this finalised ASAP."

After the call Viktor asked Kim, "You know who this cheque is gonna go to?"

Kim smiled, replying, "You know that I know that."

"They say *Trust but Verify*," he replied.

She wrote on paper and showed him as there were other people too in the room. It read, "Mom's school."

Viktor replied, "I am you and you are me. I know you this way and you too…. That's why…. crazy…. yoo-hoo…. I am for you," and kissed her, put her to sleep and went home.

∞

Two more weeks passed. Viktor's mother and other relatives from Canada joined him for his wedding in the following week.

All the rituals under Indian customs like Ladies' Sangeet (Music night) followed by his turmeric bath ceremony, etc., were performed at his home.

The last day of Viktor's bachelorhood had finally arrived. Very close friends, including Rahul and Richa, and a few relatives of Viktor and Kim were present in the hospital's auditorium.

Kim came with her friends, dressed in a white wedding gown, as per the Christian wedding rituals. It appeared as if a fairy had descended on earth. Viktor kept on looking at her as she reached the stage.

She had 'The Best Man' too with her, Greg, standing beside her. She looked at Viktor, he was dressed in a Sherwani, an Indian wedding attire for grooms. Kim was about to take the first step.

"Freeze!" said Viktor. She blushed and took her step back. Viktor came to her, expanded his arm towards Kim and whispered, "My wild queen! You are looking gorgeous."

She blushed and gave her hand in his hand replying, "Junglee King, I am happy to be yours forever."

Viktor leaned forward and picked her up in his arms. Everyone started whistling and hooting. He took her to the stage and made her sit on the decorated royal chair.

It was first of its kind, a unique wedding, where the wedding was going to happen in both types of rituals. After half an hour, they proceeded towards the mandap, a decorated place where pheras were to be performed.

Kim was happy to undergo all the rituals in her gown. In between, she was gifted gold to wear as it was treated as auspicious for the occasion. Soon Kim had adorned all the gold jewellery and an embroidered piece of shawl was put on her shoulders.

"*Sindhoor,*" said the priest and Viktor held the small box of vermilion in his hand. Kim was a bit nervous as the sindhoor was supposed to be put in her hairline on head, but she was bald.

"Raise the headscarf," said the priest.

Kim looked at Viktor and whispered, "No hairline."

Viktor's mother told Kim's mother and father to help Kim. They raised her scarf a bit.

Kim had tears in her eyes, feeling no hair on her head and she whispered, "I am sorry Viktor."

"I love you the way you are Kim," whispered Viktor.

He put the sindhoor saying, "You were, are and always will be beautiful for me."

She closed her eyes, as if her purpose of her life was met that moment.

Then they took pheras and everyone showered flowers on them.

As they were done, they proceeded to undergo Christian customs. The priest started the customs. Everyone started clicking their photos. At last, the priest asked them to kiss.

Irene came forward with a big gift-wrapped box. Viktor thanked all the patients for that great gift.

"Open it," said Irene.

As he opened, he was amazed and happy to see – it was an electric guitar.

He read a message card stuck on it that read,

"With Love...
For Guru with Guitar...

From...
Friends for Life. "

Viktor couldn't express his emotions. He tried to hold his tears back, but couldn't.

Irene's parents came forward and hugged Viktor saying, "You gave us the reason to re-live, Viktor. She smiles daily, makes others smile."

"Rock it baby," said Irene, winking. Two guys came forward and plugged the guitar in the amplifier. He strummed beautiful chords and started humming.

Almost all the patients visited them to bless and get a photo clicked too.

The Director of the Hospital too visited to greet the newly-married couple. Viktor asked his mother to take out the cheque she had got from the US distributor and asked her, along with Kim, to present that as a gift it to the Director.

"But that was for her school?" asked Kim, surprised.

"Mom is mom," Viktor replied smiling. "Mom said she has enough for the kids. She wants to extend her love to them too who gave her happiness."

"My patients....," said the director to them, "Sorry.... I mean.... Cancer fighters.... Have got a new meaning to their life."

"I now know that *love* can cure any critical disease. It is above all kinds of prayers and worships; it's the main cause of our existence," he was in tears.

Viktor asked him about Ron, the aspiring reporter and he replied that he was shifted to his home town with his grandmother and younger brother as he had no hopes of recovery, but he was content and wanted to spend his last days there only.

Later, Kim was shifted to her room. She changed and rested on her bed. Viktor was with her the whole night.

"Sleep now, you lovely lady," said Viktor touching her eyes.

She nodded a no saying, "These two hours were the best moments of my life, Viktor."

She kissed his hand, "I won't have any regret on any day if it would be my last. I don't care about my tomorrows now."

"Shh…!" Viktor put a finger on her lips, snapped softly on her cheek and said, "Dare not say anything about your life. It's mine now."

"Someone wrote," she said, "*Every TODAY has a better version called TOMORROW.*"

"Oh! Pathetic quote, who wrote that?" Viktor winked.

"Dare not say anything about him," Kim smirked. "He is my friend and an author too."

"Oh!" Viktor held her nose, "Another guy in your life?"

"He is not just another guy, he is a junglee king," she said.

"You junglee queen," he touched her lips. "You are tired. Sleep now," and he kissed her lips, "Goodnight kissi."

∞

That day onwards, Viktor continued his visits to various hospitals, medical colleges, NGOs and rehab centers.

His weeklong wedding leave was spent with Kim in the hospital itself and the day he resumed office, he started visiting her during lunch hours.

Seeing Viktor's immense love not only for Kim but for all his fellows in the hospital, the director arranged a guest room for him in the hospital.

Viktor would connect with everyone daily after office and early in the morning in the park.

∞

Months had passed and the doctors were amaze at Kim's improving health.

On a typical day, Viktor visited Kim during lunch and seeing him extraordinarily happy she asked, "Any success?"

"God!" Viktor raised his both hands, "You are face reader."

"Tell me quickly what it is?"

"My novel *10 Alone* has featured in the Limca Book of Records in India under title *First Novel with 10 Songs.*"

"Amazing," she got up and hugged Viktor.

The next moment, his cell rang. By the time Viktor was done with the call, he came back to Kim and said, "Get ready, we are going out."

"But doctors won't allow me."

"I have taken permission. Peter called me up and asked to meet."

"Peter?" Kim was surprised, "Publishing Director of AuthorsOwn?"

Viktor nodded, putting one hand on her back to help her get up.

Kim had improved a lot and so with the doctors' permission, he took her along with him.

They reached a café where Peter was waiting for them.

"Viktor! Welcome," Peter greeted as he entered.

"Glad to see you Peter." They hugged.

"Have a seat," they pulled chairs and settled.

"Congratulations on your name being featured in the Limca Book." Peter shook his hand again and opened his laptop.

"Look at this," he turned the screen towards them.

"My God!" Kim uttered out of joy seeing a steep chart of sales of *10 Alone.*

Immediately a passerby yelled, pointing at Viktor, "Are you that Guru with Guitar?"

Peter exclaimed, "Good to know about your new avatar, Viktor." He said to Kim while Viktor was giving autographs,

"Recipe of success needs tons of morale, flavour of attitude and hours or days or months or years of patience to cook."

Kim nodded and he continued, "You see! Whatever I had said, has come true."

As Viktor got free from signing autographs, the director added, "You know, I could revive my sinking business only due to sales of your novel *10 Alone*."

Kim held Viktor's hand smiling with curiosity.

"Thank you Peter, for encouraging me that time," said Viktor.

"You know," he replied, "COURAGE is the only currency, the more you spend, richer you become; by earning RESPECT. You deserve it."

∞

Viktor's life had transformed. He was hearing positive news from all around. He got promoted as VP in office and his mother had a successful school running in Delhi, India.

Later that year, he was awarded as best debutante in fiction writing in the US and was invited to address the media.

A reporter asked, "I have heard that you have failed too many times in your writing and personal life. What made you keep on going?"

"I will answer your question with a question," replied Viktor. "How did you learn bicycle? In hours? Days? Months? Didn't you fall off numerous times? But what kept you going?"

"Passion to learn," replied a guy from another corner. Viktor looked at him and was stunned to see the agility with which he has replied. But, the next moment, he got busy with other reporters who were asking questions about his future plans for writing.

After the press release, the same guy approached him during lunch party. "I guess I have seen you somewhere," said Viktor.

"I am Jeff." he replied, "Ron was my elder brother."

Viktor got the clue, but asked quickly, "Was?"

Jeff added, "He used to talk a lot about you."

Viktor smiled, but seemed more curious to know about Ron.

"Ron knew he wouldn't survive," Jeff continued. "So he thought of spending time with family and getting the treatments at home only. I was becoming an irresponsible guy day by day as mom and dad were not there to control me."

He had tears in his eyes as he spoke.

Viktor hugged him and offered him a seat. He continued after some time, "Ron asked me to take care of Granny but I won't listen, I won't go home for days."

"One day my friend called me up and said, Ron is in hospital. By the time I reached him…. He was…" Ron sobbed his heart out.

"He was a great soul," said Viktor.

"Yeah!" Jeff wiped off his tears, "That day I was cleaning his room. I came across a few of his personal diaries. He had written all the incidents from the day Mom and Dad had passed away, to the week he passed away."

"Have some water," said Viktor consoling him.

"He wrote about you too," Ron smiled. "That day onwards, all his pages were full with his to do lists. He decided to go back home from hospital, he thought to bring me on right track and make me a reporter, as at one point of time we had the same dream. He daily told me to get admission in a journalism and mass communication course, but I always ignored. He wrote everything in his log. He wrote that *Journalism is like a Guitar. You love playing it the day you tune it*."

He showed the diaries to Viktor, "See what he wrote on his last page."

Viktor opened that diary to the last page. It read, "I wish I could see Jeff as a reporter and see him reporting the best tunes of his life."

With this Jeff broke down again. Viktor hugged him again and said, "Look at me."

Jeff looked at him.

"For you, I am Ron; and today I, Ron, am happy to see you Mr. Reporter."

Jeff sobbed uncontrollably, hugging him.

As Jeff got normal he said, "Viktor! I have learnt to play the best tune of my life. Granny is going to be a happy grand-Granny. All thanks to you and to this one."

He showed the title that Ron had given to his diary. Viktor wished him and saw the diary, it read, *"Life like Guitar."*

∞

Years kept on passing. Viktor became the Director of the company. He started giving his motivational sessions with guitar to NGOs, corporates, medical colleges, educational institutions and various hospitals for free and all his sessions were titled *"Life like Guitar"*.

"Independence," he said looking at the Indian flag, while addressing an Independence day event in a cancer curing institute in Bangalore, "Independence means...enjoying the freedom and empowering others too to let them do so."

∞

His mother passed away, leaving behind her a well-established school that had various branches across rural areas in India.

Viktor used to visit the schools on every annual event of the school, and kids, their parents and their relatives used to gather in large numbers to listen to his speech.

∞

"Where are you?" asked a lady over the phone.

"Reaching there within half an hour," replied an elderly person, in his sixties. He was a well maintained guy who had grey hair, and he was quickly checking out from Amsterdam airport.

After half an hour, he reached the hotel and was received by the hotel staff, "Welcome Mr Viktor!"

Listening to this, the lady who had called him up turned back and went to him, "Viks! Where were you?"

"Honey!" Viktor went towards her with open arms, "How are you my baby?"

"I am not good, inauguration is about to happen," she replied. Next, she quickly hugged and kissed him and whispered, "How is Kim? Is she all fine?"

"Amber! Relax, she's good. Doctors asked her to rest," replied Viktor.

"Sir! Where to put this?" asked a hotel staffer holding the big wooden box, shaped like a guitar.

"Take it behind the stage," said Amber.

"Ladies and gentlemen!" said the anchor, "Please put your hands together to welcome Mr Viktor."

He went towards the red carpet and held Viktor's elbow on the right side while Amber was already walking on his left, holding his elbow.

All heads turned towards them and everyone applauded. Viktor was there to open an exhibition of paintings by Amber.

The lobby was decorated with beautiful paintings on walls.

"Thanks Viktor for making me realise my dreams," Amber whispered to Viktor. And while cheering to the photographers she said, "Thanks to you too Greg, for supporting me and asking Mom and Dad to let me paint my life myself."

Viktor inaugurated the exhibition. After that everyone settled, expecting Viktor to say a few words.

"*Life is like a painting,*" said Viktor opening his heart out.

Amber and Luke looked at each other, smiled and held each other's hand.

Viktor continued, *"It's you who has to get a canvas, I mean get an idea; choose colours, start working on the blueprint of that idea, and at last make a great art of piece, means live your dreams."*

Everyone applauded.

"Like Amber and Greg dared to paint their life," he said and everyone looked at them and applauded. They bowed in response.

"*Suppose.... It's your last day on earth. Have you done what all you wanted to do, you always dreamt of? If the answer is NO, your time starts now.*"

He looked at the audience and said with renewed vigour, "So don't wait anymore. Get ready with the colours and paint your life yourself, and paint a great one."

"But earlier you said life is like a Guitar," asked a reporter.

Viktor smiled at him and the reporter put his hand on his heart, bowed a bit and said a silent hello. It was Jeff.

"Life can be like anything that you want it to be," Viktor added coming forward. "All you need to live it, is to believe in *you.*"

He added coming a bit more forward, on the edge of the stage, "*The reverse ABC of success is Conceive, Believe and Achieve.*"

The entire hall broke into applause.

"Mr Viktor! What would be your next step?" asked another reporter.

"If I took another step," Viktor took his step ahead, in the air, "I'll fall down," as he was on the edge of the stage. Everyone laughed aloud.

"*All that falls is not bad.*" He smiled and continued, "Sometimes we should take a step back," he said and moved a few steps back, "To tune our Guitar."

As he said this, everyone started whistling and hooting, "Guitar! Guitar! Guitar!"

He smiled, went behind the podium and brought the guitar in front. The hall was full of whistles and hooting again.

He again played soulful notes and started singing.

After the song he added, "To answer your question my friend," he said, pointing at the reporter, "I would be establishing an NGO by the name *Life Beyond Living* for cancer patients across the world."

During the dinner, Jeff met him again, greeted and said, "Someone wants to meet you." Viktor nodded, "Sure!"

A little girl of 5-6 years came forward to him, holding the hand of a young lady and her other hand was behind her, as if she was hiding something.

"Your daughter? So cute," said Viktor going on his knees and raised a hand towards her, "Madam, how are you?"

"Autograph please!" she said with her cute voice bringing her hand in front.

It was a novel titled "*Life Like Guitar*".

All laughed.

"What's you name little angel?" asked Viktor.

"Kim," she replied.

Viktor was surprised to listen and he looked at Jeff.

He signed that and gave it back to her and greeted his wife too and hugged Jeff again.

"Viktor," said Jeff, "Reading Ron's story in this novel used to make me cry every time."

Viktor hugged him.

"But I won't cry today," he said, smiling. "But I feel *happy* as I made his dreams come true."

"You know," Viktor added, "Today wherever Ron, your parents and Granny is, they all are happy to see you happy."